Behind the
BUTTERFLY
GATE

Also by Merryn Corcoran

The Silent Village
The Paris Inheritance
The Peacock Room

Behind the
BUTTERFLY
GATE

MERRYN CORCORAN

CORK PUBLISHING

Published by CORK PUBLISHING (UK)

2021 Merryn Corcoran

Soft cover ISBN 978-0-9927556-8-3

Amazon KDP ISBN 9798464120013

A CIP catalogue record for this book is available at the British library.

Cover design Patrick Knowles www.patrickknowlesdesign.co.uk

Design & layout www.yourbooks.co.nz

This book has been printed using sustainably managed stock.
Printed in New Zealand by www.yourbooks.co.nz

Dedicated to the memory of the special friends
I have lost during the writing of this book.
Too many too soon.

Irene Huntley
Wael Arab
Bels King-Harman
Kay Boustridge
Diane Hudson
Betsy Tipple

Especially for my precious mother
Faith Hazel Rennie

ACKNOWLEDGEMENTS

I offer my sincere thanks to all those who have encouraged and supported me with this book. To my excellent editor Sadie Mayne whose guidance was invaluable. To the special friends who 'read' my early drafts and have given me their time, including Dame Pieter Stewart, Mary Ciurlionis, Jennifer Sutcliffe, Enid Craig, Alice Krotoff, Gillian MacGregor, Pamela Lindsay and Lynne Greenwood. An incredibly special thanks to the amazing Shirley Greene who helped me in her role as a Jewish consultant. My heartfelt gratitude to Mandy Hager who has encouraged me from my very first attempts and at writing. With all my love, I thank my daughter Emily, son in law Marc and my granddaughter Poppy for their inspiration and support. This book would never have been completed without the constant encouragement from my extraordinary husband Tim, who is always here for me.

PROLOGUE

A short life must be an important one. The symbolism of the butterfly, no longer earth bound, is believed to symbolise our next incarnation. Although colourful, the butterfly's first incarnation is as a creeping worm-like creature designed to crawl on the ground with an excess of legs – always under constant threat of being eaten by birds or stood on by larger animals. Therefore, imagine the relief when it can finally spin itself into a chrysalis and attach itself hopefully somewhere safe, then become a larva to prepare for the ultimate portion of its life journey.

From this crusty, dull chrysalis the larva has been developing, morphing into its next embodiment. It becomes irrevocably ready for the supreme entrance to the world. As a magnificent butterfly. *Un papillon magnifique.*

Once the larva has established its final metamorphosis the ultimate moment arrives. After a struggle to shed its now useless chrysalis it slowly expands its outstanding wings full of reflective, shimmering colour and stands tall ready for first flight. The next few days the butterfly has one mission only, to use its highly sensitive antennae to find a mate, then for the female to lay her eggs; it is then that her life's work is complete.

For humans who gain the visual pleasure of seeing this impressive creature gracing their garden, there is a reason. It has been the belief for many centuries across many cultures that the butterfly's incarnations are a symbol of the human spirit once it has departed its earthly skin. The butterfly passes our orbit to remind us that our loved ones are in another undefinable space; they have shed their dull, earthly existence, and are now soaring the universe in splendour with a freedom beyond our conception.

ONE

LONDON 2019

'Matilda, get in here now!'

At the shrill note in her mother's voice Tilly instinctively clutched at the silver butterfly brooch pinned to her shirt and stepped reluctantly into the kitchen.

'You have completely messed up my life with your behaviour; you are utterly useless just like your father.'

Tilly hurried across the room; eyes downward until she stood with her back to the kitchen mirror. Followed by her mother, Tilly grimaced, but then as her mother caught sight of her own reflection she paused from her tirade, drew in her cheeks and fingered her immaculately curled hair as she admired her face in the ornate glass.

Tilly knew from her childhood of living in this house full of mirrors, that if her mother was viewing herself in any available reflective device, then she would be distracted.

Every room featured some sort of mirror. Quick thinking had saved her from many extra punishments when she was a child. The diversion worked. As her mother took a second lingering look in the mirror Tilly slipped out of the kitchen and upstairs to the sanctuary of her bedroom.

Returning to her childhood home had been a massive mistake, but there had been no other option. Now, somehow, Tilly had to find a solution and the strength to escape.

As she slumped down into the large armchair beside her bed, she nervously picked at what was left of her fingernails, then her eyes fell on her cherished framed butterfly collection. Since returning to her childhood home three months previously, it had sat on the floor. It had been the only thing Tilly had taken with her when she left home five years ago. It contained several rare, precisely mounted butterflies as well as the chrysalis to match each one. The original hooks had never been removed from the wall. Tilly had been loath to put it back up. Its return to her wall would be an indication of finality; she didn't want to stay in the house any longer than she had to. In truth, she hated it here. She just wanted to go as far away as possible from the house of mirrors and her megalomaniac mother.

Oh, the memory of five years previously! What a great year turning twenty had been. Despite the sense of guilt she had experienced leaving her father, it was as if she had been born again. Tilly had felt such immense relief having escaped the orbit of an overtly opinionated, cruel woman who had a lamentable habit of dominating the whole household with her religious fanaticism.

London had been magical. She had secured the best job in the world, working beside one of the UK's most qualified lepidopterists at the Natural History Museum, dealing with glass-fronted drawers full of perfect butterflies, captured for ever in their magnificence. She had rented a room in a house with four Spanish girls in Ladbroke Grove, started dating and just like a butterfly emerging from its chrysalis Tilly believed she had experienced flight and freedom.

But things had changed dramatically. Now, as the sun sunk beyond the large oak trees in the back garden and stole the warmth from her generous bedroom bay window, a chill swished through Tilly's bones.

She had opened her wardrobe to put on a sweater and caught sight of herself in the full-length mirror. What a mess! Her jeans hung on her hips; the mousey brown hair that her ex had once told her was the delicious colour of walnuts appeared more greasy than usual and was in dire need of a cut. The past three months had taken their toll. The bright hazel eyes that had gleamed back at her previously now looked muddy texture and reflected her current mood – sad, faded and flat. Her skin was sallow from too many sleepless nights. Her fingernails were almost non-existent as she had reverted to her childhood habit of biting and picking at them. They were unsightly. But the way Tilly felt, she harboured no desire to enhance her looks. She belonged in the shadows, diminished.

As the light from the mirror offered out a shimmer on her butterfly brooch, the corners of her mouth lifted in a soft smile; it was her talisman, a gift from her beloved

Aunt Lucy who had always understood Tilly's butterfly passion. Not only had she given her the sterling silver art nouveau piece for her eighteenth birthday, but she had found her a film poster from the 1970s movie *Butterflies Are Free* starring Goldie Hawn. That poster still hung on the bedroom wall, and had been Tilly's mantra in her teenage years, to leave this house and to be as free as one of her beloved butterflies.

There was a light tap on her door, 'Matilda it's seven o'clock, let's not stir her up more, please come down for dinner.'

Tilly opened the door and faced her father. He wore his usual brown knitted cardigan with the leather woven buttons over an open-necked beige shirt and a pair of dated, loose brown corduroy trousers and his usual sad face..

'Dad I can't do it! I'm sorry, I know you will bear the brunt of it, but the fake prayers and all the supposed forgiveness that I need, I can't bear any of it anymore. Best I just eat something in my room.'

Her father reached out and squeezed her hand. 'I am so sorry. I wish I could have done more. Your mother is correct. I am a failure, but I love you.'

Tilly placed her arms around his shoulders and hugged him, 'I'm sorry too, Dad. You are not a failure and I love you heaps.' As he gently released himself from her hug, Tilly touched his damp cheek gently with her finger and lowered her voice. 'I'm going to find a solution for myself. I'm off to see Aunt Lucy tomorrow.'

Her father wiped his eyes with the back of his hand

and in his usual hushed tone replied, 'Lucy loves you; I feel sure she will help you find a way.'

Tilly had limited memories of any enjoyable childhood times with her father. The most poignant was when he bought her a butterfly net. They were on summer holiday in the Lake District. She was about ten years old; it was a rare occasion to be just the two of them, father and daughter. They chased elusive butterflies for what seemed like hours. Having her father run and laugh beside her was like magic. But the magic didn't last; once they arrived back at the holiday cottage, because they were a little late her mother had gone crazy, like a mad woman. She verbally abused them, grabbed the net off Tilly and broke it into pieces.

TWO

Despite the trauma of the previous few months, Tilly still loved London, where all the good happy things had happened for her.

As she sat down on the train, she casually picked up what she thought was a free daily *Metro* magazine on the adjoining seat. But it was a copy of *The Lady Magazine*. Not something she had ever had cause to peruse before. Flicking over the pages, mainly featuring 'Royal' stories and photographs she arrived at the International Situation Vacant column.

'Position Offered for Home Help/Companion for Elderly Lady Some French language required' Lucy read on, the location was Menton on the French Riviera and the ad stated there would be ample time off to improve your French and hobbies, all food and board provided but no mention of a wage.

Exiting Bayswater tube station, Tilly popped the

magazine into her bag. Her thoughts moved from the French Riviera back to the present. As she walked along Queensway towards Aunt Lucy's apartment she inhaled the familiar aromas being offered. A door to one of the many Chinese restaurants swung open and expelled a whiff of cured smoke from the strangulated ducks that hung in its window. She caught traces of tantalising coffee aromas as she passed Starbucks and Café Nero. Alongside these American icons she enjoyed the diversity of fragrances emanating from the apple tea being smoked in hooker pipes by white-robed gentlemen. The men relaxed outside exotic-looking cafés seated on chairs with large bright woven cushions, positioned to watch the world go by. Queensway was always busy in the summer when many Middle Eastern visitors decamped to Bayswater to escape the hot summers of their home countries.

At the far end of Queensway, she passed the Porchester Baths and approached the Porchester Hall, a favourite for low-budget events. A brightly coloured Indian wedding party spilled out on to the footpath, their foreheads bearing the red dot of their commitment to love, the women were gloriously swathed in hues of red and white saris edged in gold thread. They all seemed so very happy. Would she ever feel like that again?

Thirty years ago, when Aunt Lucy had bought her apartment with her ex-husband, this end of Bayswater had still been deemed a 'rough' area. Now it was very posh and property prices had rocketed, but Lucy had been determined never to give in and sell.

Tilly's aunt had spotted her arriving from her first-floor

balcony and promptly greeted her at the downstairs door. 'Come in my darling, I am so pleased to see you. You look so much better than last time.'

Aunt Lucy's sitting room, although small, featured two sets of tall French doors opening on to a small balcony which offered the apartment a sense of space. Tilly was very comfortable with her aunt's eclectic tastes in décor and made herself at home on a retro mint-green armchair as Aunt Lucy poured one of her exceptionally strong coffees.

'Now tell me all,' Lucy said as she took the chair facing her niece.

'I just can't stay in that house any longer! Now my situation has changed I need to leave. I do have enough savings for a deposit on a flat, but, with no job, I'm scared I wouldn't be able to pay my rent.' Lucy sighed and took a sip of her coffee.

'Are you sure you don't want to go back to the museum, you loved that job? And it appeared they were very pleased to have you. Now things have changed why not get back in touch with Maria and Alicia at your old house? I'm sure they would make room for you there,' Aunt Lucy replied.

Tilly reddened and cast her eyes downward. 'I feel such shame; I'm damaged goods, I just can't face any of them.'

Lucy leaned over and placed her hand on her niece's wrist. 'It's OK Tilly you are still very fragile; you don't need to explain to me.'

At fifty Lucy was still very attractive in a 'hippy' sort of way. Her grey-flecked blonde hair was tidied back in a ponytail, turquoise earrings dangling from her ears to showcase her long neckline. She had maintained a slim figure and the warmth of her heart was always reflected in her perpetual smile.

Tilly sighed and as she got up to use the loo she bumped her handbag. *The Lady Magazine* fell on to the floor.

'What's this? Thinking of going into service?' Lucy chuckled when Tilly returned.

'I found it on the train, an ad in the international section caught my eye, but it doesn't offer any actual wage.'

Lucy offered an odd smile as she got up and appeared to be busying herself in the kitchen. When she returned, she took a breath and then spoke in a very measured tone, 'Tilly if there is something you really wish to do to move forward, don't make money the consideration, there are ways around that.'

'Even if they offered, I would never take any money from my parents, my mother would lord it over me for ever. The practical part of me tells me I need to have some savings. The ad states a minimum of a year commitment, a year for me without a wage would really put me on the breadline.'

Lucy exhaled and appeared to gather herself somewhat before she replied. 'First, just let me say, in the past I have held my tongue in regard to my opinion of your mother; however, after twenty-five years of witnessing my brother's decline under her tyranny, and the damage I believe she has done to you, I don't want to stay silent any longer. I have decided it's too late for him, but not for you.' Lucy leaned back in her chair.

There was a prolonged silence before Tilly spoke.

'Wow! You have always been supportive of me, but I have never heard you say anything like that before!'

'Your father and I were brought up passively, taught to look for the good in people. Karen has just not been the decent mother she should have been to you. She has been odious for years now. Your father made some bad choices all those years ago. I've done some reading on the matter, and I believe she is a psychopath and a bully, this religion she follows gives her excuses to control.'

An expression of relief swept over Tilly's face as tears welled up in her eyes. 'Thank you, I feel saner just hearing you say that.'

'Actually, you need to have a new conversation with your father.' Aunt Lucy paused, and pursed her lips. 'There is something he needs to tell you.'

'What?'

'As much as I would like to, it's not my place to say. I would suggest you corner him away from Karen once you go home. I will phone him in advance.'

Tilly was puzzled but knowing how Aunt Lucy always stuck to her word, she thought better of continuing the conversation.

'Now enough of her, let's explore this position on the French Riviera which is far more enjoyable than discussing Karen.' Lucy patted Tilly's hand, then opened the magazine and read through the advertisement.

They looked up Menton on Lucy's laptop, and Google mapped their way around the town which sat directly on the border with Italy. The more Tilly thought about it, the more she started to believe it was doable.

'The only thing is my French is practically non-existent. I took French lessons for four years at school, but goofed off most of the time and have only visited France once.'

'Oh, I wouldn't let that get in your way; if that's the only barrier you will just have to learn fast!' Lucy laughed. They pondered over the French position for a while but were interrupted when Tilly's phone rang. She chatted to her former flatmate Maria for a while and when she mentioned the position in France, Maria instantly replied, 'Go for it, it's just what the doc ordered!'

'Tilly can I persuade you to stay over with your dearest aunty and we can go to my favourite eatery?'

They wandered up Queensway and shared a fragrant curry with some wine at a superb Thai restaurant. Back at the apartment, Tilly sat on the spare bed wearing her aunt's oversized T-shirt and cradled a cup of hot chocolate. It dawned on her for the first time in months that she was experiencing a sense of calm. The angst and guilt hadn't gone, but it had shifted. Just maybe she could begin to believe these terrible feelings would fade away and allow her to get on with her life.

'Good morning, how did you sleep?' Lucy asked as Tilly emerged from her bedroom the following morning.

'Better than I have in twelve months, thanks.' Tilly had offered the first real smile Lucy had seen in a very long time. 'Thank you for listening. I am still worrying about how much money I will need, but I think I will apply for that job and even if I don't get it I have decided leaving the UK for a while would be a good thing.'

'Be prepared! Karen will have an opinion and you

mustn't let anything she says alter the good things you are beginning to feel,' Lucy replied in her soft manner as she placed two crumpets and a cup of coffee in front of Tilly at the table.

Then Lucy took a little breath and a pause as she looked directly at her niece. 'I have named you sole beneficiary in my will and the main amount of money that's in there came from your grandparents. I know Karen got her hands on your father's share but I have given this some thought and I have decided to give you a portion of this now, as you maybe an old lady when you receive it otherwise.'

'No, I couldn't accept that. I hope you do live to an old age and spend it all, I'll find a way.'

'I have plenty my darling, it will be my pleasure. Anyway it is all done. I used the new-fangled way and put fifteen thousand pounds into your bank account from my online banking before breakfast.'

As Tilly was leaving, Lucy embraced her. 'Shame is something someone else dumps on you. You have nothing to be ashamed of, it is an emotion that will pass, move on and let it go,' she said then kissed Tilly's wet cheek and waved her goodbye.

As she navigated her way through the crowds at Victoria station, Tilly's heart had skipped a beat. Somewhere nearby she could hear the distinctive rapid-fire tones of Italian being spoken. She turned in the direction of the voice, her heart thumping. Could she face him? A man yelled into his phone, but dark hair and an Italian accent were the only similarities. The man wasn't tall and not beautifully dressed like her Giovanni. However, the exchange was enough to trigger the door Tilly hoped she had closed. As she hurried away from the man towards her platform, the tears streamed down her face.

Once seated on the train she managed to pull herself together. Giovanni was gone, he didn't want any part of her and, somehow, she just had to accept that.

Her thoughts hovered between her new wealth, the possibility of moving to France and to Aunt Lucy's statement about the conversation she needed to have with her father.

It had been late afternoon when she arrived back at the house and to her relief her mother was out. With focussed resolve she went upstairs to her bedroom and immediately emailed the address given in *The Lady Magazine*. She wrote along the lines her and Aunt Lucy had discussed, not actually saying anything one way or another about her lack of French language. As she hit the 'send' button, a wave of fresh optimism flooded over her.

Tilly was aware it would be near impossible to avoid dinner for a second evening without a huge row. Besides, she knew she would be leaving and wanted to be near her father as much as she could. At five minutes to seven, she took a deep breath and went down the stairs towards the dining room.

'So, Madam Matilda has deemed to grace us with her presence, has she?' her mother snarled as Tilly walked into the dining room. 'Well, go out to the kitchen and get your plate and cutlery, I've only set for the two of us.'

Karen sat at the head of the table, her head of dyed-black

hair framing her face with her dark-red lipstick highlighting her narrow lips. Edward and Tilly sat at either side of her. 'Bow your heads in prayer,' she barked as she raised her hands in the air and closed her eyes. 'Our Glorious God we ask your forgiveness for Matilda's wickedness and we ask that you give food to the poor. Amen.'

Then as Karen picked up the shiny silver knife, she held it at eye level and sucked in her cheeks, parted her highly painted lips and with her free hand patted her curls as she gave herself a smug smile before using the knife for what it was designed.

'How was Aunt Lucy?' her father asked.

'Really Edward, how do you think she would be? Still a divorced woman who conducts an immoral life. I don't know why you bother with her,' her mother snapped before Tilly could reply.

'She was on good form and offered me some comfort and sound advice,' Tilly bravely managed to get out before her mother went off on another rant.

'Comfort, why should you have comfort? Your father and I have had to suffer in front of the whole Church and our friends because of your sins.'

Tilly had resolved, no matter what, to stay till the end of the meal. So she sat, head down, as her father always did and said nothing more. She quietly cleared the first course plates away and as she was about to re-enter the dining room with the cheeseboard, she heard her father's hushed tones.

'Now Karen I am not speaking "against you" in front of Matilda, but I am saying this to you out of her earshot, whether you like it or not. You are not to say one more thing to or about my daughter and "her kind" as you put it. Imagine if she heard you?' He abruptly stopped the conversation once he was aware Tilly had returned.

It had been the first time in an age Tilly had heard her father standing up to the witch who dominated his life. And the first time she had heard him refer to her as 'my daughter'. Although Tilly really didn't know what had gone on during her five-year absence, she could clearly see her mother's obsession with 'The True Church of the Greater God' was akin to a mental illness. The past three months that Tilly had endured under this roof had been like fuel on her mother's fire. Karen deluded herself into seeing sin in everyone who didn't share her belief or fervour.

They ate their cheese in silence then, when Karen got up to answer the phone, father and daughter hastily cleared the table and tidied up in the kitchen together. They spoke in hushed tones and Tilly reassured her father she had a plan and would keep him in the loop once she had things sorted. When she asked him if Aunt Lucy had phoned, a bead of sweat emerged on his forehead and he looked down at his feet. 'I'll talk about that later,' he mumbled.

Tilly observed her mother as she spoke in contrived tones on the phone. Karen had positioned herself in front of the darkened window so she could see her full-length reflection. While she chatted, Karen sucked in her tummy and with her free hand licked her finger and wiped it across her perfectly plucked eyebrows. As Tilly quickly beat a retreat to her bedroom, she mused that perhaps her mother had missed the religious law about vanity being a sin.

Around ten o'clock Tilly heard a 'ping' indicating she had new email. It was a response from the Riviera. Dear Miss White,

I write on behalf of my landlady Madame Pollock who is elderly and does not have a computer. She has read your email and while she did have a suitable applicant for the position at the last minute this girl was unable to take it. Normally, I would set up a skype meeting but Madame dislikes anything technical. So, she would like to offer you the position on a three-month trial for both sides. You will be required to assist her with shopping and some light housework up to twenty hours per week in return for meals and board. You will have your own bedroom and bathroom. I live in the downstairs part of her house and my WiFi will reach your room so you will have use of that. We can introduce you to French teachers and we are both keen to improve our English. Madame was most impressed with your mention of 'Butterflies' hobby. Madame knows of a Riviera museum that has a wonderful collection. Madame can accommodate you as soon as possible. The house phone number and my mobile are below as well as our address. We look forward to hearing from you of your arrival date and time.

Kind regards

Enid Du Pont on behalf of Madame Rina Pollock.

THE TURRET HOUSE, 22 Rue Victor Hugo, Menton 06500, France

Tilly stared at her laptop. Then, before she could

ruminate on her decision, she immediately replied, stating once she had made her travel bookings she would be back in touch. Next, she texted Aunt Lucy, who replied with a 'Wow!!'

As Tilly trawled through the French travel sites, images of Paris kept popping up. Feeling inspired to opt for the slower, less stressful pace of train travel to the Riviera, she booked Eurostar to Paris and found a cheap hotel near to the station which she reserved for two nights. After that she would catch the fast train right through Nice to Menton on the Riviera.

Around 11 p.m. there was a light tap at her door. Her father's pallor had gone from the usual white shade to a scary shade of grey. He looked as if he'd aged ten years in the past few hours. Tilly beckoned him in, and he sat down on her bed looking at the floor.

Tilly turned her chair to face him. 'What is it Dad?'

'Karen has taken a pill, I needed to wait till I was sure she wouldn't wake.'

'Yes, so?' Tilly said.

He cleared his throat and started to wring his hands.

'For God's sake Dad! What do you want to say?'

'I always wanted to tell you, but Karen was adamant it wouldn't do any good, Ruth was dead, and Karen was here and she needed to be your mother in every sense of the word.' A tear dropped on to her father's hand as he spoke.

'Ruth? Who was Ruth?' As she spoke a shot of raw fear hit her brain.

'Ruth was my first wife, your birth mother, she died

after you were born.' He stammered, stopped then continued. 'Six months after her death I was still in a state of shock when I met Karen. She convinced me she would be a real mother to you, and as Ruth had no family, I allowed that to happen. We moved to a new area, and made new friends, no one realised you weren't Karen's daughter. My parents had passed away by then as well. Your Aunt Lucy was travelling, I wrote and told her. She phoned me as soon as she received my letter, objecting strongly to the plan. But I finally agreed I would tell you when you came of age, so she agreed to go with the plan.' His tears poured down his cheeks.

Tilly stared at him with a mixture of shock and horror. A deathly silence filled the room, then she finally found her voice.

'This is the most terrible thing I have ever heard! How could you let me believe that bitch was my mother when it was so clear how much she hated me?'

'Karen wasn't like that when you were young; it got worse when we found out she couldn't have children. Then she went through a total personality change when she took on religion. Tilly, I am a weak useless man, I have no right to ask you to forgive me.' He stood up.

'Don't you leave this room, not until you have told me a few more facts about my real mother!'

His eyes never left the floor. 'Ruth was the only daughter of a French couple who had both immigrated to London as children with their mothers just before the war. We met, fell in love and were so happy when she became pregnant. She had a condition called pre-eclampsia which killed her just after you were born.'

Her father shook with fear, and as angry as Tilly was, she could see he might keel over at any moment. With his eyes still pointed at the floor, he left the room and quietly pulled the door shut. A part of Tilly wanted to hear more, but the anger engulfed her as she fell on to the bed in shock and curled into a foetal ball.

To discover that her father and Aunt Lucy, the two people she loved and trusted the most in the world had deceived her for twenty-five years was unfathomable. That day was Tilly's apocalypse. There were no tears, only blind raging anger. The only glimmer of an upside was that Karen was no longer her mother.

It was around 2 a.m. when she finally switched her light out. Lying in the dark Tilly reflected how, once again, her world had been turned upside down. The counsellor had said her last trauma would take a few weeks to physically move on from; she trembled a little when she thought how close she had come to taking her own life. This new reveal welcomed back her suicidal thoughts.

Another hour passed, Tilly's thoughts dashed all over the place, by the time the light was awakening the day Tilly had resolved she would survive and move on. Her anger was her motivation. She had packed and would leave for a London hotel to spend the night before her early morning train trip to Paris.

After considering the temperatures in July and August, Tilly had packed mainly summer clothes. She managed to secure her framed butterfly collection amongst her clothes to protect the glass from breaking. Even with her two favourite reference books she had everything in just one manageable suitcase.

Once the sun had risen, Tilly was desperate for a coffee. Suppressing her anger, Tilly went downstairs; she had resolved not to speak to either of her parents. She would grab a coffee, then order a cab and leave. As she passed the under-stairs cupboard in the hall her skin prickled. She never looked at that door. Her sickening childhood memory was never far from the surface. She had lost count of how many times Karen had locked her in that cupboard with the threat that if she ever told her father, it would only happen again.

'You are up early, not like your usual lying in bed. Feeling sorry for yourself?' Karen stated as she walked into the kitchen. It was obvious her father had not shared his reveal with his wife. Fuelled by her anger and hurt, she was determined to not allow anyone to rattle her. Tilly made no verbal response. She offered her mother a flash of a false smile, straightened her back and returned upstairs with her coffee. By 10 a.m. she had booked a hotel near the station in London and the cab was on its way. 'And where are you going?' Karen said as Tilly arrived at the foot of the stairs with her case.

'I know you are up to something Matilda. You have always been the same, the quiet before the storm. If you are going to live here on our money and goodwill, we won't have you sneaking away and having secrets. Whatever you do always ends up in wickedness.'

Tilly put her case down and boldly eye-balled her mother. She stared directly at her but said nothing.

Staring without speaking is a dangerous act. It invites a response, like a loose thread pleading to be pulled.

Her mother's face coloured bright red, in tune with her lips. Then, without any warning, Tilly felt a sharp painful slap across her cheek as her mother stood over her.

'Stop that right now!' Edward had appeared and pulled his wife away from Tilly.

'Let me go, Edward, you failure!' Karen shouted, twisting to get out of his grasp. 'She is a rude little slut and I have God's right to punish her!'

Tilly had never witnessed this side of her father. 'Dad it's OK. She will never hit me again,' Tilly stated. 'Karen, you are not fit to be anybody's mother. From now on I will never use that word "mother" again in relation to you or speak to you, ever. I am taking my sin and my "ugly" hands away and I hope I will never see you again.'

Edward continued to restrain his wife's arms. But said nothing. She had stopped squirming; her reddened demeanour began to pale.

As Tilly left the house, she didn't catch whatever was being said between them and she no longer cared.

THREE

She had to wait outside for the cab.

When her father appeared beside her, Tilly could see he had aged overnight. He handed Tilly a chunky envelope. 'The email address on the front is a private one I use at work, and I can assure you that Karen has no access to it. So please email me when you are settled wherever you are going, and I give you my word I'll never tell her.'

'I don't want anything from you Dad.'

'Please Tilly, take it.' For the first time during this whole apocalypse he looked her straight in the face, as he thrust the envelope into her hands.

The cab pulled up.

'I understand that you will never forgive me, but please know I have always loved you.'

The cabbie put Tilly's case in the boot. She made no response to her father; she had no words. She got in the cab and didn't look back as they drove up the street.

Tilly checked into her small grotty hotel room close to St Pancras station. She wished she had changed her ticket to the later train but had decided it was better to arrive in Paris during the daylight. The time passed in a confused haze; shock was no stranger, so Tilly just lay on her bed attempting her deep breathing exercises. Although drawn to phone and vent at her aunt, she decided against it. She just wanted to leave them all behind.

The next morning Tilly wrestled her case past the rush hour morning commuters, but still she had arrived at the station in good time and settled in her forward-facing window seat.

She had only visited Paris once before, when she was seventeen, with a school group. She had studied French language at school for four years and was hopeful some of it was still nestled somewhere accessible in her memory bank.

After a breakfast of croissant and coffee from the café car, Tilly needed the loo. She flinched as she sat down – there was a mirror on the back of the door. Because of her mother's addiction to mirrors Tilly went out of her way to avoid them. But there she was, unavoidably facing herself while on the loo. It occurred to her that she looked different somehow, it must have been the dusty mirror, it softened her face a little. But she really did need to sort out her hair and resolved to buy a treatment to use on her fingernails.

When the train pulled into Gare du Nord it was heaving with people. As Tilly walked towards the exit, the babble of languages humming around her provided her with a sense of assurance that she had moved a long way away from the world that her grief, shame and deceptive parents inhabited. Tilly was grateful she had copied the walking directions from the station to her hotel, as the taxi queue appeared to go on for ever.

She was conscious of her suitcase as several beggars approached her with filthy outstretched hands. Once outside the station she was greeted by a woman with dramatic eyes and a black-toothed grimace who held a small sleeping baby, and with her free arm held her soiled palm opened towards Tilly. In that moment, her heart ached for the baby. Tilly was rooted to the spot, her mind going backwards. The woman called to her and just as Tilly stepped forward a policeman appeared, and the woman bundled the tiny baby up and ran.

Tilly moved on as fast as she could, encumbered by her case. Once away from the close proximity to the station, the environment changed, and she relaxed a little, loosening the grip on her case as she trundled along. It was lunchtime and the outside seating at the brasseries and cafés she passed was full of people enjoying plates of food and wine under an array of coloured canvas canopies to shield them from the rich midday sun. She stopped several times to study her instructions; it felt a lot longer than the ten-minute walk stated on her map. Then she finally spotted it – the Avalon Hotel.

She was delighted she had opted for a four-star hotel for the extra 10 euros per night, because, as promised, she had glass doors opening on to a tiny Juliet balcony, a 'room with a view' – even if it was on a noisy street, it was a Parisian noisy street.

Noticing several well-dressed chic women on the train and on the pavement, Tilly began to feel distinctly dowdy, and acutely aware of her bitten-down nails. After a quick shower, she put on a simple blue fitted sundress and pinned her butterfly brooch near her shoulder, then surprised herself by deciding to go in search of a hairdresser and a chemist where she could purchase a solution to sort out her nail-biting challenge. The hotel receptionist was helpful, after she had called into the bank around the corner from the hotel she found a salon. It had been all very well gathering the courage to walk in but trying to make herself understood was another matter. The girl on reception appeared to speak no English and in Tilly's usual shy way she felt she had made a fool of herself so decided to leave.

'*Pardon, Mademoiselle!*' an older woman who had been dealing with a client called out with a smile just before Tilly left the salon. 'I speak *une petite* English, maybe I can help you?'

Tilly said she needed a trim and perhaps a conditioning treatment. The hairdresser flicked her fingers through Tilly's hair. 'I think we could encourage it with a little colour as well, perhaps?'

In for a penny, in for a pound, Tilly nodded in agreement.

Previously, when she had opened the envelope her father had given her, there was a thousand pounds in cash in it. She had decided she would accept it, 'compensation for lies' she muttered under her breath as she had changed it to euros. Two hours and eighty euros' later Tilly left the salon with luxurious walnut brown coloured hair cut with short layers around her face. The other stylists in the salon all offered a smile of approval, and Tilly almost felt 'chic' as she walked out of the salon.

By eight o'clock, hunger had got the better of her. After she had applied her new lipstick and mascara along with her nail treatment, Tilly tentatively left the hotel in search of somewhere she would feel comfortable eating solo. She walked past two restaurants that displayed great window menus but couldn't spot any patrons sitting alone. At the third restaurant she could see both a single man and a single woman sitting unaccompanied at tables so, with her rumbling tummy encouraging her, she timidly walked in and in her best French requested a table for one.

She remembered the food section of her schoolgirl French and ordered confit du canard, only knowing canard was duck and having no idea what the confit part was. While waiting for her meal, to mask her embarrassment and appear busy, she googled it on her phone. It was a duck leg preserved in duck fat then quickly fried. Back in the day, less than wealthy families preserved the duck legs in jars to eat when other meats were scarce. The duck was traditionally served with potatoes fried in the duck fat as well. It was delicious.

Just as Tilly had ordered a crème brûlée for dessert a young couple came into the restaurant with a pram. They received a generous, familiar welcome from the maître d', then he seated them directly next to her. The mother bent down and lifted up a tiny baby wrapped in a pink shawl while the father looked on, completely besotted with his wife and tiny daughter. A pain shot through Tilly. It was as if she had been stabbed so hard in her heart that it had shattered all over again. She struggled to breathe. She was up on her feet as quickly as she could move. Thank goodness she had cash. She thrust 50 euros into the maître d's hand and almost lost her footing as she rushed on to the street. Clutching her handbag across her stomach, stinging tears pouring from her eyes, she hastily made her way back to the hotel.

Once inside her room Tilly released a primal scream as she fell to the floor. 'My baby, my baby,' she sobbed as she wrapped her arms across her stomach. After what seemed for ever, she forced herself to calm down. Still lying on the floor, she lifted her dress and gently rubbed her tummy. 'My chrysalis, where did you fly to when you got your wings? Are you free now my precious little girl?'

Eventually Tilly raised herself up to sit on the bed. Every part of her body and mind throbbed. Like a dull, thick, never-ending nausea of the body and soul. Desperate for relief, she scrabbled through her toilet bag and found the box of pills her doctor had said to take if needed. Until now she hadn't needed them. Until now it had all been a bad dream that she hoped she would wake from. Giovanni had been her saviour; she had experienced true love. But when she discovered her pregnancy, he flew out of the door. He didn't want her or their baby. Just as Karen had viciously predicted 'the Italian' had dumped her. She was such a sinner, should never have been born, Karen said. And now all this guilt and grief she finally had been getting under control had been compounded by the truth of her own birth.

As the medication played its role, Tilly fell into an enforced sleep with the image of a baby wrapped in pink floating above her.

She was woken in the morning with a distant knocking in her blurry brain. It was the breakfast she had ordered when she had checked in. The fresh strong coffee helped shift the residue of the sleeping pills or tranquillisers, she wasn't quite sure what they were, only knowing that they had packed the appropriate punch. In a strange way the previous night's collapse had granted her some sort of relief.

FOUR

Armed with a map of the Paris Métro and the Google map app on her phone, Tilly navigated her way, before she arrived at the Métro station Château de Vincennes. Once she had reached the Parc Floral, she sought directions to the Jardin des Papillons. The Parc Floral was twenty-eight hectares of free-flowing parkland where visitors could enjoy the gardens and share their picnics, but Tilly was only interested in the new butterfly house she had read about. It was a garden room within a greenhouse, in a corner of the park. Her early start ensured there were very few visitors when she reached her destination.

As Tilly stepped inside the warm garden room it was as if she had entered the world of her imaginings. The soft feminine creatures glided and fluttered around the diverse array of trees and bushes. She was captivated as en masse they displayed their magnificent wings, offering her a visual symphony of artistic patterns and colour.

She immediately recognised the Lycaenidae species known as 'Blues' which hovered around a thyme bush in the corner of the garden room. The butterfly known as the 'Aristocrat' floated above her showing off its colourful regal wingspan with a haughtiness befitting a queen. A small group of Delicate Silvery Argus appeared to dance to a rhythm only they could hear, darting in and around a large pot of geranium plants.

'*Bonjour,*' Tilly said to a young man in a uniform. He stood tall and reed-thin, he wore a tag on his slightly soiled work shirt, with the name 'Pierre'.

'Are you English? Do you know much about papillons?' he asked.

'Yes, to your first question, and I love everything to do with Lepidoptera, I consider it my passion, but I am by no way an expert. It has been one of my dreams to visit here,' Tilly replied.

Pierre's smile was full of warmth and his accent enchanting. Tilly levelled her stance, took a discreet breath and with bravado she didn't know she had, said, 'Would I be able to follow you while you work for a bit? I won't get in your way, just observe.'

Pierre offered another smile as he subtly scrutinised her with a longer glance.

'If you wish, let me invite you to observe some butterflies that are just about to emerge from their chrysalises. I had prepared them in anticipation of having a school group visit later today. But even though we can manipulate nature to some degree, she still does things in her own time and these beautiful creatures are ready to embrace the world now in their new reincarnation.' His English was heavily accented, but friendly.

Tilly's bravado had waned, she was at a loss for words. She nodded and followed Pierre as he walked across to a bush within a glass cage at the back of the room.

'You are very quiet, perhaps if we are to share this experience together you can tell me your name?' The formality softened as Pierre raised his eyebrows with a smile. They stood side by side at the door of the glass cage in front of the group of wiggling chrysalises.

'I am so sorry – I can be a bit vague at times. I'm Tilly, and this is just the best thing I have ever seen. I am really excited, thank you.'

The group of chrysalises looked sticky and shrivelled and to the untrained eye, just like little lumps of twig. They clung to the sparse branches of a lepo bush. Should someone pass them in their natural environment they would never be noticed as anything important. For their own protection, God had designed them to blend into nature.

Tilly stood very still next to Pierre gazing through the glass. She noticed a 'scent' about him. It wasn't exactly a fragrance, more of a musty aroma; she couldn't quite place it.

'Most of them have been struggling for about an hour now, but that one on the far left looks like it will be the first to emerge,' Pierre said as he took a small camera from his pocket. 'Please feel free to take some photos or a video but don't go any closer than this and please turn off any "sounds" from your phone,' he added.

'You must have arrived early this morning,' Tilly commented as they continued to stand in close proximity to the glass cage.

'I have been here since dawn – I must be. This institution will only continue to be funded if we can prove it is educational and the public keep visiting; it is so important I document as much as I can and disseminate our success on social media.'

'Oh! Look the chrysalis is shedding!' Tilly exclaimed. She had switched her phone to silent and clicked on the video application to check it was recording.

A tiny furry black head with delicate long antennae popped out first. It appeared as if the butterfly was shaking its head. It then gave an elongated stretch which pushed its dirty-coloured shrivelled skin down behind itself. Next, it delivered a loosening shake as it stepped away from its former shell and on to the branch. Then slowly and ceremoniously it edged out and unfolded its wings to reveal the most magnificent expanse of co-ordinated colour and perfectly matched designs.

As Tilly filmed the entire process on her camera her eyes trickled with tears. Witnessing the emergence of the butterfly had awakened her spirit and touched her heart. She felt a new sense of hope and the possibility of her own evolution and transformation.

Within a few minutes, chrysalises were being discarded all over the branches and a kaleidoscope of glorious butterflies greeted each other for the first time in their transformed states. When Pierre felt confident that all the chrysalises had completed their re-embodiment, he slid back the glass cage door to allow the resplendent 'flutter' to fly higher and investigate their new home alongside others of their kind.

Tilly stood back and watched as these colourful creatures, symbols of many things including rebirth, regeneration, and the human soul, glided nobly around her. She noted they never looked back to reflect on their withered empty husks. They seemed to instinctively understand their fate and would embrace the short life ahead of them. If they lasted ten days, that would be the equivalent of nearly a hundred human years.

Tilly's big ask to shadow Pierre was such a prize. She spent the following three hours in the Jardin des Papillons observing as he tended to the plants and photographed the butterflies. She was especially intrigued as he subtly and gently assisted crawling stripy caterpillars to new locations to help them find their special place to commence their metamorphosis.

When he shook her hand to say goodbye, she caught another trace of his aroma. She now understood exactly what it was – it was the magical fragrance of the birth of butterflies.

Tilly spent the rest of the afternoon exploring the park. Her mood elevated, and, provided she veered away from any couples with baby buggies, she began to feel some of the black cloud that had been dominating her thoughts slowly begin to drift away.

That night for the first time in months she slept soundly and awoke full of hope as she dressed, then left for the station to catch the train to Menton.

FIVE

The train travelled at up to 200 kilometres per hour as it dashed through the French countryside. Tilly gazed out the carriage window at the constantly changing scenes.. She caught glimpses of classic stone-built villages built around central churches whose tall solitary spires quickly saluted her as the train sped past.. These scenes were interspersed with snippets of the motorway where the cars appeared to move at a snail's pace in comparison to the fast- moving train. It was as if she were watching a series of moving paintings. Once they had reached Aix-en-Provence the train changed direction, slowed down and the tracks ushered them in to a more gracious pace along the coastline. Tilly was captivated by her first views of the famous French Riviera.

The train tracks in some places ran directly beside the sea, disturbing the tranquillity of the sumptuous villas which sat snugly against the cliffs. Tilly snatched peeks of their full-length dramatic windows, wide terraces and gleaming swimming pools, imagining what sort of stylish people lived inside.

After the six-hour journey the train arrived in Nice. It was so much busier than Tilly had anticipated. The hot press of humanity overwhelmed the narrow platforms, a potpourri of locals, migrants, and backpackers. Several men hassled her, feigning to assist with her case. She managed to fob them off but struggled, wrestling her case down one flight of stairs, then up another to reach the appropriate platform to board the train to Menton.

The second part of her journey proved much more impressive. The train ambled at a leisurely pace offering Tilly prolonged hints of more prestigious villas and attractive apartment buildings. She felt somewhat cheated when they stopped at Monaco only to discover the station was located within a tunnel – not even a glimpse of Casino Square. After a further ten-minute journey, the train pulled into Menton station.

Although Tilly's map showed that the Turret House was a short walk from the station, she didn't fancy hauling her case down the hill in front of the exit. She hopped in a waiting cab and handed the driver the written-out address.

They drove up a narrow steep road that looked across at the town of Menton, but the view was disturbed by the ugly mangle of train tracks directly below the road. The cab pulled up directly in front of number 22.

Tilly stood with her case at her feet in front of the rusted iron gate. The gate was waist-high and hung between two fraught stone gateposts from which loose masonry and large stones appeared be holding on for dear life. A huge unkempt hedge rose on either side completely obscuring the house from street level. A flash of insecurity whirred through Tilly's head. Had she made the right decision? She drew in a brave breath, picked up her case and pushed the gate. It took quite a shove to open it and was accompanied by a creaking groan born of years without maintenance. Tilly stepped on to the stone patchwork path and was immediately struck by the fragrance of jasmine that sweetened the air. Further up the path, to either side of the door, sat two large wooden tubs overflowing with great white sprays of the delicately scented flowers.

Looking upwards, Tilly had a full view of the Turret House. It was built with large grey stones which would have appeared depressing if the large windows hadn't been softened by faded soft-blue wooden shutters. The right-hand corner of the house was a distinct turret complete with decorative gothic-style battlements on the roof. When Tilly arrived at the entrance it was barred by a smaller black wrought-iron gate. She couldn't see any bell to ring. Hesitantly she took the two steps up and gently pushed the gate which swung open.

'Hello, *bonjour*, is anybody home?' she called out.

Several moments passed. The only sound was the background clatter of a train heading towards the Italian border on one of the many railway lines below the villa.

'*Bonjour*!' Tilly called louder this time as she walked the short distance to the base of the stairwell ahead of her.

A door opened above her.

'*Bonjour, s'il vous plait venir monter les escaliers je vous remercie,*' a voice called out.

Tilly understood the word for 'stairs' and, carrying her case, she walked upward towards the voice. The stairs were made of a dark wood and gave up a fresh gleam and a whiff of linseed. By contrast the walls of the stairwell were covered in faded old green wallpaper embossed with a fleur-de-lys symbol.

'*Je suis ici,*' the voice called from the room to the left.

Tilly stepped from the landing into a perfectly circular room, which she recognised as the distinguished turret. Sitting in a large, padded brocade chair on the far side of the room was a grey-haired old woman wearing a loose-fitting navy spotted dress. Looking out from her pale-skinned face, her eyes were extraordinary; they radiated an unusually bright aqua-blue colour. The old lady remained seated.

'Hello, I'm Tilly. I am deeply sorry, it's a long time since I've spoken French,' she stammered as stepped in front of the woman and offered her hand.

The old lady's illuminated eyes wandered up Tilly's person and rested on her face. Then she accepted Tilly's hand.

'I am Madame Pollock and I speak English – apparently quite well so people tell me.'

Her hand felt like silky butter. Tilly felt awkward; she was rooted to the spot.

'Please, pull up a chair and sit beside me so I can see you better. My vanity gets the better of me, so I don't like to wear my lunettes.' The old lady spoke in noticeably clear English.

Tilly pulled up a chair. With her fists loosely at her sides, in a bid to conceal her chewed nails, she attempted to inconspicuously study the old lady. A faint fragrance of jasmine hung throughout the room. The old lady put on her wire-framed spectacles which exaggerated her brightly coloured eyes and heightened their pronounced stare. But Tilly felt no malevolence from her, it was more a sense of intense curiosity.

'Ah! You really do like papillons! When you said in your email you were a lepidopterist, I thought perhaps you were writing that to impress. But I can see that beautiful antique brooch would only be worn by a girl your age who really does loves papillons.'

Tilly would have felt more at ease if Madame Pollock had offered a smile or even relaxed her face a little. But her facial muscles didn't appear to move in that direction.

Forgetting her nails, Tilly nervously fingered her brooch. 'Yes, I don't have many friends my age with the same interest in butterflies; however, when I worked at the museum there were several who shared my passion.'

The old lady appeared to ignore Tilly's comment and continued.

'I am a bit slow on my feet so why don't you take yourself down the hall, your bedroom is the second on the right. Please make yourself at home and unpack. You may have exclusive use of the green bathroom next door. Enid, who lives downstairs and who assists me, will be home by seven, that is when we will all sit down to a meal together and we will explain all that we expect of you.' Madame then removed her spectacles and turned her head away towards the window. Tilly felt well and truly dismissed.

The hallway was lined with the same faded-green wallpaper as the stairwell, with the addition of a dado rail. Several paintings were placed at intervals along the hall, softly illuminated by polished brass picture-lamps. The paintings appeared to be dated scenes from along the Riviera – Tilly assumed all by the same artist. The one that hung just before her bedroom door caught her eye. Under an olive tree sat a small girl in a red coat reaching out to a large colourful butterfly. 'That's a good omen!' she said out loud as she pushed open the door to her new bedroom.

As in the stairwell, the room smelt of linseed oil and wax furniture polish. It was a large space with dark polished floorboards, discoloured full-length gold linen curtains and an antique bed sat in the middle of the room. Despite its elaborate bed ends, Tilly could see the mattress dipped down in the middle. At least the white bedspread and bedding appeared clean and starched.

The view from the window looked over the rear garden where a suite of battered white cane furniture sat under a large tree; the furniture was tired but obviously loved. Tilly's attention was drawn to a bright green throw on one of the chairs, clearly someone's favourite spot.

A pleasant whiff of lavender greeted Tilly as she opened the elaborately carved free-standing wardrobe. Most of the old wooden coat hangers had an accompanying moth-repellent sachet attached to them. Everything so far was like her new boss, fragrant and old. As she hung her few dresses, she considered Madame's intense eyes, which had slightly unnerved her – but perhaps it was just a first impression. All would be revealed over dinner, and Tilly was determined to try to just take one day at a time.

The bathroom was something else – pure art deco. Linear-shaped, avocado green tiles with a key-line of black, creating a frame a few inches from the ceiling. An enormous square designer bathtub circa 1920 with stylish taps, which were in dire need of new chrome, dominated the room. Tilly was particularly uncomfortable that one wall was completely mirrored; Karen would have loved it.

'Bugger! Why did she have to pop into my thoughts?' Tilly shook her head as if to throw the thoughts away as she straightened the white fluffy towels that hung on the aged chrome towel rail.

By seven o'clock Tilly was starving and anxious to meet Enid. She pulled on a pair of denim jeans and a fresh white shirt, painted her bitten nails with the clear lacquer the pharmacist had sold her and made her way back down the hall to the Turret room. There was no sign of Madame Pollock. Tilly took the opportunity to look at the front view of the house. Sadly, the first thing she saw were the train tracks, but beyond that, the tops of Menton's pretty buildings enhanced the skyscape and Tilly caught a glimmer of the sea. To the side of the window, she had a full view of the majestic fourteenth-century old town.

'*Bonjour*, you must be Tilly?'

Tilly turned to face a rounded, short masculine-looking woman with a lopsided smile on a stern looking face framed with a sharp blonde bob. She was wearing denim jeans. Tilly put her age at mid-forties.

'Yes. Hello, you must be Enid?'

'Welcome to the Turret House, I have Madame downstairs already. We usually eat down there as the original dining room is still all in place.' Enid spoke her English with a delightful French accent.

Her demeanour was brisk. She looked like the sort of woman you would not want to mess with.

Tilly followed her new companion downstairs. Madame sat on one side of a well-set table – the old-fashioned kind, a crisp cream tablecloth laid with battered silver cutlery accompanied by cloth napkins rolled neatly into bone napkin holders beside each setting. A vase of delicate spring flowers sat to one end next to a large crystal jug of water. Enid indicated for Tilly to take the seat opposite Madame. Then Enid left the room, a delicious aroma wafting through the door.

Madame said nothing.

Tilly offered her a smile. 'This is a beautiful room, and something smells good!'

Still no response. Tilly got up and stepped through to the kitchen. 'Can I help with something?' she said.

Enid held a platter in her hands.

'No thanks, I have it all organised.' Then dropping her voice, she added, 'We will get to know you a little before we forgo the formalities.'

Tilly followed her back into the dining room, gobsmacked. What had she got herself into?

Once the three women had helped themselves to the

lamb chops, home-made potato chips and sautéed cabbage from the platter, Madame Pollock spoke her first words.

'Now Tilly, let me explain how things work here. Enid lives downstairs and works full-time in town. She cooks most nights but when she cannot for any reason you will be expected to.' Madame popped a spoonful of cabbage in her mouth while still looking directly at Tilly.

'Oh, I see. Well, I can cook simple English meals, but I am willing to try anything, if required,' Tilly replied nervously.

'Madame is not that fussy, are you?' Enid reached across and touched Madame Pollock's arm in what Tilly would term a 'calming down' gesture.

Madame gave a grunt and stabbed at a piece of lamb.

'Your primary duties are first to be nearby when Madame has her shower. She has had a fall in the past and, although she can manage, we need her to be safe. We would ask that you do all the handwashing and run any errands Madame requires in the village. A cleaning lady comes in on a Friday and does the basic cleaning and ironing. I get the groceries in the car once a week but there will be other items that will need to be bought at the market on a more regular basis,' Enid stated without altering her facial expression.

Madame added little during the course of the meal, and after a rather mumbled 'good night', she left for her bedroom. Tilly helped Enid clear the table, then to her relief Enid offered her a cup of tea and perched on one of two stools and a bench. Tilly took the tea and followed suit.

'Madame is really, how-you-say in English? "OK". You should understand, in my opinion she suffers from depression; she goes into these dark periods. She needs someone close by most of the time. It is hard to keep anybody to stay for long in this job.' Enid's voice reflected a question more than a statement.

'I am used to moods. Silence I can manage, it's malice that I find so unnecessary,' Tilly replied.

Enid nodded in acknowledgment but didn't enquire any further. 'I came here ten years ago as the tenant for downstairs, but as I run around after Madame, write her emails and do her shopping, she ceased charging me rent. Over the past couple of years, in some respects, she seems to have regressed; she has been reflecting on her childhood. I catch her looking at old photos and spending a lot of time gazing out of the window,' Enid said and took a sip of her tea, then added, 'In other respects it's as if she has lost something and is trying to find it.'

'Did she have any children?' Tilly asked.

'Yes, apparently, one son, but he died young, she never mentions him, and Monsieur Pollock died about twenty years ago. Madame was an only child, so as far as I know there is no other family. She is a very private person.'

Tilly felt some relief as Enid warmed up a bit. They chatted for a while and Enid revealed to Tilly her grandfather was from England, which explained her name and her extended English vocabulary.

'Well, I'm off to bed now, Tilly, I think you may have misled us a bit saying you spoke French! But you told the truth about the butterflies, that's what got you the job.'

As Tilly walked upstairs, she had some hope, given time, that she might defrost Enid. Her initial thoughts on the bed were correct, the mattress was ancient, and she was only able to sleep in the hollow in the middle, but for the first time in months she drifted off easily, . Just full of curious thoughts and questions about her new home with its mismatched architecture and the strange old lady with piercing aqua-blue eyes.

SIX

PARIS, 1944

I can't remember exactly when Mama starting crying in the night. I think maybe she cries because she misses Papa Hans, because she only cries the nights he goes out to his work. Once I went to her bedroom to see if I could make her happy, but she was so cross, she shouted at me. I won't do that again.

She is happy with me during the day. I was going to go to school because I turned five, but Papa Hans said I will learn more being taught by Mama at home. That was a long time ago, and now we never seem to leave the apartment much. I get bored. Some days Mama puts her dark headscarf on early in the morning and tells me I mustn't open the door to anyone while she is at the market. I have been so bored I sneak into her room and find a book in the bottom of her underwear drawer. I haven't seen it before; I think the drawings in it are ones Mama has done. Papa Hans says she is an excellent artist, but the ones in this book are not of the beautiful papillons she draws for me, they are of a man I don't know, although there is something familiar about him. I don't want her to be cross with me, so I don't ask her. Besides, I love the papillons she draws for me.

We have some special days. Like today, Mama says I am irritable, but I don't know that word. I call it bored. It is windy outside, and Mama puts me in an old coat even though it is not very cold. She pulls my hair into a brown beret, then she puts on her 'market' headscarf, so just her face peeps out. The sun is setting and it is getting dark. I can see the streets aren't as busy as usual. I hold Mama's hand and pull myself close to her. I try to skip but she pulls my hand and tells me not to draw attention to myself. I don't know what that means either, so I walk instead. I really do not want her to take me back home just yet. She sits on a bench near the children's playground in the park and I am allowed on the swing and the slide. It is lonely without anyone else to play with. When we arrive back at the building the grumpy old lady who guards the door says something mean to Mama, but she takes no notice and talks to me about the wonderful papillon gate that we go through to get into our apartment building. She always tells me how the big iron papillon watches over us.

Papa Hans arrives just after we get back from the park. Mama makes a 'shush' sign with her finger, so I know I must not tell him about our adventure. He always has a smell about him, it is the same as his hair cream I see on the bathroom shelf. I try rubbing some on my hair, but Mama catches me and then she quickly washes my hair. He has an especially important parade tomorrow and Mama is busy polishing the shiny brass buttons on his uniform, while he polishes his high black boots. He rubs his boot brush over them many more times than I brush my hair and tells me how important it is for him to look very smart when he is on parade. Before I go to bed, he tells me that I may watch the parade from the front of our building. I hope there will be animals and clowns in the parade like I remember when I was a baby girl.

SEVEN

MENTON

Tilly's first week in Menton was a rollercoaster of learning experiences. The first being just how bad her French pronunciation was, as very few of the market-stallholders seemed to understand her. She received a lot of shoulder shrugging and, in some cases, was completely ignored. Madame was noticeably clear with her about how ripe she wanted her fruit, and how crispy she wanted her vegetables, so Tilly had to express herself to the stallholders with various hand motions.

From Tilly's view, the mood had finally lightened between the three women. She had made an immense effort to gauge their moods and observe their interests.

Over dinner at the end of her first week she believed she had nearly cracked it when they both laughed at her recall of her bad French and her day struggling with the stallholders.

'I remember when we first arrived on the Riviera, my mama used to haggle with the market people; it was one of the few places she seemed to shine. I loved being with her as she always held my hand tightly,' Madame Pollock said, then stopped mid-sentence as if the memory had floated away.

Curiosity was getting the better of Tilly. 'Where were you before Menton?'

After what seemed like an age, Madame responded. 'We were in Nice, in a small apartment until Mama managed to buy this house and before that we lived in Paris. But my memory is blurry about those days. I was such a small girl back then.' Madame dabbed her chin with the napkin, thanked Enid for the meal and went off to her bedroom.

'Some days I am worried her memory is failing and then other days she is very "how-you-say in English"? Precise,' Enid commented once they had heard Madame reach the top of the stairs.

The weekends were Tilly's free time. It was a glorious sunny morning and after she had washed and blow-dried her hair, she pulled on her bright floral dress. Then armed with her swimsuit, a towel and her new French mobile phone she tapped into Google maps and walked off in the direction of the border.

She took the shortcut through the old town, which is what they called the medieval section. The narrow streets and high buildings blocked out the sun. Bed linen hung alongside all sorts of underwear on the compact washing lines outside the small windows above her. There was a lively exchange of conversation from random balconies, which appeared to be directed at two women who sat on a step smoking as Tilly walked past. A mixture of cooking smells wafted through some of the ancient doors and Tilly tried to imagine what tasty lunches were being prepared. As she stepped out into the sunlight at the end of the main lane the view was sensational. Tilly looked down at the beach, she could see families setting up with their sun-umbrellas and deckchairs against the backdrop of the azure blue sea. A fresh thread of comfort took a small hold in Tilly's psyche. There were happy families in the world and if she worked hard enough at it, maybe she could be happy too. She whispered a whistle as she navigated the steep steps down to the promenade.

Lush green hedges bordered the apartment buildings along the promenade wafting out fragrances of jasmine and mimosa. Tilly savoured both the diverse perfumes and the Riviera colours as she walked towards Italy.

When she arrived at the border, a few Italian army guards stood on one side and a couple of disinterested French gendarmes on the other side. The flow of illegal immigrants had obviously slowed down, and they didn't appear to have much to do other than pay attention to the various young women out walking.

Just across the border Tilly spotted a sign marked Balzi Rossi beach, which pointed towards a walking track. Tucked under the cliff sat a perfectly designed outdoor restaurant perched on a smart teak deck. Small white circular tables were surrounded with white cane chairs; a colourful cocktail bar was set up at the end of the deck which was shaded by canvas sails. Out in front of the deck were several rows of white sun loungers and large summer parasols.

Tilly studied the menu on a board at the top of the steps. She gasped at the price of 25 euros to rent one of the sun loungers for the day. But then, as she observed some of glam-looking people enjoying the sun and the sea, she gave into the temptation and walked down the steps. Once she was seated on the pristine white lounger Tilly relaxed and breathed in the scent of the sea. The modular mumble of Italian and French sunbathers mingled with the faint echo of the gulls overhead and gave reassurance of how far away she had come from the ordeals of the past twelve months.

Tilly and Enid had agreed to prepare a meal together for Saturday evening. Tilly had volunteered to sort out the dessert as during her visits to the market she had spotted an impressive patisserie. On her way back from the beach she bought what appeared to be an amazing torte crowned in summer berries and picked up a bottle of Prosecco that Enid had recommended from the wine stall.

Enid and Tilly had already poured a glass when Madame arrived in the dining room. Tilly felt slightly uncomfortable as Madame stared at the half-empty bottle.

'The cooks had an early glass,' Enid stated in English, ignoring Madame's disgruntled face and filling her glass. The bubbles hit the spot, with Madame taking on a pink glow and Tilly even caught a hint of a smile as Enid placed the chilled soup of melon and ginger in front of her.

After they finished the main course of honeyed chicken

and salad, Enid refilled their glasses. Madame appeared the most relaxed Tilly had seen her since she arrived.

'Tilly, I think you may be the one person I can ask to do something special for me,' Madame said.

'What would that be?' Enid was the first to ask.

Madame didn't reply. She took another sip of her bubbles.

Tilly rose and cleared the dishes, then went into the kitchen to serve the torte. On her return she gave Enid a questioning glance. Enid raised her eyebrows back in an 'I don't know' gesture.

'Thank you both for the meal,' Madame said as she stood up. 'I will think a little more about what I may ask of you, Tilly. Have patience with an old lady. Goodnight to both of you.' She waddled out of the room and up the stairs.

'What was that all about?' Tilly asked.

'I am not quite sure, but I have seen a distinct change in her since you arrived. It coincides with her going through all her old letters and documents. I guess we will find out when she is ready.'

The first month in Menton had flown by, and day by day Tilly's repressed grief slipped slowly into the distance. She managed to grow her fingernails back, and she felt more peaceful now than she had in a long time. Her thoughts seemed clearer. Although she had been deeply in love with Giovanni, she recalled her feelings were always fraught with insecurity. He said all the right words to her but in truth he never walked the walk. On reflection, it shouldn't have been a surprise that he bolted when he knew she was pregnant.

Although Tilly had kept in touch by email with her three main girlfriends, she knew she had to address the unopened emails on her laptop from her father and Aunt Lucy. She had closed her UK mobile account, so they had no way of phoning her.

Both were asking for forgiveness and her father was offering to come and visit so he could answer any questions about her real mother. After much deliberation, Tilly replied to them both giving scant details about where she was living, and her new phone number, stating that was only to be used in an extreme emergency and if they respected this, she would either return to London in a few months' time or allow them to visit. She said she needed more time away in her new life first.

Both Enid and Madame Pollock had thawed. Activities such as accompanying Madame to the doctor and short visits to one of the several botanic gardens in Menton, where Tilly would walk slowly beside her, seemed to have woven a subtle but comfortable bond between the unlikely pair. The three women often enjoyed a game of cards together in the evenings, causing Tilly to conclude that as Madame won most of their games, she was a lot more alert than she let on.

Madame had even visited Tilly in her bedroom last week. She had taken her time to study Tilly's framed butterfly collection and a faraway smile had softened the lines on her old face. Tilly appreciated the sensitivity of connecting with the old lady. The Turret House had begun to feel how she imagined a family home should feel. It was as if Madame Pollock was a relative rather than her employer.

It had been another glorious Riviera day and after lunch Madame requested that Tilly fetch a pile of folders from her bedroom and bring them out to her in the garden. Tilly had rarely been in the large bedroom alone. The air was thick with the old lady's history. The ancient bed with its ornate ends featured the same dip in the middle as Tilly's. The requested folders were sitting on the bed. A massive armoire dominated one wall and there were two curtained-off doors on either side of the room. Tilly knew that behind one was an en suite bathroom, as she often waited outside while Madame had taken her shower. She assumed the other was a dressing room. She glanced out of the window to ensure Madame was ensconced on her cane chair below, then, unable to resist, she pulled the thick red velvet curtain across to peep inside.

The room was bigger that Tilly anticipated. It harboured a mixed bouquet of lavender and camphor and was crammed full. On one side was a rail where all of Madame's clothes were hanging, a lavender sachet accompanying each hanger. Hatboxes and old leather cases were piled on a shelf above the clothes rail. On the other side was a tall and wide chest of drawers with a selection of aged black and white photos scattered on the top in front of a crackled mirror. Tilly peered down for a closer look, careful not to move anything. The photos featured a striking-looking woman and a little girl with a very solemn face who appeared to be about seven years old. There was an ancient-looking chest beside the drawers with three or four paintings stacked against it. Tilly immediately recognised the same style as those in the hallway. The one on top of the pile featured a colourful Papilio lysander butterfly. Then she felt a sweep of betrayal as she was not normally a snoop. She quickly pulled the curtain back into place, scooped up the tatty files from the bed and joined Madame in the garden.

'Pull up that chair up and sit with me, Tilly.' Madame motioned to the chair across the lawn.

There was the expected silence for a few moments after Tilly sat down then Madame spoke. 'I believe I am "reading" you correctly young lady. You seem more comfortable now than when you first arrived. I think we may be of similar minds – not one to ask too many personal questions or offer a lot about yourself. I respect that.' Her bright blue eyes regarded Tilly intensely as she spoke.

'However, I am sure there must be something you wish to ask me. I will make an agreement with you; I will ask you just one question about yourself and then in return you may ask me just one question.' Madame paused and offered what Tilly would term an ironic smile.

'I agree. So, who goes first?'

'You do.'

'Very well then, who painted the pictures that are hung on the upstairs hallway, and did they especially like butterflies?' Tilly offered a Mona Lisa smile and leaned back in her chair.

The old lady cleared her throat. 'Well, that's actually two questions but I will honour them both. They are easy ones, my mama painted them and yes, she had a love of butterflies, well more of an obsession really. Your declaration of being a lepidopterist in your first email was what attracted me to your application for this job.'

'Thank you,' Tilly said, then added, 'She was a talented painter.'

Madame Pollock clasped her hands in front of her and cleared her throat again. 'My turn! I have had several young women come to take the position you now hold; they all appeared to be escaping something and seemed intent on burdening Enid and I with it all. At my age, I have enough troubles in my mind without paying for more. But you are different. It was a profound sense of sadness you brought with you, but you have politely kept it to yourself and whether it's the sunshine of Menton or the company of two single ladies, you seem more content now.'

Tilly was momentarily astonished. She had no idea her emotions had been so transparent. She had no idea Madame was that perceptive and could articulate in English as she had just done. Tilly nodded.

'My question isn't about why you have been sad, that is not my business, but I want to ask an added task of you that involves travel to Paris, and I just need to know that you are able to extend yourself.'

'Absolutely,' Tilly said, then hesitated, 'except you know my French is not very good.'

'I feel sure you will find a way around that.'

At that vital moment, the nosey woman from the house next door walked into the garden and called to Madame. Disappointed, Tilly left them to their chatter and went up to her room.

That evening Tilly attended her French lesson at the council-run class and afterwards grabbed a quick meal in the village. When she arrived home Madame Pollock had retired, and Enid was in the kitchen.

'Yes, she mentioned to me she had asked you to go to Paris for her but didn't say why,' Enid offered once they were seated sipping their herbal teas.

'Why didn't you ask?' Tilly queried.

'Probably the same reason you didn't; I know her well enough, that she will tell me something when she is ready.'

'I would have asked but that old bat from next door arrived, so I left them to it,' Tilly said.

'Whatever it is, it's to do with the past, and I suspect her mama. She has an odd way of going about things.'

They nattered for a while, speculating over why Madame had not asked Enid to go to Paris. They concluded that her role at the house was too important to have her absent; also, Enid had a full-time job.

The old lady spent most of the following few days in her room rummaging through her papers. Tilly was beginning to wonder if she had memory loss. She could hear her rustling around in the dressing room mumbling to herself. There were now several piles of papers and photographs on the floor in her bedroom.

Taking the bull by the horns, she knocked lightly on Madame's door. 'Can I help you with something Madame Pollock? This looks like a lot of work.'

The old lady glanced up from where she sat in the armchair by the window. 'Eventually you will be able to help me, but first I must make this passage through the past, it's all in here somewhere. I must find what you will need for the Paris trip; please have patience with me.' Then she looked away and resumed reading the faded paper she held in her hand.

EIGHT

PARIS, 1944

Mama and Papa Hans are up so early my eyes are full of sleepy dust, and it's still dark when I hear the mumblings of their voices. When I join them in the kitchen, Mama is shining the silver buttons on his cap. Papa Hans has his jacket on and looks important. He is standing over her, watching and pacing by the table. Mama tells me again, even though I already know, that it is a very special parade day for Papa Hans. I ask if we will be standing down on the street to watch and wave our flags, Papa Hans snaps at me. He does not usually raise his voice, but Mama says it's his nerves, he doesn't really mean it. He says that I am too small and will feel unsafe on the street; but that we can watch from just inside the big doorway to our building. I can hear the band playing the song of the Germans and all the people are gathering on the street carrying flags.

I wish I had a flag, but I hear Papa Hans say to Mama it will be best that we do not draw attention to ourselves. I don't know what that means, but whatever it is I can only wave my hand at the parade, not a flag.

Mama and I watch as the tall straight soldiers lead the parade, sitting high up on big black horses, their shiny helmets have long feather pompoms on the top. Next, come rows and rows of foot soldiers lifting their legs straight out in front of them as they march. They looked silly and they make me giggle. Mama giggles a little as well and tells me it is called a 'goose step'. I've never seen any geese in the park walk like that.

Next, the big long shiny black cars drive by; I can see Papa Hans sitting next to the driver in the first car. He never looks across at us even once; he just looks straight ahead at the flag fluttering on the front of his car. I wait for ages for the animals and clowns. In my story book parades always have interesting animals. No animals show up. The parade is over quickly and the people on the street stop waving flags and all leave. Mama pulls me quickly back inside the butterfly gate. The horrid old woman who guards the gate from her apartment is just beside us, she sees us and I feel Mama's hand tighten on mine. The horrible woman says something I don't understand as we scurry past.

Back up in our home, Mama flops down on the big squashy sofa. Above her on the wall is the painting of a rather grumpy-looking woman. Mama agrees with me that she does look grumpy like the old lady downstairs, but says she was my great grandmama and 'it was just her way' – whatever that means.

Sometimes that happens – Mama will be looking at me in a funny way then her eyes will go all wet and I am sure she must be crying. I know because I am good at crying. But she tells me it was just that her eyes are sore. She tells me to go and play in my room. It is a wonderful room and I have a big brightly painted rocking horse, except its tail is missing some of its hair. When I was five, I suppose I really loved the horse, but now I have become quite a big girl, I am nearly seven. I am too old for a rocking horse.

When Papa Hans comes home, they think I am asleep, but I sneak to the door of the living room and hear them talking. Mama says she is frightened by the old lady guard of the gate. I hear Papa Hans say he has paid her double this month so she will keep her mouth shut. I had a double ice cream once, but I don't really understand why he would pay her, even once.

NINE

MENTON

Tilly had almost given up on Madame Pollock's suggestion that she go to Paris, when, a week later, Madame arrived at the dinner table with an old discoloured green folder. Once dinner was over the old lady ceremoniously dabbed her mouth with the cloth napkin, then picked up the folder and cleared her throat.

'I am not going to apologise for taking my time about this; as I am old it is my prerogative to do things in my own time, and my own way. I am going to tell you why I would like Tilly to visit Paris for me.' She stopped short again. Both younger women sat wide-eyed as Madame cleared her throat yet again and fingered the folder.

'I lived with my mama in an apartment in Paris during the war; I have limited memory about it or about the man I called Papa Hans; I'm not even sure he was my papa. He left us and we moved to Nice when I was about seven or eight years old; and as far as I know my mama never returned to Paris. She never spoke of Papa Hans again. It wasn't until she was on her deathbed that she gave me what I assume is the address of the apartment, as well as an entire trunk of papers and photographs of me growing up .My husband dealt with everything to do with my mama's will, but there was definitely no mention of an apartment. I want to find that apartment and try to understand more about what happened back then. This is all I have.' The folder had one piece of paper with scrawled handwriting on it. 'I would like you to go off to Paris and find it.' She pushed the folder towards Tilly. 'I realise you won't be able to read the French very well, but Enid can help you and from what I have seen you do, twiddling on your computers, you should be able to find a way to locate the apartment and discover what has happened to it.' Madame let out a big sigh, then slowly stood up and left the room.

Enid and Tilly stared at the folder.

Enid reached across first and read it. 'What does it say?' Tilly asked.

'It's just the address of what I assume is an apartment in Paris. Then after that it says I bequeath my apartment to my daughter Corrinne Estienne Pollock.' Enid looked thoughtfully at the document.

'So, technically the apartment belongs to Madame Pollock?' Tilly felt energised.

'Yes, but I am no expert. I am sure we will need more proof than an old letter from a mother to her daughter written in 1970. Maybe a family has been renting it all this time and under French laws the tenants have all the rights so it may be quite complicated. Once you have been to Paris you can see where it is and who lives there,' Enid replied with equal enthusiasm.

'I really would prefer you come with me, Enid; with my limited French it's going to be difficult.'

'I wish I could as well, but if Madame had wanted that, she would have said so; it took her long enough to instruct you. She will not be alone in the house for any length of time or with someone she has no confidence in. So, I must stay,' Enid said and then added, 'You are proficient now with your French mobile, you can text and call me as you go along, if you get into difficulty, and besides most people in Paris speak some English.'

Later in her bedroom, Tilly's mind raced; how she would approach this? As she looked closer at the paper, she was amazed to see the building was called 'Maison Papillon'. She typed the full address into Google. Scrolling down she came across a historic reference and a photograph of the building's entrance. Maison Papillon had been completed in 1870 by during Baron Haussmann final year as Prefect. The baron's controversial, extravagant, architectural vision for Paris revolutionised the structure of the city. It originally had a different name. Then in 1900 what was deemed a more modern decorative entrance was created – a tall elaborate art nouveau-style gate beside the concierge's door which led to the courtyard of the building.

Tilly was intrigued. She clicked on the old black and white photo and enlarged it on her screen. A dumpy-looking woman wearing a smock stood scowling at the camera; she appeared dwarfed by the extravagant gate behind her. The caption read 'Madame La Croix concierge of Maison Papillon 1930 to 1950'.

Tilly's heart bounced. As the pixels evened out she could clearly see a large butterfly gate, skilfully worked in wrought iron and what she assumed was enamel, that had been created as the wonderful gated entrance to the building. The copy didn't give any history of the artist who created the gate, but mentioned some of the well-known people who lived there prior to the 1960s.

The following morning, once she had completed all her errands for Madame, Tilly took her laptop to the dining room table where the light was better and, navigating with Google maps, she moved around Paris.

'I am fascinated what you can do on that computer,' Madame said as she appeared in the dining room.

Tilly was taken aback: the old lady usually napped at this time of day.

'I'm sorry, Madame. Do you need me for something? I am just looking at where your apartment building is in Paris.'

'Oh really? Can you do that? Please show me.'

Tilly pulled up a chair beside her own at the table. She went into Google Earth and typed in the address of Maison Papillon. Madame's blue eyes widened in disbelief as Tilly surfed the curser down above the Paris streets.

'I will need to find out who lives in your apartment now and then maybe we will need to obtain legal advice about possession,' Tilly said.

'I don't actually think of the apartment as mine – it was always Mama's; she never really talked about it once we left Paris. I understand the war did strange things to people, but in her last months she talked a lot about things that didn't make sense to me; but now I am getting old, I feel I need to know.' As the old woman spoke Tilly could see a fresh enthusiasm in her face, she was even walking straighter than usual; it was as if she had gained a new sense of purpose.

Tilly showed her the article on the building and enlarged the photo of the butterfly gate. Madame took a few moments to register it, then her eyes welled up and a large tear trickled down her cheek.

'My mama adored butterflies and I remember her passion for that gate; she loved it. Now I think back she also talked about it to distract me from the concierge who was always rude to us.'

Tilly read the article out loud in English. It was about the history of the building, mainly around the time it was built under Napoleon III and included a reference to the butterfly gate being added 30 years later. There were a few lines about Jews being thrown out of their apartments during the Nazi occupation when a lot were sent off to Drancy, the internment camp. Madame listened intently but said nothing.

'Would you like me to look up some photos from that time in Paris?' Tilly asked.

Madame nodded.

Tilly clicked on a site that brought up some rare colour photos from 1942 in Paris. She enlarged them; the old lady was transfixed. She appeared to be totally immersed in the time and place on the screen. Tilly slowly moved on to the next photo giving Madame time to absorb the details. In one shot a well-dressed woman sported a whole fox fur slung over her neatly tailored jacket. Another shot featured a group of older men with thick grey moustaches that lorded over their mouths. They wore cloth caps that were positioned low above their eyes and sat in a circle playing cards. The background feature of both of these photos was the presence of German soldiers in immaculate uniforms.

There was a wonderful shot of a circus; it had been hand-coloured so it stood out. It was titled *Cirque d'Hiver*.

'Oh! I went there! I remember that!' Madame declared. She didn't offer any more comment, so Tilly moved on.

The next photo was a shot of a German military parade; the photographer had captured the essence of it with what must have been an exceptional camera for that time. The soldiers' boots gleamed in the sun, their free arms in full swing with their other arms tightly clutching their polished rifles. Tilly could clearly see that Madame's expression had changed from reminisce to distress as another big tear ran down her cheek and she clutched at the collar of her dress. Tilly minimised the screen and put her arm around the old woman. It was the first time she had ever touched her. For just a short moment the old lady leaned her head on Tilly's shoulder. Then she sat up, took her handkerchief from her cuff and blew her nose. 'I am sorry Tilly – I am struggling with memories I can't quite get into focus. I was about seven when we left Paris and Mama forbade me to speak about what I had seen so I must have blanked it out; but now I have a compelling need to remember.' Madame stood up. 'The photographs seem to have unearthed things that had been tucked away. I think I will go and have a nap now.' Her eyes glazed over as she left the room.

TEN

PARIS, 1944

I have been so excited as Papa Hans is taking me to a circus. I can't remember ever going before, but Mama says I did when I was a little girl. Mama isn't coming with us, which I was sad about this for a little while, but Papa Hans holds my hand and as I haven't been out of our apartment for ages, I can't wait.

Mama puts one of her berets on my head; it is a bit big, but it matches the new navy coat Papa Hans has brought home for me. I like my red beret best, but he tells Mama it will stand out – whatever that means – so, I wear her dull, navy one instead. Both Mama and Papa tell me I mustn't speak to any of Papa Hans's work friends, they say they will all be in uniforms like his and if they talk to me, I must only smile back; not talk. They say this to me about five times.

Mama has wet eyes when we leave; she is such a silly billy sometimes – circuses are for children, she knows that. We go in the back of a big shiny black car that a man with a pointy moustache drives. Papa Hans talks to the man in a strange language; Mama has told me, Papa Hans is from Germany, so I think he is talking that language. But I stay very quiet. We arrive at a big round building with a sign saying 'Cirque d'Hiver'; we walk through two tall iron gates and on to a red carpet. How funny, to have a carpet outside. Inside we walk up lots of steps; I sit next to Papa Hans and another man in a uniform like Papa Hans sits on the other side of me. He has a boy with him who looks a bit bigger than me. But I know I must not talk to them, so I look straight ahead.

Oh, it is all so magical! First, a man comes out in the brightest red suit and cap and makes loud announcements. Then next, a whole row of white horses; I count six of them – they walk backwards and do things all in a line at the same time. But then, my favourite – the clowns. They are so funny even Papa Hans laughs. Then, after that I watch a lady swinging from high up near the ceiling. I grab Papa Hans's hand I feel so scared she will fall. He tells me she is called a 'trapeze artist' and she practises a lot so she won't fall. Then, the best of the circus is last – two tigers. They are like big stripy cats and I love looking at them. But I am pleased we are not in the front row as that would scare me; I am safe up in the stand. It is all over too soon. Papa Hans seems to be in a hurry to get me back to the shiny car, he pulls my hand a little too hard. Another man stops him and bends down and talks to me in the same funny language. But I do not talk, I just smile like Mama said. Then we walk out to the car.

ELEVEN

MENTON

After their interlude at the computer, Tilly was more aware
of Madame's vulnerability. She had caught a glimpse of
the child, the teenager and the wife she would have been.
It occurred to Tilly how much she now identified with
Madame Pollock's pain; how terrible it must have been
for her to grow up without a father, to have lost memories
of the Occupation during the war in Paris. Madame
harboured this furtive need to rediscover her heritage, and
clearly believed the Paris apartment would return some
of her early memories. Tilly felt valued; it was as if this
intriguing old woman had chosen her to be the guardian
of her quest. Tilly reflected how eventually she would
have to face her own mystery mother's background. But
not just yet.

She talked through her plans for Paris with Enid. They

agreed in the first instance that she should visit Maison Papillon to see if she could gain entry and find out who lived there now. If she was unable to achieve that, she would visit the Pavillon de l'Arsenal where building plans of Paris were stored. They had sourced online the name of a law firm who specialised in historic property law and she would make an appointment with one of their solicitors. The law firm's website stated they worked in both French and English and Madame agreed to the quoted hourly charges.

'I enjoyed the train trip here, but you are right, Enid, the easyJet flight is not only cheaper, it's faster if I go to Orly airport,' Tilly chatted as she surfed the net for some affordable accommodation near Maison Papillon.

'I've booked four nights through this Airbnb site as I can get an entire studio for less cost than a cheap hotel.'

'You keep your mobile with you at all times and call me if you don't understand anything.'

'I'll be OK. I can always type out what I need to say on my phone then hit Google Translate and show it, rather than try to speak it with my dreadful French.' They laughed; Tilly's bad French accent was a daily joke with her new friends.

A week later, as Enid pulled up at the departure terminal, Tilly's bravado had begun to wane. She hesitantly kissed Enid goodbye and as she was already checked in online and only had a wheelie bag, she went straight to the security check. Away from her new home and the daily rhythms of Madame and Enid, Tilly's insecurities came flooding back. There was a thirty-minute delay in the flight before they were seated on the plane. A woman with a small baby arrived to sit in the seat beside her; she was struggling with the front-pack that the baby was cocooned in. It took all Tilly's strength not to walk away, but there were no other seats and it would have looked like a snub.

Once the woman had the baby out of the front-pack she took a bottle from her bag. She gently rocked her precious bundle as she offered the bottle to the wriggling baby who immediately latched on and with obvious delight made enjoyable sucking sounds.

Tilly couldn't hold back; the emotion overwhelmed her. She wrestled for a tissue from the side-pocket of her bag as she left her seat for the toilet. Once inside the cubicle she sat and let the tears flow.

The speaker system called for everyone to return to their seats. She had no option. As she sat back down, her emotions seemed finally under control, and she managed to return the cute baby's gazes with an appreciative smile and made small talk with the mother.

On arrival into Paris, Tilly's taxi arrived outside the address of her rented studio. It was a pleasant street but a very weary looking building. There was no concierge. Tilly pressed the first of the door codes she had received by text from Airbnb. It took a big shove to open the heavy wooden door. Once inside the unremarkable foyer it became apparent there was no lift. It was a steep hike up the four floors of narrow winding staircase until she finally came to the door she was looking for. She referred to the second code she was given, punched it in and entered a tiny but tidy bright studio apartment with a great view over the Parisian rooftops.

It was only early afternoon so with her Google map pulled up on her phone she went back down the four flights of stairs to find Maison Papillon.

At the end of her very narrow street with its tall slim buildings, she turned into Rue Brocit, a very wide boulevard with large square buildings – distinctly Haussmann architecture. Looking at Paris through the eyes of her recent research she could see what a difference Haussmann had made to what would otherwise have been a very cluttered city. Google told her to turn left. Rue Dout was a more discreet street with just enough room for two-way traffic and leafy trees softening the building façades that offered shade to her walk.

It was a little confusing as some of the building numbers weren't obvious, so after three laps of the street Tilly worked out the number sequence and finally found number 22. As with many Parisian buildings there were two giant wooden doors safeguarding and hiding whatever lay behind them. Tilly pushed the buzzer, and there was an immediate click; she pushed the tall door open and stepped into a paved space. It was very clear she had arrived at the correct building because the butterfly gate was directly in front of her. It stood about three metres tall, and as if by heavenly appointment it heralded the courtyard beyond. Although sculpted from heavy wrought iron, the butterfly appeared ethereal with its classic art nouveau lines and dabs of red and turquoise enamelling to authenticate its provenance. There were apartments on all three sides looking into the courtyard.

Tilly's eyes then moved to the glass-fronted door to

the side of the butterfly gate; it was swathed on the inside with dated lace curtains, the type that twitch in domestic neighbourhoods. Located at eye-level there was a highly polished brass sign saying 'Concierge' with a plastic buzzer beside it.

After savouring the majesty of the gate for a few more moments, she stepped forward and pressed the buzzer. The door was immediately opened by an old, small stout woman with short grey hair, wearing a green work smock. Tilly's eyes rested on a large black mole beside the woman's mouth.

The woman glared at Tilly.

'*Oui?*' she said in a raspy voice that sounded like it'd been dry-cured by years of unfiltered French cigarettes.

Tilly referred to her prepared translating notes; she took a large gulp before delivering her rehearsed French.

'Bonjour, désolée je ne parle pas français. Je cherche une amie pour l'appartement 59. Elle en a hérité. J'ai les papiers légaux ici. Merci.'

The woman swiftly replied, her voice raised a notch; the black mole quivering as she barked.

'Il n'y a pas de numéro 59. Vous avez le mauvais bâtiment. Au revoir.'

Then she abruptly closed the door.

Tilly's heart was thumping; she felt so frustrated. What was her comeback now?

She dialled Enid's mobile number. It seemed an age before she answered.

'Tilly, what's happening?'

'The concierge is an old dragon who told me there is no

number 59 in the building and then slammed the door in my face. I feel a bit useless.'

'Hmm. OK. So, knock on the door again; keep me on the line and hand her the phone.'

Tilly stepped up to the door again and pressed the buzzer. This time there was no immediate reply.

'She's not answering, Enid!'

'Press the bell for a long ring this time. I know this type of woman; if you aggravate her, she won't be able to help herself – she will open the door to tell you off.'

Tilly held her finger on the buzzer.

The old woman whipped the door open and hurled a string of abuse at Tilly.

Tilly handed her the phone. The concierge flung her hand up and flicked it, clearly indicating a 'no go' situation.

Tilly could hear Enid call out, 'Hold your ground, Tilly, put the phone in her hand!'

Tilly stepped right up beside the old woman and pushed the phone in her hand. The woman reluctantly put it to her ear. Enid spoke in rapid fire French with the old woman barking what sounded like orders back at her.

She then thrust the phone back to Tilly and stormed inside, slamming the door.

'So, tell me all?' Tilly said as she stepped into the shadow of the wonderful gate.

'She told me the numbers of the apartments don't run numerically as the building is old and things have changed over the years as some apartments have been combined into one. The old witch has been the concierge at Maison Papillon for forty-five years, as was her mother and grandmother before her. She told me she has never known a number 59. I asked if you could go in and have a look and she said absolutely not. She is ignorant and won't be any help. I think now we need to go to phase two and perhaps visit Pavillon de l'Arsenal and see if you can do some sort of building search,' Enid explained, then told Tilly that she must get back to work; best to call her that evening.

Tilly took a photo of the impressive butterfly gate and peered in between the bars and took another of the courtyard and the entrance to the building beyond.

Once back in her apartment she checked the opening hours for the Pavillon de l'Arsenal and realised her visit would need to wait until tomorrow.

TWELVE

With an evening to herself in Paris, Tilly decided to visit the Left Bank and do the tourist thing. Recalling her recent French lesson, she was intrigued to discover the Left Bank in French is La Rive Gauche – she had always assumed that was just a name for a YSL perfume.

Once happily snug in the corner of a busy, cheap brasserie, mainly populated with students, Tilly's reflections had shifted to the new events of her life: her new home in Menton, the feeling of contentment with her relationship with Madame Pollock and Enid. Her deliberations were interrupted by the handsome smiling waiter delivering her steak and frites. As Tilly eyed his attractive physique via his tight black jeans and beautifully fitted T-shirt, for the first time in months a flutter of lust passed through her body.

'I must be on the mend, with thoughts like that!' she muttered to herself as she tucked into her steak.

The following morning, Tilly took the Métro and exited at the Sully-Morland station. The Pavillon de l'Arsenal opened at 10 a.m. and she was keen to beat the queues. When she found the relevant department, the first assistant handed her to another who spoke English. Tilly explained her quest. The woman she was addressing wore an extremely conservative navy dress, her hair was tied back tight in a severe ponytail and she wore oversized Harry Potter spectacles. She showed no expression as she listened without interrupting. Once Tilly had finished, she handed Tilly a form and stated: 'All requests for building plans must be applied for in writing and paid for in advance. We will notify you by email, informing you if we have the plans and how long it will take to deliver them; this may take up to six weeks. Thank you.'

The assistant dismissed her then moved on to the next customer.

Irritated, Tilly moved over to a bench with a chair and began to trawl her way through the French document, filling in what she could. She dropped her pen muttering 'shit' under her breath. Suddenly she was aware of a presence beside her.

'May I help you?' he said in charming accented English.

The first aspect of this man Tilly noticed was that his faded blue jeans were pressed with a crease in the middle. He wore an immaculate white cotton button-down shirt and brown brogues – a little like her father's but far more European. His hair was a tad long to be fashionable, his eyes were framed in silver wire-rimmed spectacles and he smelt nice.

'I do apologise, I should have introduced myself. I am Jean-Luc but my friends call me JL. I work here and noticed that this form may be a challenge for you?' As he spoke his subtle lisp added to the charm of his French-accented English.

Tilly blushed.

'Thank you, I am Matilda, but please call me Tilly. I can probably fill it in OK; I was just getting frustrated at how long the process may take as the friend I am acting for is over eighty years old and not in great health.' She offered Jean-Luc a smile.

'Well, I may be able to help speed the process along. We are keen to offer good service here. My role is more with architecture, but I have a friend in the department you require. Perhaps tell me what you need to achieve?'

He sounded hesitant, but Tilly felt flattered he was trying his best to be confident and she needed all the help she could get.

She found herself not only telling him about Madame Pollock and the apartment but revealing where she lived and her job. He listened silently and nodded occasionally. When she finally stopped for a breather, there was an elongated pause; Tilly was patient, assuming he was thinking through his English.

He cleared his throat. 'I suggest you finish filling in the document and give it to me; I would be happy to help you.' He moved awkwardly from one foot to the other as he spoke.

Tilly completed the form with all Madame Pollock's details, her late mother's details, the address of the apartment, and then feeling assertive, wrote her own mobile phone number down before handing the paper to Jean-Luc.

'I have written my phone number there; I am here in Paris for a couple of days. Perhaps you could send me a quick text when it's complete and I'll come back and collect it; I realise you must be very busy.'

Tilly noticed a slight tremor in his hand as he took the form.

'I am sorry I can't be of more help right now, but I must return to my office. It's been a pleasure to meet you.' A tiny bead of sweat had manifested on Jean-Luc's upper lip as he spoke.

He reached out and shook Tilly's hand.

'Thank you! I hope I hear from you soon,' she said as they parted.

Tilly returned to her apartment and, as it was the lunch hour, she figured it was an appropriate time to call Enid with an update.

After sharing the details of her visit to the Pavillon de l'Arsenal, Enid was quick to pick up the change in Tilly's tone when she mentioned the helpful chap Jean-Luc.

'He sounds nice, was he handsome?'

'I didn't notice!'

'Oh Tilly! I've known you long enough now to "hear" a smile in your voice.' Enid laughed.

'Well yes, he was attractive in a nervous French sort of way. I am not sure if I should change my flight to tomorrow or wait it out a couple of days and see if he comes back with any information.'

'You have paid for two more nights' accommodation, so you might as well stay, as I don't think it is worth contacting the lawyer until you have the information on what apartments exist in the building. And besides they will have to go through the same search method and charge Madame for doing it.' Enid had to cut the conversation short as her boss was calling to her.

Tilly wandered around the area near her apartment and found a café that offered an array of pastries. She chose a caramel éclair and took an outdoor table to enjoy her coffee and cake, with a view of the passing Parisians and tourists. She was looking at Maison Papillon on Google when her phone lit up with an incoming call from a number she didn't recognise.

'*Bonjour* Tilly?'

'Oh hello! This is Tilly.'

'*Bonjour* this is Jean-Luc.' He paused.

'Hello there?' Tilly responded to the silence and checked her watch, surprised to see it was already 4 p.m.

'Uumm, I found some information about "Maison Papillon" and uumm, wondered if perhaps you were available this evening to meet me?' he stammered.

Tilly took a deep breath, before responding.

'Yes, I would love to meet with you,' she said, then taking the initiative, she added, 'Would you allow me to buy you dinner for being so helpful?'

Once again, a silence on the end of the phone.

'Oh my! Yes, that would be wonderful, uumm having dinner with you but as you are a visitor in Paris I couldn't possibly allow you to pay.'

Tilly gave him her address and they agreed they would meet outside the main door at 7.30 p.m.

Tilly practically skipped back to her apartment. Thank goodness she had squashed her 'no-ironing-needed' little black dress into her bag as well as her heeled sandals. This was a date!

After she had showered, washed and carefully blow-dried her hair, Tilly closely inspected her face in the mirror. She looked like a different woman than the one who left London. The eyes that glistened back at her from the mirror were full of joy and anticipation. She no longer felt diminished to the shadows. It was now over six months since she had originally arrived in Paris, her French had improved and so much had happened.

Thanks to the initial conspiracy with Aunt Lucy, this completely new life in France suited her well. She had managed her grief and had become to come to terms with the loss of her baby. Previously, just thinking about that had invoked fear and shame. She had long forgiven Giovanni. There were even stirrings of forgiveness towards her father for a lifetime of hiding the truth about her mother. And tonight, she had a date! He was no 'beef steak' like the waiter from the previous evening, but he had something about him that she couldn't quite define.

Jean-Luc was waiting at the entrance door when Tilly arrived downstairs. She was five minutes early, so she was impressed by his enthusiasm.

'*Bonsoir* Tilly,' he said and then quickly averted his eyes towards the roll of paper he had tucked firmly under his arm.

'He's nervous,' Tilly thought.

'*Bonsoir* Jean-Luc.'

'Uumm, I have booked a table in a small restaurant not far from here, if that pleases you?'

Tilly smiled at his precise use of the English language.

'It pleases me very well, thank you,' she replied as she stepped in beside him on the footpath.

Jean-Luc offered very little conversation as they walked. This gave Tilly the opportunity to study her date. He wore what she suspected were his trademark trousers the immaculately ironed blue jeans, this time with navy suede loafers – she assumed they were Gucci – and he sported a navy blazer over his crisp white shirt. He was definitely the most conservative dresser she had ever dated.

To Tilly's English eye, the ambience of the restaurant was what she would term 'traditional Parisian'. Distinguished in its faded glory, with well-worn wooden floors, individual seating booths that could sit up to four people, crisply starched white linen tablecloths. However, very disconcerting for Tilly, there was an abundance of bevelled mirrors adorning the walls.

The maître d', sporting a giant moustache which appeared mismatched with his roughly shaved head, greeted Jean-Luc with warm familiarity. He pulled him into his ample chest and loudly kissed each of his cheeks, before standing back to appreciate Tilly.

'This is Tilly, she is English. Tilly, this is Klute – the owner,' Jean-Luc managed to say before Klute started again.

'You are such a beautiful Anglaise woman! Welcome to

L'Auberge Bressane,' Klute rapidly replied in English as he took Tilly's hand and gently kissed it.

Tilly blushed brighter than a bowl of raspberries and Jean-Luc stepped towards her and reassuringly patted her back urging her to their reserved booth.

'He is a wonderful host, but a little overwhelming at times,' Jean-Luc said as they nestled into the deep-buttoned green velvet banquette.

Tilly smiled. 'That's OK, I'd much rather a happy host, than a grumpy one; now tell me what is great to eat here?'

Jean-Luc placed his rolled-up document on the seat between them and appeared to relax as he picked up the menu and began to explain it to Tilly.

As the L'Auberge Bressane specialised in soufflés, Tilly ordered both of her host's recommendations: cheese soufflé with a side salad as a main and a chocolate soufflé for dessert.

Once the wine had been poured, Jean-Luc cleared his throat, which Tilly had deduced was his preparation to say something of importance.

'I spoke with my colleague whose department contains some of the original plans from the buildings of Georges-Eugène Haussmann's time as city designer. Maison Papillon was completed in 1870 and the elaborate papillon gate was added around 30 years later. There were notes in the file that stated one of the residents had commissioned it, and, as the Haussmann establishment didn't approve of the art nouveau design, the residents paid to have it made and installed.'

Jean-Luc then cleared the side of their table and

proceeded to unroll the plans. He anchored down each end with the heavy glass salt and pepper shakers.

'This is a copy of the original plan – we reduced it down; it doesn't show specific numbered apartments, but this is the original configuration. Over the last 100 years people have extended their apartments, by purchasing the next door one and then sometimes dividing them up again in different configurations, to sell off as smaller spaces. I couldn't gain access to the latest blueprint for any alterations.' He paused and looked at Tilly.

'So which floor would you think number 59 would be on?'

'Well, logic would tell us the fifth floor – which is the second from the top. The very top floor had small box rooms for storage and for maids' quarters.' Jean-Luc ran his finger to the fifth floor.

Tilly counted six apartments on every floor on each of the three sides of the courtyard.

'What I need to provide you with next is the list of original owners as well as the owners since then. This may take a couple of weeks,' Jean-Luc said and then cleared his throat.

'Oh, that would be great! That's weeks earlier than indicated by the woman I spoke to at the desk yesterday,' Tilly replied.

The waiter appeared at the table holding two magnificent soufflés – they appeared as fragrant, heavenly 'clouds' of temptation.

Jean-Luc rolled up the plans and placed them back on the seat.

'A perfect soufflé will stand up for a minimum of four minutes from the time it leaves the oven,' Jean-Luc announced.

Tilly watched as he dug his knife into the soufflé expelling the air and causing the supple rich velvety cheese to run out; she followed his lead. The sophisticated soufflés had a subtle but delicious taste, with hints of fresh thyme and rosemary accompanying the flow of the cheese.

'I am pleased to see you enjoy food like a French person!' Jean-Luc said with the first relaxed smile Tilly had seen since they met.

'This is so good! The best I have ever tasted.' She smiled back.

'Wait until you taste the dessert!' he replied, then popped another fork of soufflé into his mouth.

After the second glass of wine, they both loosened up. Between courses Tilly shared some of her previous life. She told him about her passion for lepidopterology, and how coincidently Madame Pollock's mother, from whom she had inherited the apartment, loved to paint butterflies. She was less candid as to why she had left London – she said she wished to learn a new language and have an adventure.

Jean-Luc told her he was a qualified architect and that his parents had put enormous pressure on him to work in a company designing buildings or houses. He admitted not only to a lack of confidence with this, but that his passion was in 'old buildings' and the study of architecture. So, he was grateful to have the position at the Pavillon de l'Arsenal as it gave him access to Paris's architectural mysteries and secrets. As he relaxed his lisp was less noticeable.

The waiter carefully carried out the chocolate soufflé desserts; he was followed closely by Klute who held two glasses of champagne and placed them in front of the couple.

'On the house! To celebrate the beautiful Anglaise Tilly's first visit to my restaurant!'

They dipped their forks into the fragrant chocolate clouds and Tilly was in heaven as the delicate chocolate oozed on to her plate and she savoured the divine taste.

'You must eat here often to get such brilliant treatment!' Tilly said as she sipped the last of the chilled bubbles.

'Well, it's my parents! They have been returning here on a weekly basis for twenty years. I have often come with them. I was nervous about trying anywhere new with you as I would never wish you to be disappointed.'

'Are you generally nervous?' Tilly probed.

'Is it the wrong English word?' Jean-Luc said with a worried look.

'No, not at all; I understand. I have felt insecure most of my life; like I didn't match up to my mother's expectation. It's only in the past six months I am feeling any confidence at all about myself.'

Jean-Luc looked at her without responding.

It didn't seem long before they had finished a second glass of champagne and declined the coffee. Klute made another big fuss of saying goodnight.

'Shall we walk through the park? It's such a beautiful evening,' Jean-Luc said, offering Tilly his arm. She slipped her arm through his and enjoyed the ripple of warmth as they connected.

'You were very frank with me, back in the restaurant about your insecurity and your mother. I find people… maybe it's just the French don't often say what they feel. I really appreciate it.' Jean-Luc spoke so softly Tilly strained to hear him.

They arrived at the park. He pushed the low gate open.

'If I hadn't had the wine and champagne, I may not have said anything!' Tilly laughed.

The moon was high and illuminated the small fountain that centred the park.

'Look, I am sure the architect who designed this park knew the moon would shine on this bench at precisely this time for us to sit on!' Jean-Luc took Tilly's hand and they sat down on the ancient wooden seat spot-lit by a beam of moonshine.

'Is your mother very critical of you?' Jean-Luc asked.

Tilly was a little taken back but answered. 'That is an understatement! I think she is mentally ill. She is my stepmother, but I only just found that out.' The second she had said the words, she regretted it. What would he think of her?

Jean-Luc stroked her hand.

'I understand family drama and disappointments. I have overheard my mother telling all her friends that I'm on "the spectrum". She is so disappointed I haven't achieved like my sister.'

Tilly was wide-eyed.

He continued, 'I am obsessive about some things

like ironing and the neatness of my clothes. I went to a therapist that cost my parents a fortune. It didn't really help, other than to understand this is who I am, and now I have learned to accept myself.'

'Wow! That's a lot to say on a first date!' Tilly leaned over and brushed his cheek with her lips.

Jean-Luc smiled. 'I am very pleased you said the word "date" as I was concerned you just thought I was only here to help you with Madame Pollock's quest.'

As they walked, he put his arm around Tilly and left it there until they had arrived at the door.

'May I ask you something before we say goodnight?' Jean-Luc said, looking directly at Tilly.

She nodded.

'Do you have a boyfriend?'

She shook her head.

'Great! Then will you come out again with me tomorrow?'

Then he handed her the building plan.

Tilly raised her eyebrows, nodded a 'yes', leaned across and kissed him, said 'goodnight', then walked into her building.

THIRTEEN

Tilly floated up the stairs. Jean-Luc had stirred something within her; she identified with his damage, with his battle to please his mother. For the previous twelve months, before arriving in France, Tilly hadn't been living – she had been existing. Meeting this awkward Frenchman offered her a new sense of comfort. The next morning, Tilly could hear her mobile phone ringing in the other room. Rushing out of the shower without a towel, she grabbed the phone.

'*Bonjour* Tilly, this is JL. Did you sleep well?'

A shiver of pleasure shot through Tilly's naked body.

'Brilliantly! And thank you so much for dinner last night; it was great.'

'Would you join me again this evening? I may have some more information on Maison Papillon by then.' He sounded hesitant, but Tilly understood the signs now.

'I would be delighted; shall I meet you at my door at the same time as last night?'

'Yes, and Tilly I have a more casual idea for this evening so perhaps you would be more comfortable in a pair of slacks.'

It was all Tilly could do to suppress her laughter as she said goodbye and clicked off the phone. 'Who calls jeans, slacks nowadays!' She laughed aloud as she returned to the bathroom to get dressed.

Tilly treated herself to a leisurely coffee and croissant, sitting at the pavement table of a busy brasserie. She unrolled the building plan Jean-Luc had given her and studied each floor with a less distracted eye than the previous evening, then headed off in the direction of Maison Papillon.

She stood across the street from the building and counted to the fifth floor, then worked her way across from one side towards the other, studying the window configuration. She needed to get inside the courtyard beyond the butterfly gate to compare the other configurations. As much as Tilly wanted to gain entry inside, she was reluctant to have another encounter with the old concierge until she had more proof of Madame's claim. She took a few more snaps on her camera so she could compare them once she was at her laptop. Then, unnoticed, she observed the old lady leave her apartment and waddle down the street with her grocery cart.

Tilly rushed across the road. She pushed the tall outer door – it opened! Then just as she was about to take a photo through the butterfly gate, a middle-aged man came towards her from the courtyard. Tilly quickly put her phone in her bag and pretended to look for her keys.

'*Bonjour*,' she said and offered what she believed was her sexiest smile as the man opened the gate.

'*Bonjour*,' he replied and held the gate as she walked in.

Tilly's heart pounded; finally she was inside the courtyard! It was beautifully manicured, edged with neatly clipped hedging, and with several large potted palms placed to give a softness to the cobbles that covered the ground. On each of the three surrounding sides looking into the courtyard were elegant green doors – the entrances to the three separate buildings. Tilly tried the first door, which was locked; the security was good. She would need a key to gain entry. She looked up and photographed each of the buildings, ensuring she captured all six floors in her shots. She was gathering her confidence, so decided to attempt her previous deception of looking for her key in her bag. She waited near the door, for what seemed an age, for someone to enter or leave the building. But then she heard the raspy French tones of the old concierge across the courtyard. Tilly panicked. What if the old bag called the police? The concierge was chatting to a tall refined woman who appeared to be on her way into the courtyard. Tilly needed to get as close to the gate as she could, so she could slip out when the elegant woman entered. As the old lady turned her back to unlock her own door the tall lady opened the gate. Tilly seized the moment and rushed past, murmuring a '*Merci*' as she passed. She wasn't sure if the concierge saw or heard her. She didn't wait to find out. Adrenaline pumping, she legged it up the street and, once out of view, stopped, clutching her side and laughing aloud.

Back at the apartment Tilly reasoned, after her James Bond-style attempt to enter the building, there wasn't a lot more she could accomplish with her Maison Papillon quest, until she met with Jean-Luc. She decided it was time to indulge in some 'me' time.

Tilly's mission was to visit Deyrolle, a unique Parisian taxidermy store; it had been around since 1831 and its website boasted an impressive butterfly collection.

It was a joy to stroll along Boulevard St Germain. As Tilly passed the Fragonard perfume boutique, she was lured inside by the window display. The enticing spectacle was brimming with ornate bottles and cosmetic purses. The brand theme was based around colourful, fantasy butterflies. Tilly stood in front of a row of tester decanters and vigilantly sniffed until she found the one she liked best. Then, realising the cost of two bottles was out of her league, she purchased soaps and hand creams which were also sold with the wonderful promotional butterfly purse. She considered it was important she took a gift home – not just for Madame, but for Enid as well.

After gazing at more window displays, she resisted any more temptations and eventually arrived in Rue du Bac where Deyrolle was located. The ground floor of this old store was ordinary – mainly selling vintage French clothing and gardening accessories.

Tilly walked up the wooden staircase and was greeted by a fully-grown majestic stuffed white polar bear. A towering giraffe was poised in the corner of the room, as if any minute it would walk across and give her a lick. Two menacing tigers accompanied the giraffe, one sitting and one primed as if about to attack. A large round table in the middle of the store was home to an astonishing array of small rodents, exotic birds and large insects.

After numerous 'stuffed' distractions of nature, Tilly walked through to the next room. There were various small animals sitting on tables and a huge crocodile standing low-bellied on the floor. At the rear of the room sat a man busy with his head down at a long, cluttered desk. Tilly edged her way over. He had an angular-looking face and was thin with a neat narrow moustache and ink black hair. Her excitement grew once she could see what he was doing.

He was surrounded by butterflies. They sat delicately and perfectly still waiting to be mounted and given everlasting life behind glass. Tilly was transfixed. The work required massive concentration and precise actions to anchor each tiny leg to the board.

She felt intrusive. So, although riveted by his skill, she moved into the next room.

It was heaven – the papillon sector! Her non-PC attitude towards the mounting of dead butterflies sometimes jarred with other butterfly lovers, but it didn't affect her. Adorning one wall were row after row of framed captivating papillons, their iridescent feathery wings shimmering under the halogen lights. On the adjoining wall were rows of framed insects, beetles, praying mantises, large ants and spiders.

She moved back to the row of frames and, beginning at one end, carefully scrutinised, read and considered the names – savouring her delight as she viewed each one; some creatures she had only previously ever seen photos of. In the middle of the room were rows of butterflies under glass with stacks of drawers underneath. Customers were pointing out to the assistant what they liked, and she would carefully remove them from a drawer and place them on a flocked tray.

'*Bonjour, puis-je vous aider?*'

Tilly looked up to see a casually dressed man smiling at her.

'I'm just looking,' she replied.

'Oh! You are English. Hello, I am Thomas,' he replied in English with a gleaming white smile.

'If I buy a selection of butterflies, do you mount them as well?'

'Yes, and we include the work in the price. But you must pay for the frame; there are many to choose from.'

He picked up a tray and shadowed her as she pointed to various species.

'Do you have any chrysalises or pupae?' she asked without looking up. Thomas moved in front of her and opened a low drawer. Tilly noticed his tattoos – three beautiful butterflies cascading down his arm, framed by the word 'Papillon'.

The opened drawer contained several chrysalises which were triple the price of the butterflies; but there was no holding back now. Tilly pointed to the one she knew was the forebear to the most expensive butterfly she had chosen.

'Ah, you have excellent taste! I can see you are a true

lepidopterist; perhaps you would like one of these as well?'

He moved along and opened another drawer full of stripy caterpillars.

'Wow, how wonderful!' Tilly knew exactly which one was the antecedent of her chrysalis and her butterfly.

'Now I am very impressed!' he said as he flashed another gleaming smile.

As Tilly paid the hefty bill, with courier postage added, she reflected how the money her father had given her was coming in handy.

Now she had a legitimate reason to engage with the interesting man mounting the butterflies. She decided to have the 'set' of the three stages in one frame and the other butterflies in a separate frame.

Sadly, Monsieur Georges did not speak English, so the conversation was limited, but he seemed to understand exactly what Tilly wanted. She understood when he assured her they would arrive on the Riviera within two weeks.

Back at her apartment, Tilly slipped into her best matching underwear, and pulled on her 'slacks' with a smile as she thought of Jean-Luc; they were in fact her black jeans, accompanied by a flattering white T-shirt she had hastily purchased on the way back. She studied herself in the mirror, an activity that six months ago was a complete no-go area. She felt like an entirely new person. She realised she was learning about how to feel fine, and maybe there would come a time where she could finally learn to live alongside her grief and hurt.

FOURTEEN

Jean-Luc was waiting when Tilly opened the door to the street; he offered a delicate but welcoming smile. He wore his signature blue jeans, this time accompanied with pristine white Nike trainers and a pale blue three-button shirt. Tilly figured this maybe was casual as it got. He had a slim leather bag under his arm.

'I had some good luck today with news of Maison Papillon,' he said as he kissed both Tilly's cheeks.

'Great! Tell me.'

'Uumm, best we wait until we are settled with our picnic,' Jean-Luc replied.

Tilly looked puzzled. 'Picnic! Is it in that thin satchel?'

'No, we are going to choose it together.' He beamed.

They went down into the Métro then exited at École Militaire. Almost directly outside the Métro station was an impressive patisserie/delicatessen called Arnaud Nicolas.

'I am not a very good cook, so this wonderful store serves me well. But you must choose anything that you like,' Jean-Luc said.

Tilly walked along the glass-fronted chilled savoury section. It was a stunning display of immaculately presented foods. After deliberation she chose a duck thigh, a bean salad that looked fresh and moist as well as some salmon gravlax.

'Good choices, now, with your permission, may I select a patisserie and the wine?' He looked anxious.

Tilly smiled and nodded.

Jean-Luc ordered two portions of the same food Tilly had selected as well as a small baguette and two Paris-Brests which were doughnut-shaped circles of choux pastry stuffed with a caramel-coloured cream and topped with the same coloured icing. He chose a bottle of Chablis, stating it was his favourite.

The assistant packed everything neatly into boxes, accompanied by a wad of paper napkins, two paper plates, plastic knives and forks and a couple of plastic disposable wine goblets.

As they had travelled underground, Tilly didn't quite have her bearings until they turned the corner just outside the delicatessen. There, gazing down on them in all its steely glory loomed the magnificent Eiffel Tower.

Jean-Luc led her on to the park that stretched out in front of the massive monument that symbolised Paris. Couples and groups of young people were eating and drinking and largely enjoying themselves under the shadow of the giant tower. Tilly followed him to the far end of the park, the furthest away from the crowds and the pushy souvenir men selling mini Eiffel's with flashing lights.

Inside his leather satchel, next to a file of papers, Jean-Luc had carefully folded up a fine sheet of plastic that he strategically lay on the ground and invited her to sit on. He then proceeded to unpack the food. He took a small cork screw out of his satchel,opened the wine and poured them each a glass.

'À votre santé! Or, how-you-say "cheers"! To Madame Pollock's quest!' He raised his glass to Tilly's.

'I can't wait to see what you have found out.' Tilly flicked her index finger with nervous excitement.

'Uumm, well it's not a lot; I still have to wait for my colleague to go through the correct procedures.' Then he paused.

Tilly knew the drill, so she bit her tongue. She knew from her own lack of confidence to give him time to collect his thoughts. Once he had ritualistically laid the food out, he handed her a plate, then he picked up the file.

'I have here a copy of the original purchasers' paperwork relating to the apartments in Maison Papillon, which was on completion of being built known as Maison Parc. The first owners of apartment 59 were Monsieur and Madame Cohen.' He stopped and picked up the duck leg and took a bite.

Tilly ripped a piece of baguette off, added a slither of the tangy salmon and attempted to eat it in as lady-like a way as she could. Then she replied.

'But Madame's mother's name was Estienne. Cohen sounds Jewish.'

'Ah, well this is what is so interesting.' Jean-Luc pointed to the bottom of the page. 'There is a handwritten note here dated 1938 that says the ownership of the Cohen apartment was passed to Monsieur and Madame Jacob Estienne. No financial consideration passed as it states Madame Estienne was the Cohens' daughter.' He paused and ate a few mouthfuls of his bean salad.

'Does this prove ownership?' Tilly asked.

'Unfortunately, not exactly. The more recent documents are in a location in our building being used on a more regular basis, so that is my next mission, to see if I can access any Memoranda of Transfer from 1938 to the present day.'

He poured Tilly a second glass of wine.

'This is delicious, a good choice!' Tilly said as she raised her glass to Jean-Luc. He moved closer to her and smiled.

'I did some reading about artists who were working in Paris during the art nouveau period, specifically to look for the origins of the artist who designed the papillon gate.' He smiled with his eyes and raised his eyebrows.

'Go on!' Tilly gave him a gentle poke.

'Well, it was designed by a jeweller who was with the famous jewellery company Georges Auger which specialised in art nouveau design at that time. But the interesting thing is that it was commissioned and paid for by one of the residents of the building.' He beamed.

'Wow! They must have been quite wealthy to afford to build the gate. I wonder if it was Madame's parents or grandparents?' Tilly said, then took a big sip of her wine.

'Going from their names, yes, I believe they were

Jewish. This brings me to the next point I need to warn you about, as it may cause some delays.' He paused.

Tilly was feeling impatient but waited without speaking until he had sipped his wine.

'Because many homes and businesses were taken from the Parisian Jews when the Nazis ordered them into camps, there is still a process going through the courts now, of descendants trying to prove ownership and retrieve what is rightfully theirs.'

'Ah yes. I read about some of these cases regarding the provenance of precious art that was stolen during the war.' As she spoke, she felt Jean-Luc's hand brush across hers. It ignited a gentle spark. She continued talking.

'Funny, Madame and Enid have never mentioned that Madame is Jewish.'

'Ah, well there is still some strong anti-Semitism in parts of France and people of Madame Pollock's generation will remember the horrors of what happen to the Jews. A lot of them still stay quiet even today, out of fear.' Jean-Luc stroked her hand; he moved as close as he possibly could and kissed her mouth.

The late afternoon light had gone, and the onset of the evening lights had begun to twinkle around them.

The gentle kiss had sparked a fire! Tilly put down her almost empty wine glass and rested her hand on his shoulder, then kissed him back. He tasted of Chablis, with hints of limes and lemons.

When they were ready to go, Jean-Luc packed up the picnic in much quicker time than he had taken to lay it out. He threw all the remains in a nearby rubbish bin and as they passed a taxi stand on their way to the Métro, he opened a taxi door, ushered Tilly in and gave the driver the address of her apartment.

'You are keen!' Tilly said beaming at him as he rested his arm firmly across her back.

'It's a special treat for me catch a taxi, and tonight is such a treat,' he said then kissed her again.

Once they had arrived at her building, the sun had long set and some of his bravado had dissipated.

'You do want to come up for coffee, don't you Jean-Luc?' Tilly said tilting her head to one side with a lustful thought.

'Uumm, well yes, but I don't want you to do anything you may regret later.' He shifted from one foot to the other.

'Never! However, there are four full flights of steep stairs ahead of us so I am hoping you will still be interested once we get to the top!'

Jean-Luc hadn't heard the final part of what she had said. He had grabbed Tilly's hand and pulled her up the stairs.

They fell on to Tilly's bed with the curtains open and the moonlight illuminating the room.

Nine months had passed since Tilly's pregnancy ended and over a year since she had made love to anyone. For two years prior to that, it had only been Giovanni. She hadn't spoken about the pregnancy and what had happened with anybody, other than the counsellor that the hospital had appointed for her.

She didn't want to tell Jean-Luc – well, not yet anyway. Her body had returned to its former shape.

There was none of the Italian verbal cascade that Giovanni spilled out as he had seduced her. Jean-Luc was quite a different man.

He removed his glasses and held her face in his hands, looking directly at her; his eyes shone with warmth and longing. Very gently he stroked her neck and the top of her arms. They kissed for what seemed an age, then he carefully removed his clothes, down to his underpants. Tilly smiled at his immaculate boxer shorts. As she took off her T-shirt and unbuttoned her jeans, she revealed her pure white lacy underwear and his excitement was obvious. He kissed her cleavage and reached around to her back to unbutton her bra, then gently ran his lips across her nipples.

Tilly was so aroused it was all she could do to stop herself grabbing him to her. Then, once Jean-Luc was inside her, the heavens opened, and it was their love making liberating her from all the grief and pain of Giovanni. She was engulfed in a whole new sensation of love as she lay in his arms.

He whispered French words she could not quite catch and stroked her hair as he held her in both his arms.

By early morning when Tilly floated to the kitchen to make them coffee, they had made love three times. The third time was less desperate and more adventurous.

'I wish you didn't have to leave today,' Jean-Luc said as they sat side by side in the bed clutching their coffee cups.

'I wish I didn't as well, but I am sure once we have the new information, I will have to return. Besides, you are welcome to come and visit me on the Riviera – I have weekends off,' Tilly replied, with a thought dashing through her mind as to what Enid would say.

After Jean-Luc had had a quick shower and dressed, he sat quietly on the bed.

'Are you OK? *Ça va?*' Tilly said.

She had pulled her short black nightdress on. He took both her hands in his.

'It's at this point, when something wonderful has happened to me, my bravado drops and my insecurities creep in.'

'What do you mean?'

'I think, what would a beautiful woman like you want long-term with an architectural geek like me?' He hung his head.

Tilly dropped their hands, and gently tipped his chin upwards until their eyes met.

'Don't you ever say that to me again. It's what a girl thinks when she is sixteen, not a man of nearly thirty. I fancy you madly, and I suspect I am probably as much a geek when it comes to butterflies, so that should work!'

FIFTEEN

PARIS, 1944

Mama seems so grumpy with me most days. I know it is because we are not allowed to go outdoors. I do not understand why. Papa Hans also seems angry all the time when he comes home and starts shouting at Mama. She stays quiet but when he goes away to his army, I hear her crying in the bedroom. Papa Hans says awfully bad words against people called the British and the Americans. He seems to be angry all the time. I know Mickey Mouse is from America. I don't believe he is bad, just a cartoon. Sometimes Papa Hans does not come home for a few days and Mama is too scared to go outside so we just eat boring food from tins in the pantry. Most of the time I feel happy in our apartment; Mama plays cards with me and we do jigsaw puzzles together. Sometimes she lets me in her bedroom; it is so beautiful. It is much bigger than mine with a huge bed with a gold crown above it. Thick gold curtains hang down from the crown; it looks like a bed for a queen. My mama is a queen. Although Papa Hans doesn't seem like a king to me. Mama's dressing table is laden with beautiful bottles with silver tops on them; she tells me they are crystal and her mama gave them to her on her wedding day. She has a special silver brush and comb and sometimes she lets me brush her hair with them. It makes her eyes go all dreamy.

I am forbidden to go in her dressing room. Mama allowed it once; it smelt lovely, sweet, like a vanilla cake that we used to eat a long time ago. All her beautiful gowns hang on one side, but she never wears them any more. There is an animal lying over the chair; I get a fright and squeal. Mama laughs; it was one of the few times I have seen her laugh. She tells it is just a fox fur and she wore it on her shoulders to keep warm. I think that is horrible, but I don't say anything as I don't want to spoil Mama's laughter. She keeps the door to her dressing room locked now and I don't know where she hides the key.

SIXTEEN

MENTON

'You look happy, did you find the apartment?' Enid asked as she greeted Tilly at the airport.

'Not yet, but I am hot on its trail; why don't I wait and tell you what I know over dinner with Madame?'

'So, how was your date?' Enid poked Tilly's arm affectionately.

'Just about perfect.' Tilly beamed, then went on to tell Enid all about Jean-Luc.

'His mother sounds like a witch! Watch out for French mothers! Do you really think he's odd?' Enid said as she negotiated the motorway.

'No, not at all; he's just been misunderstood. I recognise the symptoms; and he's a bit eccentric like a lot of people I worked with at the museum.'

When Madame arrived at the dinner table, she offered

Tilly a wonderful rare smile; she stood more upright and seemed to be moving much faster than usual.

Tilly told her story carefully, so Madame could absorb each piece of information; she omitted any reference to her romance. When she came to the final details of the gate, the tears trickled down the old lady's face.

'Yes, my mama's family was Jewish, but she never spoke about or practised the religion with me. Anything to do with what happened to us in Paris during the war was never spoken about once we arrived on the Riviera,' Madame Pollock said in a very soft voice, then continued, 'I have read about these cases where homes and businesses were stolen from Jewish families, I do so hope that is not the case with my mother's apartment.'

'I feel confident Jean-Luc will be able to hurry the next part of the process along and we will know soon.' As Tilly replied, she heard her mobile ring from the kitchen worktop.

She had only recently responded to Aunt Lucy's email and included her new French number.

'Aunt Lucy, what's wrong?' she said, then after a couple of minutes' listening, almost dropped the phone as she clutched her cheek and let out a cry.

Enid was swiftly at her side.

'Yes, yes I will get the next available flight back,' she said, as the tears poured down her cheeks.

'Oh Enid, it's my dad! He's had a heart attack and I need to go back as soon as possible as the doctors say he's not in very good shape!'

Tilly quickly went online and found a flight leaving the

next morning at 8 a.m. She texted Aunt Lucy who replied that she would collect her at Heathrow.

Enid and Madame had stayed at the table while Tilly made her calls, and once she had re-joined them Enid popped a cup of camomile tea in front of her.

'That will help soothe you and I will drive you to the airport in the morning.'

On hearing those words Tilly burst into tears. Between her sobs she managed to get out a few words. 'You have both been so kind to me, I don't really want to leave; but despite what Dad has done, he is still my father. My stepmother is such a cow I can't bear to think of her looking after him.'

Madame Pollock pulled her chair up next to Tilly's and patted her shoulder.

'Tilly, you go and do what is needed with your father. Whatever he has done to distress you, please consider forgiveness. We will be here, your room will be here, and the Paris assignment will wait. It's taken me a lifetime to decide to find the Paris apartment, so a few weeks more won't matter.'

Tilly couldn't stop crying; the others sat patiently until she had dried her eyes then Enid poured out three small glasses of brandy.

Tilly threw hers back, then cleared her throat. 'I just feel I need to tell you both something I have never spoken about.' She paused, took a deep breath, then continued: 'I had a two-year relationship with an Italian man in London. I was madly in love with him, then I became pregnant. He was furious and demanded I have an abortion. I just couldn't go through with it. When my parents found out my stepmother went ballistic. She was already unhinged but it sent her off completely. Calling me a "slut" and a "sinner".'

After a long pause Madame finally spoke.

'What happened to your baby, Tilly?'

A fresh tear welled in Tilly's eye.

'I stayed in my flat in London; my flatmates were very supportive and at eight months into the pregnancy, I collapsed and was rushed to hospital. My daughter had died in the womb and I had to give birth to her knowing she was dead.'

Madame dabbed her eyes with a napkin and Enid gave a big sniff. Tilly took another breath and continued.

'She was a tiny angel; her face was as perfect and pure as a pearl. The hospital helped me have a funeral in the hospital chapel. Only my Aunt Lucy came; I didn't want anyone else. Apparently because I was so disturbed, the hospital social worker contacted my father who took me home; but my stepmother verbally abused me every day. Once I was well enough, I knew I had to move on, then I saw your advertisement. I discussed it with my aunt whom I was awfully close to. She eluded to something my father needed to tell me.' Tilly patted her eyes with her napkin, then continued. 'As a result of pressure from my aunt, after twenty-five years my father was forced to tell me my real mother had died as a result of giving birth to me and the woman that I had always believed to be my mother, wasn't.'

There was a silence in the group. Then Madame spoke.

'I lost my young son, I have never been able to discuss it, and no matter what anyone says you never fully recover, but somehow you learn to cope,' Madame said and then looked to Enid before she continued.

'We felt you had brought something special with you when you arrived, didn't we, Enid?'

Enid smiled and nodded.

'We were chatting about it this morning before you arrived back.' Enid leaned over and squeezed Tilly's hand.

'Now I need to go to bed. I will say goodbye to you now Tilly, as I won't be up early enough in the morning. Please keep us informed about your father,' Madame said before she left the other two sitting at the table.

'Will you have another brandy?' Enid asked as she poured herself one.

Tilly nodded.

'I was in love once as well, and I remember the pain when she finally ended it,' Enid said.

'She, don't you mean he?' Tilly interjected, assuming Enid had mistaken her English.

'No, I'm gay and I had been through so much with my parents not accepting it. I made the decision to come out, then six months later she left me for another woman. That's when Madame offered me the position here.' It was Enid's turn to throw back her brandy.

'I guess no one goes unscathed in this world; we all have our secrets. I think I had better go up and repack. Thanks, Enid, for everything,' Tilly said, then kissed her friend on the cheek.

Tilly's thoughts oscillated from the fear she felt that

she might lose her father, to how she was going to cope facing him after all that had transpired. She pondered on the revelation of Madame's child and how it offered her more insight into the old lady's behaviour. Enid being gay wasn't much of a surprise, and it did explain a few things.

Madame Pollock's compassion and generosity towards her and Enid's friendship had lifted her spirits; she really did want to return to this old turret house which she now regarded as home.

SEVENTEEN

Aunt Lucy had aged ten years in the past six months. She wore a forced smile as she greeted Tilly at the terminal.

'I am so pleased you are here!' she said as she pulled her niece into her arms.

'How is Dad?' Tilly stiffened at the embrace.

'Well, he's conscious; I sat with him all night. He knows you are coming. Karen is with him now, but he has told her she must leave before you arrive as he wants to see you alone.'

At the mention of Karen, Tilly experienced a cold shudder – as if someone had walked on her grave.

The drive from Heathrow into central London seemed to take for ever. Tilly could see how tired and stressed her aunt was, so chose not to distract her with too many questions.

They pulled into the Royal Brompton Hospital carpark on Fulham Road; everything seemed grey and morbid compared to the sunlit environment of Tilly's newly adopted home.

Her heart pounded as they walked along the never-ending corridor. The smell of antiseptic and the squeaking of the nurses' rubber soles on the shiny linoleum triggered recollections of her own hospital stay and her dead baby girl.

Tilly's father lay behind a glass wall in a brightly lit high-tech room. He was lying on his back propped up with pillows with his eyes closed. A heart monitor gave out a multitude of details about his vital signs on a screen that could be easily viewed through the glass; he had a drip in his arm. As Tilly had entered the room, he opened his eyes.

At first he seemed a little confused, but once his eyes had registered Tilly's face, he gave a soft smile and beckoned her over.

'Come sit right beside me on the bed, love.' Tilly had to strain to hear his fragile voice.

'Oh Dad, I am so sorry, I wish I could have been here sooner!' Tilly eyes welled up.

'Now, now don't be silly. I am just so happy you have been having a wonderful time on the French Riviera.'

They made small talk for a bit, then Aunt Lucy, who had been sitting on the seat beside the bed, spoke. 'Your father and I need you to know how sorry we both are about the deception of your birth.'

Her father strained to speak. 'I have no right to ask you to forgive me but perhaps you could pretend to forgive me?' He looked directly into Tilly's eyes.

Tilly squeezed his hand. 'Dad I don't have to pretend, I needed to answer your emails in a brisk manner as I was so angry, but I've done quite a bit of growing up in the past few months and I am learning about forgiveness; regardless, I do love you.'

Aunt Lucy let out a loud sob. 'You too, Aunt Lucy,' Tilly said as she reached out and held both their hands.

Her father dropped his hand then clutched his chest and his voice dropped to a whisper. 'Thank you my darling, I love you for ever.'

The graph on the monitor moved faster. As shocked as she felt, she knew she had to keep calm as her father was barely coping.

The monitor had started to beep and within seconds there were three nurses at the bedside ushering Tilly out. She resisted. Although her father was struggling, she could see his eyes hadn't left her. She pushed in beside the nurse who was placing the oxygen mask on him and squeezed his hand.

'Dad I love you,' she said as she kissed his blue lips, then allowed the nurse to guide her to the door.

Aunt Lucy put her arms around her as they both anxiously watched the nurses through the glass administer CPR to Tilly's father. They swiftly used the resus paddles on his chest, but when there was no response they stopped and reverently turned off all the equipment.

'I've killed him! I've killed him!' Tilly shouted as she rushed into the room.

The nurse who was attending Tilly's father's body, made room for Tilly to hold her father's hand. Grief was a familiar acquaintance. She waited until Tilly had quietened before she spoke.

'I have been your father's nurse since he was admitted. There wasn't much hope; he had suffered a major heart attack and there was nothing much we could do, except keep him comfortable. It's amazing he lasted until you arrived; but he was determined to. He told me he needed to talk you.' It sounded like a question.

'My heart is broken,' Tilly replied as she held her father's hand to her cheek and sobbed.

With the sounds of the monitor gone, the quiet air in the room suggested finality. The cloud of silence offered sanctity to Tilly's father. Eventually Aunt Lucy took her brother's other limp hand in hers and kissed his face. He was her only sibling. This was goodbye for ever. She then gently coaxed Tilly, the only child either sibling had ever had, to let go and leave the room. As aunt and niece both looked back through the glass, the nurse respectfully shrouded Tilly's dead father's face with a stark, white sheet.

Aunt Lucy drove Tilly back to her apartment. She made a pot of tea and added sugar to both cups.

'Apparently sweet tea is best for shock,' Aunt Lucy said handing Tilly a cup.

Tilly felt an anger welling up inside of her; she was shaking as she tried to hold the hot cup of tea.

'You knew! You knew that bitch wasn't my mother and despite all I went through you never said a word!'

Aunt Lucy put her cup down and hung her head in her hands. Between sobs she attempted to speak. Her voice was shaky.

'I so wanted to tell you many times; but your father assured me it was for him to do; then he would "bottle" it. He was terrified of Karen. But I can see now that was no excuse.' She blew her nose and avoided looking Tilly in the eye.

'What I don't get is why bloody Karen would care? She has always hated me. She was continually cruel to me as a child and I didn't know any better; I just accepted that was how mothers were, locking me in the dark in the hall cupboard, hitting me with a leather strap!' Tilly stood up and shoved her hands down by her sides.

Lucy gasped. 'I didn't know any of this, or how you felt. I am certain your father didn't know how bad it was. Why didn't you tell him?'

'She told me if I told anyone about her strapping my backside, she would lock me in the hall cupboard and she did lock me in, frequently. So, I believed she would carry out any threats; even back then I must have sensed Dad was weak when it came to Karen.' Tilly threw herself down on the sofa and pulled at her fingernails.

'I just wanted to please, and for her to be pleasant. But she only ever was when Dad was there, so I didn't know I had any option. I was only a child; she was the only mother I had ever known!'

Aunt Lucy stared at Tilly and clasped her cheeks. 'Oh my God Tilly, we never knew she was so wicked. I am so, so sorry.'

Lucy's mobile buzzed from her handbag, and she picked it up. 'It's Karen; I'm not going to take that.'

Tilly sat rigidly on the sofa, alternately struggling with waves of grief and floods of anger.

'So, what happens with the funeral? Do I organise it?' Tilly spat the words at her aunt.

'If you wish, or I can do it. No doubt Karen will want to hold it at The True Church of the Greater God.'

'Over my dead body!' Tilly retorted.

An hour or so passed without either woman speaking. Aunt Lucy busied herself in the kitchen cleaning up and putting a snack together.

Tilly's mind was racing. She didn't want to ever see Karen again, but she wanted to play some role in her father's final farewell.

'Tilly, please just eat something! You haven't had anything except the tea all day.' Aunt Lucy had laid out various nibbles and pitta bread.

'I'm not hungry and I would prefer to go and stay in a hotel, but I don't think I am capable of doing anything right now. Just two days ago, when I was in Paris, I thought my life was all sorted; I thought I was in love and so happy in my new home. Now this!'

She stormed off to the spare bedroom and slammed the door. Although exhausted, Tilly wasn't ready for sleep. She had bitten her nails as far down as she could. She turned her phone on and two messages beeped. The first was from Enid, checking in and saying they were thinking of her. The second was from Jean-Luc.

'I am missing you Tilly! No further info on Maison Papillon yet as a lot of sensitivity around any building where there is uncertainty of ownership resulting from the Occupation. I will get there, but it will take time. Love JL. Xxx.'

This day had been horrific; how would she ever recover? She so hoped that her feelings for Jean-Luc and the relationship with her friends in Menton would be strong enough to bring her out the other side to some sort of sane future.

EIGHTEEN

Tilly didn't wake until late. She had been up most of the night. Aunt Lucy knocked, opened the bedroom door and placed a tray with a cup of coffee and a piece of toast on Tilly's lap and then stepped back.

'I am not asking you to like me, but please don't close me out of your life. You are my only living relative, and I know it's selfish to ask, but I couldn't bear never to see you again!' Aunt Lucy said as she pulled a chair up beside her niece.

The long night had taken Tilly's emotions to many different places; she had finally drifted off at 3 a.m. with one reassurance that she had to keep reminding herself: '*I am not and have never been Karen's daughter.*'

'It will take a lot more time for me to work through this. I am going back to France as soon as I can sort Dad's funeral out.' She took a sip of her coffee and a bite of the toast as a gesture of goodwill.

'I had a heated argument with your mother—' Aunt Lucy stopped, then corrected herself. 'Sorry, I had a heated argument with Karen last night about the funeral; however, your father apparently knew his heart was playing up and went to the lawyer and made a new will, as well as declaring what he wished for his own funeral arrangements.'

'And?' Tilly raised her eyebrows. 'Well, I don't know. He didn't tell me what he wanted, just that when he died, I was to phone the lawyer, which I did a half an hour ago. The lawyer is a chap your father was at school with; his name is Andrew McKenzie and he was phoning Karen this morning and unless we hear otherwise, we are to be at his office, all three of us, at 3 p.m. today.' Aunt Lucy sighed.

Tilly realised she was starving, so she politely asked if she might have some more toast. Her aunt was delighted and boiled her an egg, before testing the emotional waters.

They moved through to sit at the kitchen table.

'I know we are both in a bad way, but you mentioned Paris and love last night? Your father would be so pleased, it was very important to him that you are happy.'

Tilly managed to put her anger at her aunt to one side; she realised it had been her father's place to tell her about her birth mother. She couldn't be angry at him any more. But Karen was still alive, and Tilly believed, without any guilt, that she was at liberty to hate her.

Then with the mention of Paris, a welcome trickle of warmth tickled her heart.

'On my quest to help Madame Pollock find her Paris

apartment I met a man who works in the city buildings records office; as dull as that sounds, he's interesting and a kindred spirit. Dad would approve.'

Aunt Lucy smiled, kissed Tilly's cheek, and offered a silent prayer of thanks.

At 2 p.m. the two women caught the underground to Holborn where her father's lawyer had his office. On the tube Tilly noticed her hands for the first time since she had left France – her beautifully restored fingernails were broken, picked-at and looked disgusting.

'Don't fret! You grew them once, you will grow them again,' Aunt Lucy said as she rubbed Tilly's arm.

Tilly was in a state of high anxiety by the time they arrived at the lawyer's reception area. They were ushered directly into a boardroom and offered coffee. Andrew McKenzie was bald with prominent tortoiseshell square-framed glasses, and slightly prominent front teeth. He offered his hand and, as Tilly responded, he placed his other hand over hers. 'I am so sorry for your loss! I was very fond of your father; we had a great time together when we were at college.'

As Mr McKenzie spoke, the door opened, and the entire atmosphere of the room changed as Karen appeared.

She had really pushed the boat out for the occasion. She wore a knee-length fitted black skirt and a black shirt, black tights and pointy-toed black high heels and black gloves, which would have been OK, but the accompanying small hat with black netting sitting over her eyes above the scarlet red lips was just too much. Tilly and Aunt Lucy were momentarily speechless. Karen would have been right at home as a grieving black widow in a Jackie Collins novel.

Mr McKenzie was quick to take control.

'Mrs White please sit over here!' He indicated to Karen to sit at a chair on the opposite side of the table to Tilly. Then he sat at the top of the table between the three women.

He got straight to the point.

'Edward was very clear that on his passing I would read out his instructions as soon as possible as he knew Tilly would only wish to be here in London for a short time.'

'This is not about "her"!' Karen interrupted, her cheeks beginning to take on the same hue as her lips. 'I was his wife; I bore the brunt of all her sin!' At this point in her rant, she caught her reflection in the window and momentarily paused, to fiddle with the net from her hat.

'Please Mrs White. This meeting is about Edward White's wishes and I am the only one here who knows what they are. He came to see me two weeks before his heart attack and we drew this up together.'

Karen mumbled under her breath; the lawyer continued.

'It was Edward's wish to be cremated at the funeral home as soon as possible without a service and only his direct family in attendance – that is, you three ladies. And then, if you can all agree, to hold a small memorial service later in a non-religious venue.'

'What do you mean a non-religious venue? Of course, it will be at our church!' Karen shouted.

'Mrs White I must implore you to calm down. I

reiterate, this is about your husband's wishes which he dictated to me when he was of sound mind.'

Karen pursed her lips and glared at the lawyer, who returned to his seat.

'Probate will need to be granted, but Edward said that while you were all present, I was to read out his will.'

Karen straightened in her seat and directed her stare at Tilly.

'The house and the hundred thousand pounds life insurance policy will go to Karen; the funds in his HSBC bank account will go to Matilda and he would ask that all his first wife's jewellery, that his sister Lucy has been keeping for him, will pass to Matilda.'

Now Karen was on her feet. 'What HSBC account? Any money that man had is now rightfully mine. I'm glad you now know who you really are, Matilda. You and your kind! I would never have given birth to someone like you.'

Tilly stood up and walked around to the other side of the table to confront her.

'Karen, don't you dare speak about my father like that. Listen to yourself! This is me you're screaming at. I am the one that suffered when you hit me and locked me in a cupboard when I was just a little girl. You would go to prison for less nowadays. So, shut up, or I will go to the police and report it as a "historic" crime of child abuse. Even if I didn't win, your precious church friends might raise their eyebrows a little!'

Karen stepped back as Tilly's words sunk in. She grabbed her handbag.

'I never liked you; you were a horrible child; your father

always put you first. I am not interested in being at that man's cremation. You two are welcome to it; I will hold my own memorial service. But I will be seeking my own legal advice and believe me Mr McKenzie I know my rights!' With that she stomped out of the room; her façade had truly fallen as they noticed a large hole and a run in the back of her black stockings.

'Bravo Tilly,' Aunt Lucy said and lightly clapped her hands.

Tilly sat down; she was shattered. Mr McKenzie poured her a glass of water and put it down in front of her.

'Did you mean that, about going to the police?' he asked.

'No, not if she just leaves things how Dad wanted them. Anyway, I cannot imagine he had much money in this "secret" bank account, as from what I observed, Karen controlled and spent everything.'

As Tilly spoke, she caught a collaborative glance pass between her aunt and the lawyer.

Mr McKenzie cleared his throat. 'As I said before, we need to go through the probate process and check there are no outstanding debts – there certainly weren't two weeks ago when I had the meeting with your father. After probate, you will have access to the funds. What Mrs White doesn't know is that bank account was opened in your father's and your name when you were born; your parents had taken life insurance out on each other as, at the time, it was a prerequisite for a mortgage. When your mother died, your father put your mother's life insurance money into that account. All that transpired before his second marriage. He was the signatory until you came of age. He never disclosed exactly how much he earned to Karen and regularly put further money into the account.' He paused as if to give Tilly time to absorb this information.

'Am I allowed to know how much there is?' Tilly asked.

'As of two weeks ago, around £300,000,' said the lawyer with a smile on his face.

Both Tilly and Aunt Lucy gasped.

'What! He kept that quiet,' Lucy said, managing a chuckle.

Mr McKenzie continued. 'He was very good with stocks and shares, but very discreet. Also, twenty-five years has been a good length of time for the compounded interest to build up. He said when we last spoke that he was keen for you to feel you had financial security and to do whatever you chose to do with the money.'

Tilly was speechless; the tears ran down her cheeks. Aunt Lucy's eyes were welling up too as she reached over and put her arm around Tilly.

Once she had eventually composed herself, Tilly thanked the lawyer. He said he had already spoken to the funeral directors as per her father's instructions and, if it was OK with her and Lucy, they could schedule the cremation for Monday afternoon in four days' time. He also handed her a thick manila envelope.

'Your father asked me to give you this. I don't know what's inside, but he was very clear I was to give it to you out of sight of Mrs White.'

Tilly thanked the lawyer and tucked the envelope under her arm.

'Let's just hope Karen is as good as her word and doesn't show up at the funeral,' Aunt Lucy said as they left the building.

Tilly was very subdued but nodded in agreement when Aunt Lucy offered to take her to Sketch for lunch.

Lucy hailed a cab and they were soon in Mayfair, pulling up outside the restored Conduit Street building. They were ushered up to the Gallery restaurant which was a sea of dusty pink velvet banquette sofas and matching chairs shaped like upright lozenges. Every round table was draped in a crisp white damask tablecloth all in stark contrast to the striking zigzag carpet. Very modern chic art decorated the walls.

Once they had ordered and Tilly had taken a mouthful of wine she finally spoke.

'I am going through such extreme emotions. I really don't care about his money. I only wish he had been honest with me about my real mother.'

'I do too, Tilly, but it seemed to me as if he felt he had made his bed with Karen and he had to lie in it. But I promise you he never had an inkling of the cruelty she had inflicted on you. I am sure he wouldn't have tolerated it.' Aunt Lucy's eyes welled as she spoke.

'I want to believe you; but he must have been totally blind to the bitch.'

They were interrupted as the waitress brought out the salads they had ordered.

After a second glass of wine, Aunt Lucy looked relieved when Tilly loosened up and started firing questions at her.

'So, what is this jewellery you have of my mother's?'

'That silver butterfly brooch you are wearing is the key piece to the collection; I also have matching earrings as well as a necklace.'

Tilly fingered her brooch; she could feel the anger rising again as she considered all the time she had worn it she had no idea it was her late mother's. But after another gulp of wine, curiosity got the better of the anger.

'So, who were her parents? Dad said they were French.'

'Her name was Ruth Goldsmith; she was the only child of a Jewish French couple who both arrived as children in London just before the German occupation in 1940. I think both their fathers must have been killed and somehow the mothers and children managed to get to safety in London. Ruth was born around 1963, I think. Her parents died relatively young, and soon after Ruth married your father.' Aunt Lucy rested to allow Tilly time to absorb things.

Tilly felt very strange, as if her brain were on the cusp of a revolution. 'So, I'm Jewish?'

'Technically yes. As I am sure you know, being Jewish is passed down through the mother, but Ruth wasn't what you would term a "practising" Jew.'

'As well as half French! What a day of new revelations this is turning out to be!' Tilly said then placed a fork full of the Roquefort salad into her mouth.

'Anything else I should know?' she said sarcastically.

'I feel your pain, Tilly. I know this isn't about me, but I love you and this was all out of my control. I promise I will do all that I can to acquaint you with your mother's history.'

They ate for the next few moments in silence.

'I suspect that envelope Mr McKenzie gave you may be information about Ruth.' Aunt Lucy indicated Tilly's tote bag.

Tilly put her hand down and fingered the envelope.

'I don't want to spill any more emotion in public today, so I think I will keep it till we get back to your place.'

Tilly sat on the bed in Aunt Lucy's spare bedroom and cautiously opened the large envelope the lawyer had given her. There was a letter from her father, along with her mother's birth, marriage and death certificates. Tilly unfolded the letter.

Dear Tilly,

As I write this you are sixteen years old and I am full of guilt. I know I should tell you this in person, but you are going through adolescence and it's a very awkward time for us all. The best I can manage is to write it down. I believed when my Ruth died, and Karen appeared, that marrying her and giving you a new mother was the best thing for both of us. But now I am having my doubts, and everything seems out of control. So, I am putting this down in this letter; if anything should happen to me before I tell you in person you will have some understanding and I hope you will have some forgiveness for me.

My love for your real mother Ruth was true love; she was the only child of very protective older parents who had suffered much in France because of the war. I was her first and only love. When I married Karen, I was still in shock and very grieved, but I can only now see that in retrospect.

Karen insisted that we said you were her daughter and I agreed, but as time passed and she couldn't conceive, it was as if she began to resent both of us. I suspect Karen has been horrid to you at times, but she has fulfilled her motherly duties in other ways.

I am not brave enough to leave her now. Maybe I will be in the future. Please forgive me for not telling you all this sooner.

Your loving father

Edward White

Tilly's tears dripped on to the letter. Her father had always used a proper fountain pen and the ink began to smudge. In that moment Tilly never wanted to read those words again. She wanted to banish all thoughts of her father and his cowardly and deceptive deed. Her blood boiled in anger. But although she had given him her forgiveness, she screwed the letter up and threw it on the floor.

Ruth's birth certificate confirmed what Aunt Lucy had told her: she was born in 1963, her full name was Ruth Matilda Goldsmith, her parents were Hannah and Jean-Pierre Goldsmith.

Was it ironic, or was it fate, that the happiest place Tilly had found in her twenty-five years of life was in the French home of a French Jew?

As she had opened the marriage certificate three photos fell out. First, a black and white one of a small girl with a shock of black hair holding hands with a man and a woman. By what they were wearing it looked like the 1960s. Tilly turned the photo over. There were names and dates written. 'These are my grandparents and my mother,' Tilly said out loud as she stroked the photo with her forefinger.

The next was a colour photo of a wedding party; her father was smiling proudly at the camera, holding his beautiful bride's hand. Tilly had never seen him look so happy. His bride wore a simple full-length white gown with a long tulle traditional veil edged in what looked like handmade embroidery. She held a bunch of lilac-coloured flowers. Tilly experienced a tingle through her entire body as she recognised familiar traits of herself in the face of the woman in the photo.

The third was a portrait-type shot of Ruth. Tilly turned the photo over – the date 1995 was written on the back. This was the year Tilly was born; the year Ruth had died. Wiping her tears, Tilly studied her mother's face. The familiarity was so obvious. She could see herself, mainly in the eyes. What was Ruth thinking when this photo was taken? Was she pregnant then?

So many unanswered questions, such big gaps in her history. All of which her father had chosen to hide. Tilly clenched her fists, punched the pillows and then, muffling her scream with the blanket over her head, she eventually sobbed herself to sleep.

The next morning Aunt Lucy appeared at the bedroom door with tea and toast. 'You look like you had a rough night. Once you are up and sorted, I have some things to give you.'

When Tilly emerged from the bedroom, there was a flat brown box with a lilac ribbon, a white plastic old-fashioned photo album and a large worn black velvet jewellery box sitting on the table.

'I'm not going to keep telling you how guilty I feel as it will serve no purpose now. I agreed to keep these in my home all this time out of loyalty to my brother rather than disloyalty to you.'

Tilly made no response to her aunt's comment; she sat down at the table staring at the articles, not knowing which to touch first.

Aunt Lucy took the chair beside her and gently placed the black velvet box in front of her. 'These came from your maternal grandmother's family in France.'

Tilly slowly opened the old battered box; the velvet felt soft and welcoming, how she imagined a mother's touch should be. Inside was a heavy silver chain with a large stylised butterfly sitting in the centre. It wasn't the same as her brooch, but Tilly could see they had been made by the same person in the art nouveau style. This was accompanied by a set of beautiful delicate butterfly earrings. Tilly was momentarily distracted from her anguish as she placed them in the palm of her hand and examined them from both sides, marvelling at their intricate craftmanship. She sensed a strong connection.

As Tilly placed the velvet box to one side she noticed a faded logo in the lid 'Georges Auger', but couldn't quite place how she knew that name.

Next, she opened the plastic photo album; it was full of pictures of her mother at all stages of her life and some of her grandparents. There was a whole series of her parents' wedding photos. Tucked in a pocket at the back of the album were two very old faded black and white pictures. One featured a young woman – going by the background it was taken in Paris; the other was what looked like a family shot with a man, a woman and two small girls. It also looked very French.

'I think they were brought over from France when Ruth's grandparents escaped; the jewellery that's now yours was the only thing of value that they managed to bring with them.'

Tilly still offered no response. She undid the lilac satin ribbon that was around the box, lifted the lid and sensitively peeled back the tissue paper. It was her mother's wedding veil. A delicate confection of soft tulle edged in the most refined, intricate embroidery – clearly handmade. On closer inspection, Tilly could see tiny Stars of David and Crucifixes had been worked into the soft floral pattern.

'Your mother did all that embroidery herself; she told me she wanted a symbol of both religions present at the nuptials and this seemed a subtle way to express it,' Aunt Lucy said, hoping for a response.

Tilly remained silent, so Aunt Lucy busied herself in the kitchen making a snack. Tilly looked back through the photo album, then carefully packed the veil and the jewellery back in their boxes.

She had taken a bite of the pitta bread and hummus Aunt Lucy had served before she finally spoke.

'Aunt Lucy I respect your loyalty to your brother, although I don't really understand it, given your history of fighting causes and "doing the right thing".' She sighed, then continued.

'For me, to only now discover a major part of my history and where I came from in these two boxes and photo album is pathetic. I wonder what my mother would think about her beloved husband hiding her memory from her daughter. I imagine she is up there in heaven looking down with relief that you all finally came clean about her existence and my heritage. I wonder what my grandparents would think, having lost their fathers, fled their country to stay alive, to then have their only surviving descendant spend her youth believing she was the daughter of a radical religious nutcase,' Tilly said, then took a gulp of her water to quell her anger.

Aunt Lucy dropped her hands to her lap and hung her head.

They both nibbled at the food in mutual silence before Tilly spoke again. She had to get it all out.

'I was made to feel such shame as far back as I can remember by Karen, shame for everything from my fascination with butterflies to the way I looked and, in the end, shame about my pregnancy. Why did my father never stand up for me?'

Once again, Aunt Lucy's eyes were wet with her own sense of shame as she struggled with her response.

'I always sensed Karen was a bitch; it was only in later years that she exposed her anti-Semitism. She was sneaky – she never said or did anything in front of me. I thought you were just a quiet little girl. I can't speak for your father. I can only tell you how sorry I am,' she said as she sniffed back her tears.

As distressed and angry as Tilly was, she still felt for

her aunt. Her guilt was obvious. She was, after all, now her only living relative.

'As I don't really have anyone else, would you mind keeping these things for a while longer? I don't wish at this point to take them to France with me.'

'Of course,' Aunt Lucy replied as a huge sense of reprieve swept over her.

'I will take the earrings as they are so wonderful and a few photos,' Tilly said as she flicked through the album.

The next few days were very awkward between the two women and Tilly had even considered going to stay in a hotel. But Tilly really wanted to move forward, and she must honour 'her forgiveness'.

True to her word, and to Tilly's relief, Karen didn't show up at the cremation. Aunt Lucy sobbed as the coffin slid through the curtains. But Tilly had shed enough tears. All her initial fear and sadness when she first received the call about her father, had been replaced by anger. No matter how much money he had left her, she would only ever view her father's silence about her mother's existence as selfish and a personal betrayal.

The following day Aunt Lucy drove Tilly to Heathrow airport.

Aunt Lucy's black-ringed eyes and the sudden sallowness of her cheeks reflected the pain of losing her brother and the fear that she would lose her only niece.

'Aunt Lucy, I will always stay in touch and always love you, but I won't be returning for Dad's memorial service or anything that Karen organises. I just want to return to France and move forward.'

Tilly hugged her aunt and walked through the departure gates.

NINETEEN

Tilly was brimming with emotional contrasts as she sat down at the dinner table with Enid and Madame Pollock. The realisation that she was an orphan had impacted on her psyche; the usual restraints on her thoughts and edits on her conversations no longer applied. Her companions were so warm and welcoming, it felt better than any home Tilly had ever known. She had managed to disguise her anger as grief and initially was reluctant to share. But Madame with her piercing aqua-blue eyes seemed to see beyond her façade. She asked her a direct question about her mother. This activated the floodgates. Tilly had no control, and she sobbed as the other two women waited patiently.

'Once you have been touched by evil it doesn't leave you easily. That woman made my father the man he was when he died. They were equally complicit in their decision to keep me from the truth,' Tilly stated once she had regained her composure.

After Enid had poured her a brandy and the emotional landscape had calmed, Tilly showed her friends the photos and the earrings, and shared the outline of her father's and stepmother's betrayal with them.

Madame's eyes welled as she cleared her throat to speak. 'I always believe things happen for a reason, and I knew you were special from the minute you spoke such bad French to me on your first day. Now, to discover you are both half French and Jewish, it is definitely fate that brought you here to us.' She reached across and took both Tilly's hands in hers and squeezed them.

Madame eventually made her way to bed, but Enid stayed up; as a distraction, she updated her friend on all the domestic comings and goings.

'Madame has been so much happier and alert since your trip to Paris; she has been anticipating more news from Jean-Luc.' She raised her eyebrows in a question.

'I emailed him to tell him my father had died and said once I had returned to Menton I would let him know, so best he kept any new information on locating the Paris apartment until then. I will contact him tomorrow,' Tilly said. Then Enid spontaneously hugged her before they both went off to bed.

It was a glorious Riviera morning when Tilly opened her curtains. The sun had risen just far enough to cast a ray on Madame's battered wicker furniture in the garden below. The chairs looked a little marooned, now that the large tree that offered Madame welcome shade in the heat of the summer had shed most of its foliage. The last of the leaves looked as if they had been brushed with gold. Tilly felt a fresh sense of stillness solidifying below her anger, a sense of familiarity and belonging.

Before she went downstairs, she sent off a short email to Jean-Luc saying she was back in Menton and asking whether he had more information that could help with Madame Pollock's quest.

After breakfast, and once Madame was installed in her chair in the Turret room, Tilly left the house under the pretence of buying some fresh vegetables in the market. She just needed to walk and breathe in the fresh sea air. She was desperate to navigate a way through the choppy waves of emotion that kept threatening to upend her.

The constant emotional pain had taken up permanent residency in her head. Was she grieving for a mother she never knew, or for a father she couldn't forgive?

When Tilly returned an hour later there was an email from Jean-Luc waiting in her inbox.

Dear Tilly, I am so pleased to know you are home with your friends in Menton. I cannot begin to imagine what it must be like for you losing your father. I do have some more information on Madame Pollock's apartment; perhaps it would be best if I called you this evening to discuss? JL x

This frustrated Tilly. She needed traction on the quest – new information; it was the vehicle for her to override her rage and grief. She would have preferred to know there and then but considered Jean-Luc's approach to things and respectfully replied that she looked forward to his call.

It was 8 p.m. when Tilly's phone buzzed. Madame

Pollock had stayed downstairs especially. So, with the other two women pretending not to listen, Tilly had to keep the conversation professional.

'Hi Jean-Luc, Madame Pollock and Enid are here with me!'

'I understand!' he replied; she could hear the subtle laughter in his voice.

'I am putting you on speaker phone,' Tilly responded.

'Madame Pollock will receive an official communication from our office about this, so, until then please keep this information confidential. A friend of mine who works in the relevant department here gave a push, and our people have liaised with the Mémorial de la Shoah, which is the Jewish organisation that assists with these matters in Paris. It has been agreed by both organisations that the documentation shows that a Jewish family by the name of Estienne did own an apartment in the Maison Papillon prior to World War II.'

He paused, and Tilly could imagine how his expression would be; he struggled to say the next part of the sentence. Madame Pollock sat bolt upright; she was totally riveted by the phone call. Jean-Luc continued.

'They go to great lengths to prove that someone is really who they purport to be. As Madame Pollock was very young when she left Paris, she will need to show evidence such as her birth certificate and her parents' marriage certificate plus any other documentation she has to connect her to the apartment; a deed would be excellent or perhaps photos or a key?'

Madame Pollock cleared her throat then replied in

French, thanking him and saying she would look through her mother's papers and see what she could find. Then, without a word, she went up to her room.

Tilly took Jean-Luc off speaker phone as Enid discreetly went into the kitchen.

'Thanks Jean-Luc, I guess we have more research to do. What about the concierge saying there is no apartment number 59 in the building? What was the apartment number your office found for the Estienne family?'

'There was no apartment number in the records they found, but apparently that isn't uncommon. A hundred years ago, the apartments were identified by the owners' names rather than a number. Remember it looks like Madame's grandparents may have been the first owners.'

He paused then continued.

'Tilly, do you think you will return to Paris again soon? I really would like to see you.'

Tilly let out a small sigh.

'I would love to, but I need to help Madame find these documents and hopefully a key. Also, I have been in a rather fragile state, with my dad's death,' Tilly replied.

'Oh! I am so sorry; I was being quite selfish. Of course, you must grieve. It's just I have been thinking of you all the time and can't wait to see you again.'

Tilly alluded briefly to other upsetting facts that had been revealed. She didn't wish to discuss these with Jean-Luc yet.

The next morning, after Madame had been through her bathroom routine, Tilly approached her in the Turret room.

'Do you think perhaps I should assist you with looking for the other evidence required by the officials on your mother's apartment?' Tilly said softly, not knowing which way Madame would respond.

After a protracted silence, Madame replied, 'I suppose so; I'm loath to burden you with all this. I really thought I could manage it myself, but I now realise, if I want to complete this "quest" as you and Enid call it, I will need your help in most aspects.'

The old lady hauled herself up from her low-slung armchair and Tilly followed her down the hall to her bedroom. Once in the room, she pulled back the dusty velvet curtains to her dressing room and pointed to the big chest that sat in the middle of the small space. It was surrounded by discarded clothes and a variety of ancient battered boxes. As Tilly stepped towards the chest, the faint aroma of lavender and camphor tickled her nose. Then, as she attempted to open the lid of the chest, the years of old dust swished up and both women sneezed. She quickly shut the lid and grabbed a tissue from her sleeve.

'I never let anyone clean in here; it's always been very private to me, so I think I will sneeze a bit; best to expect a few resident moths to greet us as well,' Madame Pollock said in a faraway voice.

'Don't fret! I'll be very careful. Why don't you sit on a chair and I'll go through each paper one by one and you can tell me what you wish done with each of them,' Tilly said as she pulled a desk chair into the dressing room and encouraged her to sit down. She dragged open the old window to help get rid of the dust.

Once Tilly had stacked the scattered papers from around the chest, she looked at each one and told Madame what she thought it was – at least reading French was easier than speaking it. Most were old receipts for work done on what must have been Madame's former home in Nice and receipts for things for the Menton house. Tilly put them into logical piles; most of them were so old she was sure they could be thrown away.

For a second time, she opened the chest; it still smelt musty but this time she managed not to sneeze. The papers on the top were yellowed and damp, and some were completely faded and stuck together.

By lunch time they had only been through a third of the contents. Tilly was determined not to miss anything relevant. There were more old receipts, and various magazines from the 1960s and 1970s that Madame's mother had kept. The most impressive things so far were her mother's sketchbooks and, to Tilly's delight, there were several wonderful drawings of fantasy butterflies.

'Oh! Why is there so much stuff?' Madame Pollock said, clearly exasperated by the chaos of the chest. 'None of this is what we are looking for – it needs to be prior to the liberation in 1944.'

By late afternoon they had worked their way through half of the papers and magazines in the old chest. As they had dug deeper, the dates of the various papers went down into the 1950s. Tilly could see Madame was becoming agitated.

'Let's continue this tomorrow! I can hear Enid is home. Why don't you have a lie-down and I will come and fetch you when supper is ready?' Tilly said, then gently guided the old lady over to the sunken bed.

TWENTY

PARIS, 1944

Everyday Papa Hans is angry, and Mama cries. When Mama makes the dinner, it is not very nice; she used to always give me yummy things to eat. Sometimes it is only a baguette with no cheese. She says I must be grateful, but I don't really understand because my tummy rumbles, and I am hungry. I cannot sleep very well at night and I keep feeling like something bad is going to happen. Papa Hans and Mama talk quietly for a long time, and when I go into the room they stop talking. No one smiles any more. It is a good thing I cannot go outside as I have become too big for my shoes; they pinch my toes. So I just wear my socks. My pinafore seems too short, so I know I have grown taller. I wish Mama would get me some new shoes and a new dress for my birthday.

Papa Hans is getting grumpier every day; he is out at

work for a long time and only comes home late at night. Mama cries a lot and when I cuddle her, she is not as soft any more; I can feel her bones. When I tell her, she gives a little laugh and tells me it is her new diet.

TWENTY-ONE

MENTON

Tilly eventually went up the stairs to check on Madame. It was unlike her to not come down on her own in time for supper. She was sitting on her bed with her head in her hands.

'Madame, are you OK?' Tilly asked as she sat down beside the old lady on her crumpled bed.

'Probably not, maybe I am getting dementia?' she replied as she sat upright and rubbed her bright eyes with her hands.

'I don't think so; I am sure Enid and I would have noticed.'

'Well, I hope not; it's just that I am struggling to remember what I can about Mama's Paris apartment. I lie down and concentrate and try to cast my mind back; but then it seems like I have fallen asleep and I'm dreaming.

It is all so real and I'm not sure what is factual and what is a dream.' She dropped her hands to her lap.

'Is what you remember very unpleasant?' Tilly asked.

'Well, I was only seven or so at the time we left Paris, and I could only grasp what my parents told me or what I saw. I am sure they hid a lot from me. Mama was constant in her care for me, but after Paris, she never spoke of Papa Hans other than to say my papa died during the war.' Madame stood up and Tilly followed her out.

Over supper Tilly attempted to bring up the subject of Madame's dream again, but to no avail. She said very little before returning to her bedroom.

The official letter to Madame from the land registry arrived the next day and confirmed that the records showed that in 1938 Joseph Cohen had signed the apartment over to the ownership of his daughter, Elsie Estienne, and son-in-law, Jacob. The registry's records had no evidence that the apartment had legally changed hands since then.

Madame Pollock would need to provide proof of who she was, including her mother's birth and marriage certificates as well as her own birth certificate. Given the registry's experience with what had happened to similar properties during the German occupation, the letter from the land registry also included the contact details of the Mémorial de la Shoah and advised Madame to get in touch with them as well.

'Well, now I have an option of two fathers, Papa Hans or this Jacob. It is frightening to think I don't know who my real father was. Maybe Mama told me, and I have blanked it out,' Madame said as she dropped the letter on to her lap, sinking into the chair while clutching her cheeks.

Enid and Tilly both thought it best not to pursue this conversation. Madame would need time to digest the information.

The next day Tilly and Madame returned to the chest. Amongst the papers, they found several incomplete sketches that Madame's mother had started. Tilly thought it was strange she had kept them. Maybe she had been interrupted and thought one day she would finish them. Maybe they had a special meaning.

Right at the bottom of the chest, inside a folder, was a sketch quite different from the others. It was of a woman in a drab overcoat with a paisley-patterned scarf over her head, tied tightly under the chin; she was holding hands with a little girl who looked equally as drab.

'This doesn't look like your mama's style; do you know anything about it?' Tilly asked as she handed the sketch to Madame.

Madame's bright aqua-blue eyes widened as she took the sketch in both hands and peered at it. After what seemed an age, she looked up.

'I think it is her work; I remember that when she was sad, she drew sad pictures, but often tore them up sometime afterwards. I am fairly sure the girl is me with Mama, when we first came on the train from Paris.' Then the old lady carefully returned the drawing to the folder.

They had drawn a blank. No legal papers at all referring to the Paris apartment, no key, none of her parents' certificates; it was frustrating.

Tilly started looking around the cramped space in Madame's bedroom; there were big round boxes of old hats from an era when a well-dressed French woman always wore a smart hat. There was a box of old handbags; clearly Madame didn't believe in parting with much.

'What's in that box over there?' Tilly asked, pointing to a closed brown box in the far corner.

'Oh, just old books; there are no loose papers or documents in there. I think we are going to have to contact this Mémorial de la Shoah place and see if they can help us.'

'Well, we have your marriage certificate which shows your maiden name as Estienne, but what I can't work out is why you don't have your birth certificate,' Tilly said.

'I don't ever remember having my birth certificate, a lot of people lost a lot of important papers during the war so maybe I didn't need it sixty years ago when I got married. Being realistic I think it's because of who my father was.' Madame paused, then added, 'Or who he wasn't?'

Tilly took their lunch, which consisted of a fresh baguette, some wonderful goat's cheese and a bowl of salad greens, on a tray out to Madame's favourite spot on the cane chairs under the tree in the garden. It was still warm enough to sit outdoors.

Although disappointed they hadn't achieved much in nearly two days of searching, Madame's demeanour had changed from last evening's lapse; she seemed more alert and motivated.

'Tilly, how are you feeling now, about your father and his revelations?' Madame asked as they sipped their coffee.

Tilly wasn't used to Madame asking her direct personal questions; it took her a few moments to gather her composure.

'Well, I feel extremely sad, but also a bit guilty. The sadness is for me and the mother I never knew. My guilt is about the anger towards my father. I had figured I would harbour it for a few years, but now he's dead, it's grief I feel. However, to be honest, I think the relief is greater. I feel safe now from Karen – her accusations, her overt narcissism and her caustic tongue. Relief, knowing she was never my real mother, if that makes sense?'

'I can identify somewhat, as I know nothing about my papa. However, my mama was such a loving woman it wasn't until I was in my twenties and getting married that I started to ask questions. But she would just shut the subject off.' Madame reached over and affectionately patted Tilly's hand, then continued.

'I just want to know if you feel up to another trip to Paris, and to this organisation Mémorial de la Shoah. If I understand things correctly, it is there to solve Jewish problems from the war, and I thought, if I gave you a letter giving you authority, you could go and speak to them on my behalf...' She paused, then added, '...but if you need to wait a while I understand.'

Tilly was impressed by Madame's proactivity.

'I think it will be a good distraction and I really need to be busy; so yes, I am definitely keen to go.'

Mid-afternoon, Madame went to have a rest and Tilly went for walk along the sea front. Once she reached the border, she made her way round to her favourite secluded beach; a light breeze wafted autumn scents of wood smoke from a large garden at the front of one of the villas that sat regally on the hill overhead.

The commercial operations of the beach were finished for the year. It felt strange being the only person on this coveted stretch of sand that belonged both to French Menton and to Italy. Tilly removed her shoes and paddled, allowing the chilled, crisp water to purify and refresh her feet. As she sat down on the sand a vast flock of tiny birds clustered overhead, soaring and swooping to make strange shapes in the sky as they feasted on an influx of minuscule insects that favoured that time of day. The pure azure-blue sea reminded her of the colour of Madame Pollock's eyes.

Despite recent traumatic events that had knocked her confidence, the essence of this French town and the Turret House offered Tilly sanctuary. Menton had nothing to do with her past, and everything to do with her future.

TWENTY-TWO

Tilly had emailed Jean-Luc about her proposed visit to Paris and he had immediately responded by inviting her to stay on with him for the weekend, so they could share some free time together.

'I just don't want to appear "easy" by agreeing to stay with him so soon after we have met,' Tilly said as she sat sipping fresh mint tea after dinner with her companions.

'I am sure he will have a second bedroom,' Madame quipped with a deadpan face, then winked at Enid.

This gesture seemed so funny and out of character, it made Tilly giggle. It was the first time since her father's death that she had experienced any inclination to humour or laughter. The giggles grew into an infectious laugh and soon the other two had joined in.

'Well, I think I have said enough for now,' Madame murmured, still smiling as she went off to bed.

'What an amazing change in Madame!' Enid said once

they heard her reach the top of the stairs. 'Her quest and response to your new situation appear to have activated a part of her I've never seen before. She has always been on the verge of depression since I have known her.'

'Well, I am grateful for her "quest" as I have this big struggle going on inside me between anger and grief, so being able to focus on how to reunite Madame with her birth right will help me work through my own hang-ups,' Tilly said with a shrug.

'And I am sure seeing a certain Jean-Luc again will be a pleasant distraction!' Enid added as she tapped the side of her nose.

Madame had reassured Tilly that, once in Paris, if she wanted to move to a hotel, that was fine with her. She wanted her to know that all her expenses were covered. They had agreed Tilly would leave the following week, allowing four days for further research of Maison Papillon, and then stay for the weekend with Jean-Luc.

Even though Tilly had been insistent that Jean-Luc didn't meet her from the plane, he had positioned himself as close as anyone could get to the arrival gate. Although he appeared subdued and formal with the familiar ironed crease in his jeans and his button-down pale blue shirt, Tilly experienced a whole new surge of love as she saw the corners of his eyes were creased with a special warmth above his subtle smile.

Jean-Luc took her case from the baggage carousel.

'I think it will be easier to catch a cab with this case rather than the train,' he said as he politely led her out of the building in the direction of the taxi rank.

'Sorry it's so big! I just wanted to be sure I had enough choices of what to wear,' Tilly said once they were in the cab.

Jean-Luc put his arm around her, kissed her cheek and whispered, 'I am flattered you want to look wonderful for me.'

The cab circled the famous Republique square with its striking central monument before turning into a narrow side street.

'This seems so close to everything! How wonderful!' Tilly declared as they pulled up outside a *brocante* shop. The footpath in front was festooned with old chairs, light fittings and other French junk.

Jean-Luc wore a somewhat serious face as he led her to an entrance adjacent to the shop. He produced a key and pushed the tall heavy door which opened into a courtyard full of overgrown shrubs. Once inside the adjoining foyer, the interior revealed itself to be much more impressive than the outside of the building suggested. The black and white marble floor tiles, although old, were gleaming in welcome and the freshly polished dark panelled walls offered a whiff of lemon-scented furniture polish. A neat row of nine letter boxes were mounted to the wall, and beside the curved staircase was an ancient looking lift with a metal gate. Jean-Luc pulled open the gate, which gave a loud creak; it was a real squash for the two of them and the suitcase – they were literally nose-to-nose as they made the slow cramped ride upwards. Tilly kissed Jean-Luc's cheek. He looked momentarily a little taken back, but then finally responded with a warm smile, still clutching her suitcase. The geriatric lift gave a bump as it came to a halt at the first floor.

The front door of his apartment led them directly into a spacious living room; Tilly was surprised by how much light there was, considering they had entered the building from a shaded narrow street. The room they walked into featured two floor-to-ceiling glass doors opening out on to a small balcony with wrought-iron decorative railings. Jean-Luc put her case down. His demeanour had totally turned around, and he was beaming. 'Welcome to my humble home!' he announced as he pulled the balcony doors open. A small white metal table had been squeezed on to the outdoor space, with a pink potted geranium positioned in the centre and two very small chairs on either side.

Tilly walked out on to the balcony. 'Jean-Luc this is wonderful! Just how us English would imagine a typical Parisian apartment.'

'It took me ages to find; I didn't really want a modernised building or apartment. This one is so meticulously kept, and it's mainly French people who live here. The rules of the building do not allow short-lets, so we don't get lots of American and English tourists coming and going.'

'Well, you have an "English tourist" here now! I hope you can cope!' Tilly responded with a poker face.

The poor man's face completely fell. 'Oh, I didn't mean anything against the English!' he blurted out.

Tilly took his hand and smiled. 'Calm down, I'm just joking,' she said, then added, 'Now come on, give me a tour.'

Jean-Luc had painted all the tall walls and high ceilings a chalky white. For Tilly, after living in the Turret House in Menton with its busy interior full of old furniture, textured wallpaper and numerous knick-knacks, she was intrigued that this apartment was the complete opposite. Other than one similarity – the architecture of both buildings was late nineteenth century – the interior was completely masculine and minimalist.

In the corner of the living room was a door leading to a tiny unmodernised kitchen. 'My mother keeps insisting I put in a new kitchen, but this works perfectly for me,' Jean-Luc said as he picked up her case and walked across to the hallway.

The entire apartment featured original, wide, dark wood polished floorboards. The hallway was devoid of any paintings but there were three doors leading off it. A huge brushed-metal lamp hung from an original rosette on the ceiling.

'You can hang your clothes in here,' Jean-Luc said as they entered a smallish bedroom that had a single bed draped with a pristine white cotton bedspread and was accompanied by a beautiful antique free-standing wardrobe and duchess dressing table.

'I'll enjoy sleeping in here – it's very cosy looking,' Tilly replied, tongue firmly in her cheek.

'I am a fast learner – I know this is your humour. This is your dressing room; however, I am very hopeful you will be sleeping with me!'

In Jean-Luc's bedroom a king-size bed sat proudly centred in the middle of the room overseen by a stylised, leather, designer headboard against the wall. The bed was swathed in a soft grey quilted bedspread which reached to the floor on all three sides. The bed faced two outside doors the same as in the living room but only one had a small Juliet balcony. There were no curtains, only the wooden shutters on the outside. In contrast to the masculine brutalist lamp in the hallway, a very impressive modern circle of crystal and bulbs hung on taut wire from the ceiling plaster rosette, directly above the bed.

There were two doors on one side of the room. Jean-Luc appeared pleased by her curiosity as Tilly opened the first door to reveal an austere, grey-tiled bathroom with an ancient tin bathtub that looked as if it'd been fully restored. The second door took her into Jean-Luc's wardrobe – no surprises here! He had a lower rail of immaculately pressed jeans and trousers, shelves of perfectly pressed shirts, and a top rail of several rather serious jackets.

'Are you happy to sit out on my balcony and have a glass of wine? I think it is warm enough?' Jean-Luc asked as he walked back to the kitchen.

He opened a bottle of chilled Chablis and, after some superficial chat, Jean-Luc expressed how sorry he was that she had lost her papa.

Tilly had been on her second glass of wine when it seemed to deactivate her self-protection barrier. All the emotion hit her at once; between sobs she found herself pouring out her entire life story; everything about her family's deception, Karen's cruelty and who her real mother was. Jean-Luc reached over and held her hand without saying a word until she had let it all out.

Then he leaned over, put his arm around her and handed her an immaculately ironed and folded white handkerchief from his pocket.

A large tear had appeared in each of his eyes, then Tilly sobbed. Once she had quietened, he responded.

'I cannot begin to imagine how bad you must feel; I can understand the betrayal is the worst part of it all. Tilly, please know I am here for you. Anything I can do to ease your pain I will do, and maybe this is just the right thing to be helping Madame Pollock with her quest. It's a worthwhile distraction.' He took her cheeks in his hands and kissed her.

Tilly felt quite conscious of her red face and her panda eyes from the smudged mascara, but the sensation of passion offered her a form of comfort. She kissed him back. He stood up, took her hand and led her to the bedroom. In one quick motion he pulled the grey bedspread off the bed, which revealed the pure white, starched and ironed sheets. Tilly was appropriately diverted to focus on her lover and surrendered to his slow sensual touch.

Part of the burden had moved by sharing everything about her parents, and Jean-Luc's response had soothed her. However, there was a niggle in the back of her thoughts that she should also disclose about Giovanni and the baby. But she reasoned there was probably plenty he hadn't told her, so that episode of her life could wait.

Shining with the glow of freshly made love, they walked out hand in hand into the crisp Paris early-evening air, and arrived at Centenaire, a small busy bistro just a short walk from Jean-Luc's apartment.

'Do you have the photos you captured of the Maison Papillon?' Jean-Luc asked once they were settled at their table.

'Gosh! I haven't even looked at them since I took them, I've been so self-absorbed in my own drama,' Tilly replied as she pulled up the photo gallery on her phone.

They both peered at the screen, but it was difficult to see many details. Jean-Luc offered to enlarge them later on his computer.

Over a wonderful mushroom risotto their chat moved to her new circumstances; Tilly managed to talk without further tears. She told Jean-Luc it was such a coincidence that she was not only half French but, like Madame Pollock, also officially Jewish.

'How do you feel about that?' Jean-Luc asked.

'In the first instance, frustrated, as I have so much catching up to do. In the second, I'm wildly curious about it all and, once this mission is over, I think I will read up on what it means to be a Jewish woman in this day and age.'

Once back at the apartment Jean-Luc transferred Tilly's photos to his computer; it had a wonderful big screen and the butterfly gate came to life.

'It is impressive!' he said.

'Yes, so is the courtyard. See, there is a main door to each building, but I didn't get a chance to check which apartment numbers were on which buildings,' Tilly replied as Jean-Luc scrolled through the shots.

Once they enlarged the back building, they could see it was like the others, except on the fifth floor – there were only four windows, not six. The others had two front-facing windows each, but there the similarity ended – there was just a blank space. But as he enlarged it further, they could see the faint outline of two sills where you would have expected to see windows. On closer inspection, although painted a dirty cream like the rest of the building, the space above the sills was a completely different texture. The original windows must have been filled in!

Jean-Luc then referred back to a map on Google. They could see there was a tall commercial building at the back of that side of Maison Papillon so there wouldn't now be much of a view of the back building, but, by the same token, there wouldn't be much to see from the outside.

Jean-Luc gently stroked Tilly's neck as they scrutinised the screen. This led to some intense kissing and before long they were back on the bed.

A serene sense of peace filled Tilly after they had made love for a second time that day. A lot of her anger had softened by this pleasurable physical and emotional act. She smiled as Jean-Luc brought in two cups of herbal tea on a small silver tray, then sat naked next to her on the bed. Despite the lightness of his build and his relatively narrow shoulders, he wasn't in any way frail. His muscular body gave her a striking impression of graceful strength.

Her lustful thoughts were distracted by Jean-Luc who had moved back to the business of the 'quest'.

'I feel sure where those two sills are is where Madame's apartment must be; but gaining legal access is going to be quite a process, then proving ownership is going to take some investigating.'

'Tomorrow I have an appointment with the *Fils et Filles des Déportés juifs de France* association; even though Madame and her mama were not deported from France Enid found this organisation online and thought they may be able to help,' said Tilly.

TWENTY-THREE

It took Tilly some time to find the *Fils et Filles des Déportés* association. Its priority appeared to be recording concentration camp deaths. The section of its website which she hoped would help gave more information about finding stolen Jewish artwork than property, as most property had been returned to family survivors soon after the war. After a twenty-minute wait in a busy office with chatter in both French and what Tilly assumed was Hebrew an unsmiling middle-aged woman, with her black hair pulled back in a severe ponytail, called her name and invited her into an office.

She politely introduced herself as Miriam, then sat down and placed her clasped hands on her desk.

'How can we help you?' she said in English without a trace of sentiment.

Tilly stammered her way through Madame's story; as she went on, Miriam's interest level appeared to increase.

Once Tilly had finished, she paused to gauge the reaction.

'Curious, very curious!' Miriam finally stated as she rubbed her nose. 'I haven't come across a case like this before. I think, in the first instance, we should do a search for Madame Pollock's parents; we will look in the Central Synagogue registry for their birth and marriage certificates and then do what we can to source a death certificate for Jacob Estienne.'

'Thank you,' Tilly said.

Miriam continued, 'Then we can see if those names correspond with the ownership details of the apartment and if they do, we can move forward offering support from there.' She took a breath. 'I just feel I have to mention at this point, Tilly, that you should be aware that thousands of babies were conceived by the occupying forces during the Occupation and this can often add an extra level of complexity as to how services can be accessed.'

'But Madame was at least seven at the time the war ended,' Tilly quickly responded.

'Well, she may believe that, but I have met people who have at least a five-year age difference from their real age. This may not be the case here; I just believe it is best to be open about all possibilities. I will email you as soon as I have followed these lines of enquiry.' Miriam offered what probably constituted a smile, then stood up, and Tilly was clearly made aware that the meeting was over.

As she left the building, it occurred to Tilly for the first time that this quest may not have the happy ending she had hoped for. It also triggered thoughts of her birth mother's missing grandfathers.

Her next appointment was the following day at the Pavillon de l'Arsenal, Jean-Luc's building. It was not at Jean-Luc's department she needed to present herself as Madame Pollock's representative, she must ensure she had all the supporting documentation they had prepared.

Tilly didn't have any other appointments until 5.30 p.m. when she was to meet Jean-Luc back at the apartment. She couldn't help herself; she wanted to find out if she could see more of the fifth floor of the building from within the courtyard at Maison Papillon and get some clearer photos.

Tilly knew the route and Métro off by heart now. When she arrived at the outside doors her entry was thwarted; the tall door was open, but the concierge was standing chatting to a well-dressed man. So, she scooted past unnoticed and made her way to the rear building in the middle of the other two. The four sides of the building extended further than Tilly could see. There were several sets of tall doors. It took her some time to locate the rear of Maison Papillon, or where she thought it was.

There was a narrow alleyway between the rear of the commercial building that overlooked the back of Maison Papillon – it was less than two metres wide. She walked halfway along and looked up. The windows on the Maison Papillon side were all quite small. Clearly all the light and view were to the front, overlooking the attractive courtyard and the butterfly gate. It was quite dark, so she switched on the flash of her camera and held her arms as high as she could and took several photos.

After further inspection she could see that five floors

up on the commercial building there were some small windows looking directly across at the rear of Maison Papillon. It would be a perfect spot to take some more photos. So, she followed the building around to the front to see if she could gain entry.

The front of the building was on a busy street with lots of retail shops. There was a large set of doors and a buzzer halfway along, so Tilly pressed it and immediately gained entry. The foyer was highly polished and slick with a very official-looking man sitting at a desk at the base of the stairs and next to a set of lifts.

'*Puis-je vous aider?*'

'Uumm, I would like to go to the fifth floor please,' Tilly blurted out.

'Do you have an appointment?' the man responded in English.

'What company is on the fifth floor please?' Tilly said, and as soon as the words were out she knew she had blown it, and this wasn't going to work.

'I am not allowed to let you in without an appointment,' the man said as he stood up and glared at her. Tilly figured she had done enough so better to leave and regroup with more information.

Once outside the door, she took a quick photo of the sign beside the buzzer which featured the business names in the building; she would inspect it more closely later.

Just as she finished, her phone beeped.

'Hello Tilly, it's Andrew McKenzie. I'm just giving you a quick call to say we are working through the probate process, but Karen has requested details of the bank account he held in your joint names. I feel confident she has no claim, but I must provide them to her and wait to see her reaction, so I'm afraid none of the funds can be released until that happens.'

'I don't need the money, so timing is not important; but I definitely don't want that woman getting her hands on any of it so, please do whatever you need to,' Tilly replied.

With the mention of Karen, her world suddenly turned upside down again. Spotting a café a couple of doors along, she plonked herself down on an outdoor seat and although initially intending to order a coffee, she found herself asking for a glass of rosé instead.

The memory of Karen and the dark days of her childhood had reignited her anger. The worst time for her was after she got home from school before her father returned from work. Those two hours would be torture; Karen would find fault with everything, from a spot on her school uniform to her unruly hair. If Tilly answered back, she would get a wallop from Karen's leather belt on the upper part of her legs. On reflection it was as if Karen wanted any reason to hit her.

The waiter interrupted her thoughts as he placed the wine and some nuts in front of her. She must try to shake these thoughts off. The wine disappeared quite quickly and by the time her phone beeped for the second time that day she had polished off two full glasses.

'Tilly, where are you?' Jean-Luc sounded desperate.

'Oh sorry, I'm having a glass of wine in a café over near Maison Papillon.' She let out a loud hiccup then continued. 'I had a phone call from my lawyer in London and it triggered all the memories of my horrid stepmother.'

'Tell me the name of the café?' was all Jean-Luc said.

Tilly checked the name on the wine list in front of her, and he said he would see her in around half an hour.

By the time he arrived Tilly had slowed down a bit and was only halfway through her third glass.

'Did they let you leave work early?' Tilly asked.

'No, I arrived home from work at my normal time and you weren't there as we had discussed, so I worried,' he replied abruptly, then added in a softer tone, 'It's now 6.30 p.m. Tilly, how long have you been here?'

'Oh shit! I thought it was about four o'clock! I am so sorry.'

'Do you want to tell me what the lawyer's call was about?' He placed his hand on hers.

Tilly's eyes were red, fuelled by the wine. She made a small gasping sound then managed to respond. 'Karen, my stepmother, is objecting to me having the money my father specifically left me in his will; the lawyer tells me he is confident she hasn't got a claim. It's not the money I want, it's just that it only exists because my mother died giving birth to me. It's her life insurance payment. That was all my father did for me, in defiance of his horrid wife. A bank account! It feels like the only positive memory I have of him.' Jean-Luc took his immaculate white hanky from his pocket and caught the tear before it rolled off Tilly's cheek.

'I feel the shame that woman inflicted on me all over again. I'm sorry, Jean-Luc, I will understand if you can't cope with these outbursts.'

He pulled her towards him; she rested her head on his shoulder.

'Don't speak like that Tilly! I'm also well-schooled in the shame department, so I can identify with what you are feeling. Come on, let's go back to the apartment and eat; I want to hear all about your adventures with the "quest".'

TWENTY-FOUR

By the time they had returned to the apartment, Tilly had sobered up. Jean-Luc made them a cheese and ham omelette with an impressive salad. They ate it on his small balcony.

'I love all the diverse things you have put in this salad and the honey and mustard dressing is delicious.' Tilly was delighted that he thrived on her compliments.

She told him all about her visit to the *Fils et Filles des Déportés* association, then about her failed attempt to photograph the rear of Maison Papillon from the commercial building.

After they had finished the meal they moved inside, and Jean-Luc put the photos from her day into the computer.

'I didn't think I would capture much from down in that alleyway,' Tilly said as they enlarged the shots.

'Let's see which company is on the fifth floor of the commercial building.' Jean-Luc reviewed the photo she had taken of the entry sign.

'It looks like a biotech company of some kind called Medi-Alert Paris.'

Tilly quickly googled the name and hit 'Translate'; it led her to the website which stated that its function was drug discovery.

'I wonder what excuse I can make to visit their offices,' Tilly said as she randomly scrolled through the complex scientific details packed on to the page.

'Why not just phone up and explain what you are doing and that you only wish to use their rear room for a few moments to take some photographs.' Jean-Luc raised his eyebrows.

The next morning, he called in late for work and phoned the biotech company. He really had to stretch himself to sound confident in convincing the secretary to allow Tilly access to what he had established from his conversation was in fact a small storeroom. He assured her that Tilly wasn't a spy but an eccentric English woman with a camera and a passion for Haussmann architecture. Tilly had agreed with him that the whole World War II Jewish story might sound a bit much and a bit far-fetched.

Tilly had put some effort into looking smart, with her version of 'English' – flat leather walking shoes, jeans and a white shirt. The snooty secretary was on the wrong side of fifty and greeted her with a scowl, stating that she thought Jean-Luc, the gentleman who had phoned, would have been accompanying her. Tilly responded that as an architect he was a very busy man with important engagements today.

She followed the secretary into a cramped room that

housed piles of printer paper, boxes of files and, to Tilly's dismay, a window of frosted glass!

'Would it be OK if I open the window please?'

The secretary offered another scowl then replied in English, 'We have never had that window open; you may try but you must not disturb any of our important papers!'

Tilly clutched the bottom of the window frame; it was a sash window and she could see from the dust that it hadn't been opened for years. The secretary stood at the door the entire time while Tilly tried to push the window up. After three big shoves she managed to move it. A wind blew in and there was a collective flap of the loose papers on the storeroom shelves.

'*Merde*! You must close that window *toute suite*!' the secretary barked as she dramatically threw her hands on piles of the papers.

Tilly moved like lightning. She lowered the window fractionally to offer some reassurance to the frantic woman, then swiftly pulled out her phone camera and leaned out of the window. She took a moment to aim clearly at the part of Maison Papillon she believed was her target and managed to take several shots before the secretary literally pulled her away and slammed the window down.

'You will leave now!' she barked.

Tilly figured this was all she was going to get. She thanked her and scooted out of the offices as quickly as she could.

She made her way to Jean-Luc's building for her meeting with the department that housed the original plans for the

Haussmann buildings together with the records of sales and purchases. She had suspected that, although he wasn't directly involved with that department, Jean-Luc would be about. He was hovering near the entrance when she arrived.

'*Bonjour ma Cherie*! You look as beautiful as the first day I saw you in this same foyer.' Then as soon as the words were out, he blushed a bright red hue. He accompanied her to where she needed to be and left her to it. The man that greeted her stood very upright and had a head of thick grey hair, which he had heavily gelled to a slick on his head. He introduced himself as Monsieur Yves and stated in English that he was the director of the department of historic plans.

He opened the palm of his hand and indicated for Tilly to sit down.

'Mademoiselle Tilly, we can confirm now that there was, or is, an apartment in Maison Parc the building which had its name changed to Maison Papillon, that belonged, or belongs, to the family of Elsie and Jacob Estienne. It was purchased by Elsie Estienne's grandparents, the Cohens, in 1905 and signed over to the Estiennes in 1938 and we have no record of it ever being sold. There are technically three buildings, as each side overlooking the courtyard is a separate building. The only documentation we have is that the Cohens purchased an apartment on the fifth floor of one of these buildings.'

'Thank you,' Tilly replied, then he continued.

'We have no ability to grant you or Madame Pollock access to Maison Papillon – you must achieve that through the normal legal channels, but I can inform you that Madame Pollock will need a copy of her birth certificate and the relevant documentation of her parents' ownership.'

Tilly told him they were looking for that but as it was over eighty years ago it was proving difficult. He agreed that getting the *Fils et Filles des Déportés* association involved would help, as they had powers of investigation that surpassed the usual channels.

Jean-Luc caught up with her again as she left Monsieur Yves's office. She asked him if she could use his home laptop to view the morning's photos. He reassured her whatever was his, was hers to share. As Tilly walked away, she basked in his gesture, and how romantic it sounded, said with his delicious French accent. Nothing like the multi-layered bullshit her former lover, Giovanni, had spun her.

Although she was very enthusiastic to get back to inspect the photos, Tilly wanted to express her thanks and show some token of her affection to Jean-Luc. Knowing her cooking wasn't up to much and that to pay for a meal for him would offend his sense of propriety, she opted to call in to a delicatessen she had passed with some rather extravagant-looking food on display. As the automatic doors opened and Tilly walked into the air-conditioned store, the aromas offered the first seduction of her senses. Then the visual symphony kicked in. This food was art, the presentation immaculate, the food types and colours working in perfect harmony. The meats were presented in delicate aspics with subtle sauces in separate side containers. A whole cooked salmon lay on a mirror garnished with symmetrically cut lemon and bundles of parsley that had been intricately tied with twine.

She perused the comprehensive array of savoury dishes, then moved on to an equally mesmerising display of mouth-watering pastries and chocolates. Surely this was food for love!

Tilly left the store cautiously carrying the two boxes that housed the dinner she had carefully selected as her gift for Jean-Luc. She had managed to squash the bottle of champagne in her tote bag; the shop assistant had assured her, although not one of the famous brands, it was both delectable and affordable. Once back at the apartment she left the food in the boxes on the kitchen bench, put the bubbles in the fridge, then after a search through his linen cupboard she set the small dining table with the arty looking place mats and two precisely ironed white linen napkins. The small posy of miniature white roses she had bought en route she placed in a water glass in the centre of the table. Then, before she sat down at the laptop, she lit the Maharaja scented candle that Jean-Luc had lit on her first evening. This distinct, musky fragrance would always belong, exclusively, to her special French man.

Tilly logged the photos on the laptop and was deep in thought about the possible permutations of the fifth floor of Maison Papillon when Jean-Luc returned home.

His first glance was one of slight puzzlement, then a smile crossed his lips as Tilly got up and greeted him with a soft kiss on his mouth, then said, 'It's my treat this evening, I have a meal prepared.'

Jean-Luc was clearly impressed. He chose his best crystal glasses and poured their champagne as Tilly undid the food boxes and he retrieved the appropriate serving plates. The small version of the salmon Tilly had chosen had lost some of its allure, with the lack of the mirror, but she carefully placed the garnish and the sauce with it and felt her presentation would pass muster after the second glass of champagne had been consumed. The salmon was accompanied with thick, white asparagus spears that had been drizzled in unsalted butter with tiny new potatoes festooned with finely chopped mint.

The crescendo to this gourmet feast was the mille feuille; it was the most delicate and creamy Tilly had ever tasted. Layers of light flaky pastry with both cream and custard between each, then topped with a slither of vanilla icing.

'I am somewhat of an expert on this pastry,' Jean-Luc said as he topped up Tilly's glass with the Sauterne he had offered to accompany the dessert. 'My mother's cook used to make it for us for very special Sunday lunches when I was young. Although originally made in Napoleon's time, it was updated and modernised by a chef called Marie-Antoine Carême.'

Tilly smiled, it sounded like something an architect would say; she reached out and gave his hand a stroke.

After a perfect 'dinner-of-love', their love making went to a new level; it took Tilly to a place of intimacy and trust. In the afterglow as they lay naked on the crisp white sheets, she reflected that the sting of her immediate grief had subsided. They talked easily about everything and nothing, intending to return to the photos on the computer, but drifted off in each other's arms. They only awakened as the sun offered its countenance through the still-open shutters.

'I have something planned for you this morning – you need to be ready by 10.30 a.m.,' Jean-Luc said as they sat drinking coffee on the small balcony.

'I need us to look at those photos I took yesterday first, please?' Tilly replied. 'That's why I am here, to solve Madame's mystery.'

'Oh really! Here was I deluded into thinking this beautiful English woman was mad about me and all the time she was just after my laptop!' he retorted as he moved inside and turned the computer on.

Tilly had captured what they hoped was the back wall of the apartments on the fifth floor and as Jean-Luc enlarged and endeavoured to sharpen the images they could see that they were all smallish back windows. They didn't have any obvious way of opening and didn't offer them any insight as to what the configuration of apartments was within.

'*Ma Cherie*, I think that may have been a wasted mission. I am sorry.'

'Oh well, this is such a slow process, I just wish we could gain entry to the inside. Even possibly get to chat to an elderly resident who might remember Madame's family.' Tilly sighed as she replied. Then added, 'It's a waiting game now until Miriam from the *Fils et Filles des Déportés* gets back to me with any of the Jewish records of Madame's family.'

'Well, now it is really up to Madame to supply proof of

her identity, previous to her marriage and a key or some other connection to the apartment; once the lawyers get involved it will become very expensive,' Jean-Luc said, then sat up straight as if he had an announcement to make.

Tilly straightened as well and folded her hands in her lap.

'Now, I hope I have done the correct thing?' Jean-Luc finally said.

'Yes, what?' Tilly replied.

'Well, after our conversation about your new-found Jewishness I thought it would be of interest to go to the Grand Synagogue this morning?' He had stood up and apprehensively shifted on his feet.

Tilly reached out and motioned for him to sit down. 'For goodness' sake, don't act so nervous, it's a wonderful idea! I would love to and it's the Jewish Sabbath so there should be a service on.'

Jean-Luc sat back down and gave a smile of relief. 'Yes, I phoned them yesterday to check if I needed to wear one of those small hats and if we could get in. I had noticed the security around the Synagogue so thought I had better check.'

TWENTY-FIVE

The Synagogue service commenced at 9.30 a.m. so they hurriedly dressed; Tilly made sure she had on a knee-length dress and so her arms could be covered if need be, she grabbed a light jacket. After arriving from the Métro Jean-Luc led her into a rather drab side street. A strange place for the entrance to something called 'The Grand Synagogue'. They were required to show their passports on entry and the level of security felt slightly unnerving on entering a place of worship. It passed through Tilly's mind how sad it was that after all that was fought for in the last World War, terrorism and anti-Semitism were still part of their lives and even now, Jews didn't have total freedom of worship.

They had arrived a little late and stood looking at the situation inside. There were clearly divided seating areas for women and men. Non-Jewish visitors were only required to dress modestly and didn't need to cover their heads. There was a smattering of Orthodox Jews in their full regalia, but mainly smartly dressed Parisians.

Tilly was surprised at the lack of a grand entrance. Jean-Luc quietly explained that when the building opened in 1874, the entrance did open out on to the main street but due to the politics of that time it had to be shifted to an insignificant side street, to minimise what was perceived at the time as social embarrassment to non-Jews living in the area.

The space was very large, but in no way opulent as a French or Italian Catholic cathedral might be. A series of twelve striking, stained-glass windows towered over the congregation, each symbolising one of the twelve tribes of Israel.

Beyond what Tilly assumed was the altar were a few steps upwards where a curtain had been pulled open to reveal the Torah, the holy scrolls.

Tilly took a seat in the 'women's' area. The service was mainly in Yiddish and while Tilly had no recognition of its strange tones, as she looked around her and studied the sincerity of the worshippers, she considered that her grandparents and the generations before them would have possibly worshipped in this place, practised the sacred rituals in their everyday lives. This was all something she was keen to explore. The emotion crept up on her; it arrived from a place that she hadn't visited before; it wasn't grief or anger, but a colossal slice of sadness from being deprived of and never knowing 50 per cent of her heritage. A heritage that came through her dead mother's blood; it offered so much history and so much colour.

Tilly knew that her mother would have wished her to have understood the deep love that had created her only child – something her father had kept from her. She sat upright and fought hard against the tears, then the anger began to slip through. Yes, her father had been grieved by his beloved wife's death; but Tilly knew grief too, under no circumstances would she have treated her own daughter that way.

As the first tear began to fall, Tilly wished Jean-Luc was beside her. She could only see the back of his head in the 'men's' section. But by the time he greeted her at the end of the service she had managed to get her emotions under control.

As they left the Synagogue Jean-Luc translated what was written above the inside of the entrance door.

'This is none other than the House of God, the very gateway to Heaven.'

Then as they stepped back out on to the narrow street he added, 'Not the entrance I imagined Heaven should have!'

'Are you OK, *ma Cherie*?' Jean-Luc asked as he put his arm around Tilly. 'You have gone very quiet; do you wish to share with me?'

Tilly couldn't help but smile at his formal English which jolted her away from her thoughts of regret.

'Yes, I'm fine thanks. Where are we going now?'

As they arrived on the Métro at Concorde, the midday sun added a luminosity to this instantly familiar part of Paris. Jean-Luc held Tilly's hand as they walked towards the Tuileries Garden.

They found an outdoor table at the Café des Marronniers and Tilly was appreciative of Jean-Luc not asking her any questions about her emotion in the Synagogue. However, he was very enthusiastic to share his knowledge about their surroundings.

'Catherine de Medici created these magnificent gardens in 1564 for her own amusement and pleasure. By 1667 they were opened to the public and have been enjoyed by Parisians ever since.'

He was interrupted when the waitress arrived to take their order. He persuaded Tilly to try the escargots; she agreed to share an entrée of them with him if he agreed to share an English special, fish and chips, with her as a main.

'Now please tell me more about these beautiful gardens,' Tilly said once they had ordered.

Jean-Luc straightened in his seat and smiled. 'What I like the most is the perfect symmetry that André Le Nôtre, who designed them, created. I enjoy its formality. He reflected self-control and discipline way back then in seventeenth century.'

The escargots arrived and, while they mainly tasted of garlic, to Tilly's surprise she enjoyed them; washing them down with a perfectly chilled glass of Chablis certainly enhanced the experience.

After lunch they walked past the small lake, or large pond, depending on one's view. Jean-Luc, with his architectural hat on, explained in detail how the octagonal shape was unique, and that the pond measured sixty metres across.

Back at the apartment, once they were seated on the balcony sipping an espresso, Tilly's conversation returned to Madame's quest. She expressed her frustration that it felt as if she had not moved forward at all; waiting for people to get back to her was an annoyance.

'If only we could take a sneak peek inside the apartment building and at least see which apartment it might be; I'd feel I'd achieved something before I return,' she sighed.

The following morning Tilly woke with Jean-Luc sitting up in the bed beside her, with an odd look on his face.

'What's going on in your head this morning?' Tilly asked as she sat up and kissed his cheek.

'Well, I must be breaking out, as they say on American TV shows. I am thinking about a plan that will be illegal, and with considerable risk, all to help overcome your "frustration and annoyance", to quote your own words.'

'Tell me!'

'No, not until we have our coffee and the croissants that I have heating in the oven.' He took his empty coffee cup out to the kitchen, returning with the breakfast on a large tray.

Tilly smiled at his precision as he studiously placed the tray on her side of the bed, then propped several pillows to lean against. He manoeuvred the tray so they could eat over it avoiding crumbs in the bed, then he sat up even straighter and cleared his throat.

'As it is Sunday, no doubt the old concierge at Maison Papillon will be off to church or visiting her family, so I thought we could "stake out" the building to ensure she isn't there, then loiter by the gate to repeat what you did and gain entry when a resident comes in or out. We will improvise once we are in to gain entry to the back part of the building where we think the apartment may be,' he said, then picked up his coffee cup, took a sip and looked expectantly at Tilly.

Tilly laughed. 'I love it! But what if the old bat has her family over for Sunday lunch or to visit?'

'I thought of that! If she has guests, she won't be paying attention to the comings and goings of the residents.'

There was a pregnant pause while they both contemplated the plan. Then Tilly laughed again. 'Shall we dress in black and wear knitted beanies?'

Jean-Luc raised his eyebrows. 'I am not familiar with beanies; it wasn't in the American detective series I learned the word "stake out" from.'

'I was making a joke. A beanie is a knitted hat that burglars wear in American detective TV programmes.'

He smiled. 'I think the idea is to dress as if we belong in that apartment building, so are you up for my plan?'

'Yes, I am definitely up for it. What do we have to lose!'

Their jokes about what to wear and the laughter continued as they showered and dressed for their adventure. Tilly was seeing a whole new side to her French man and was also pleased that she had experienced a swifter recovery from her emotional upheaval during their Synagogue visit. It was as if she was learning the meaning of moving forward.

TWENTY-SIX

They arrived outside Maison Papillon around mid-morning. The large outside door was open and during the ten minutes they loitered across the street, they observed several people coming in and out.

After attempting to blend in for around twenty minutes they finally spotted the old lady. She was clearly dressed in her Sunday best. She wore a smart jacket with a fitted skirt and carried a white cardboard box neatly tied with a piece of string.

'She will be going to her family; and I bet those are her home-baked pastries in that box,' Jean-Luc spoke directly into Tilly's ear.

As soon as they saw her back as she waddled up the street they slipped through the large outside door. They commenced a charade of chatting by the butterfly gate. Jean-Luc cast his eyes down the list of names by the buzzers. Then he turned and studied the gate.

'It is much more impressive than in the photos. I like the fact it is an architectural contradiction to the early Haussmann style.'

They were just about to engage with a young man who was walking towards the gate when the old concierge reappeared. They panicked. Then Jean-Luc grabbed Tilly, so her back was to the old lady, and holding her in a strong embrace he swiftly kissed her full on the mouth. The old woman looked over and muttered something along the lines of 'disgusting' but was thankfully distracted by the fact she had forgotten something. Once she went into her apartment, they scurried out to the street and concealed themselves behind a large tree. Within a couple of minutes, she came out again carrying a small tote bag.

'I do apologise for grabbing you that way, Tilly, but as we are doing very illegal things and the concierge has already encountered you before, I needed to conceal your face,' Jean-Luc said as he raised his eyebrows and smiled.

Tilly laughed and pecked his lips. 'Any time!'

They returned through the door to continue their ruse by the gate. They didn't have to wait long before a middle-aged man wearing smart but casual attire walked in with a newspaper under his arm, holding a bag of fresh pastries.

Tilly nudged Jean-Luc. He gave a puzzled look then sprang into action. He said he had misplaced the fob his grandmother had given him for the gate and that he had rung her buzzer, but she was very deaf and couldn't hear it.

The man was clearly in no mood to chat. He opened the gate, held it for a moment while the duo hurried through, then briskly walked off in front of them to the door which gave entry to the left side of the complex.

'What would you have said if he had asked who your grandmother was?' Tilly said.

'I looked at the most worn-looking name on the buzzer list and spotted a Mme DeFoud so I assumed she would be elderly and alone.'

'Good thinking Batman! Now we have to crack the next door.'

Jean-Luc frowned. 'What is this "Batman"?'

Tilly laughed out loud. 'Sorry, I assumed you would know about Batman! I loved watching the Batman TV series—' Then she stopped. 'Look, I'll tell you later; we are on a mission and don't have time for cultural explanations just now.'

They stood in front of the door at the back of the building; there were no numbers, just another line of names and buzzers. It was obvious the only entry was via a fob, or if someone from the inside buzzed you in.

'I see Mme DeFoud lives in this block. Do you think it's worth buzzing and bluffing for her to let us in?' Tilly asked.

'Well, if she is old, I feel that it would be unfair to take advantage or confuse her. Let's see who turns up in the next few minutes before we attempt that.' As he spoke a young woman wearing an odd-looking sun hat, slightly too baggy jeans and a sweatshirt with the word 'Paris' written on it, came through the gate and headed towards the door of the building to the right of them. Tilly called out '*bonjour*'.

The woman replied in very bad French, asking if she could help them.

Tilly quickly answered in English.

'Hi, my old aunt who is rather deaf can't hear us ringing her buzzer and I have misplaced my key.' She offered the woman a big smile.

'Oh, no problem. I think I can help. I'm Jackie by the way.'

'Are you American?' Jean-Luc asked and managed a smile as well.

'Sure am! I'm just here staying in a short let for a week; I leave tomorrow. I love old French buildings, so I have had a snoop around. I'm up on the fourth floor but found that if you take the lift to the fifth floor then walk up the stairs to the sixth floor, to what were previously storage rooms, there is a connecting stairway to your aunt's side of the building.'

Jackie spoke very fast with a strong southern American accent and Tilly could see Jean-Luc having trouble grasping everything she said. She quietly whispered, 'I've got this, just follow my lead!'

'Oh, that would be wonderful Jackie, thank you,' Tilly responded as they followed her into the building.

They stepped into the small foyer which had a highly polished black and white tiled floor. Jackie walked over and opened the aged iron gates to the lift.

'It will be a tight squeeze, but it beats the stairs,' she said as the three of them pressed into the intimate space. The ancient lift jolted to a halt at the fourth floor and Jackie got out.

'Good luck!'

'Thank you,' Tilly said as Jean-Luc went to press the button to the sixth floor. Tilly reached over to stop him.

'No, she said it's better to take the stairs from the fifth as that's where there is a passageway across; I think the door across to the back building is off the stairwell.'

'OK. I just couldn't understand what she was saying; was it a dialect?' Jean-Luc said.

'I guess you could call it that!'

Another jolt and they were at the fifth floor. Close to the lift was a faded, barely legible sign saying *'Escalier'*. The door creaked as they opened it. Unlike the rest of the building and gardens, the staircase had clearly not been updated and was a bit grubby. It was nevertheless impressive with its wrought-iron bannister and chunky polished solid wood handrail. Once at the top of the stairwell, they could see the door that led out to the hallway of the apartments. They looked more closely, then registered that the seam in the wall wasn't a panel but was in fact a second door. It had no handle or lintels and was painted to blend in with the wall. Jean-Luc pushed the panel and it swung open to reveal a narrow rustic-looking wood-panelled hallway. It was devoid of light. Tilly turned on the torch on her mobile phone and just a few steps in they pushed a further panel and arrived on the sixth floor of the building. They then located the stairwell and made their way down to the fifth floor.

They found themselves in a long empty corridor. They could now understand why there were no useful windows at the back of the building – the hallway ran along the back wall. The corridor had a very sad, brown faded flocked wallpaper above a painted dado rail. From the staircase door to the first apartment door there was an expansive space that was out of kilter with the doors along the hall. After that, there were four apartment doors evenly spaced six metres apart.

They both stood, still and thoughtful, taking in the bland colourless hallway. Tilly followed as Jean-Luc walked along studying the area before the first apartment door. Tilly was silent, not quite sure what they were looking at.

Jean-Luc stopped and whispered to her.

'I think this apartment was built or was altered to be double the size of the other two, which accounts for this wide expanse of space.'

Tilly nodded. 'So, what do you suggest we do now?'

'I think we have to be brave and knock at a door and see what we can find out.'

'So now we just have to choose which door!' Tilly sidled beside him as she spoke. In this morbid-looking hallway, her bravado was waning.

They stood in front of the first door they came to and gave a gentle knock. But there was no answer.

There was no answer at the next two doors.

Finally, their knock to the fourth door at the far end of the hallway was opened by a young-looking Asian woman in a white nurse's smock.

Jean-Luc quickly explained they were looking for an apartment that had been owned by the Cohen and Estienne families prior to the last war and queried whether there was an elderly resident who might be able to assist. Before the young nurse could respond a very old white-haired lady holding two sticks appeared beside her. She looked very dishevelled and irreverently shoved the nurse to one side and hobbled directly up to Jean-Luc.

'Who the hell are you?' she demanded in rapid French and poked his foot with one of her sticks.

Jean-Luc recovered quickly and asked if she had known the Estienne family who had a small daughter called Corrinne and left Paris during the war.

The old woman blinked several times. She flicked her walking stick again. This time Jean-Luc stepped back.

'You shouldn't be in here! You are trespassing! Bugger off or I will call the concierge and the old bag will call the police.' She turned, pushed past the nurse and went back inside.

The nurse stayed put. 'I am so sorry! Madame DeFoud has some dementia now and probably doesn't remember. She is rude to everyone, so don't take it personally. She should know who has lived on this floor as she has been here all her life. She is over 90 years old. She was born here and has never married.'

This had all been said in French and Tilly was only grasping the gist of it.

Jean-Luc wrote down his phone number and email address and said if Madame revealed anything about the Estiennes, they would be most grateful if she could inform him as they were helping their elderly aunt to find her old home.

'Well, we have made some progress, I guess. Let's

photograph the hallway and the other doors in case it jolts Madame Pollock's memory.' Tilly took a video on her phone as well.

They walked to the end of the hallway, pressed for the lift and returned to the foyer in thoughtful silence.

'Madame Pollock's apartment could be one of the three where no one was at home,' Jean-Luc said as they stood on the polished floor, not quite ready to venture into the openness of the courtyard.

'Yes, but I also think Madame DeFoud knew something. As soon as you mentioned the Estiennes she reacted differently; and she didn't deny knowing them.' Tilly sighed.

'Well I guess, she is older than Madame Pollock and would have known what was happening back then to Jewish property when they were sent off; maybe she is living in the Estiennes' apartment?' Jean-Luc took Tilly's hand and gave it a squeeze as he spoke.

They decided there wasn't much more they could do so, after taking a few more photos of the outside of the building, they returned to Jean-Luc's apartment.

TWENTY-SEVEN

'I am sorry you feel disappointed with your progress with Madame's quest; I wish I could do more to help,' Jean-Luc said as he sat with Tilly on the train to Orly airport.

'You have been brilliant! I saw a whole new side to you yesterday; it's a waiting game now till Miriam from the *Déportés* gets back to us. I also need to research Madame's boxes and papers,' Tilly said as she placed her hand on his.

Just before Tilly left through the departure gate, she agreed with Jean-Luc that they would next see each other in Menton. As the plane roared into life, she suddenly felt very alone; grief tapped her on the shoulder and nudged the insecurity she fought daily.

As it was Monday morning and Enid was working, Tilly humped her case for the ten minutes it took her to walk from Nice airport to the Gare de Nice Saint-Augustin train station. As the train ambled along the coast towards Menton, Tilly's mood swung the other way. The memory of her first arrival on the Riviera over eight months ago reminded her of how far she had journeyed emotionally, and how much happier she was now. Even carrying her grief and the discovery of her father's deception, deep down she knew the knowledge that Karen wasn't any real relation to her offered her a way out: it offered her liberation. She just had to grasp it and move on.

When Tilly walked into the upstairs Turret room, Madame's blue eyes sparkled as if the sun had just kissed them. Tilly was amazed when the old woman practically jumped up from her armchair and walked towards her. She hugged her and then holding Tilly's face in both hands kissed her cheeks, proffering a delicate fragrance of mothballs and lavender.

'We have missed you, Tilly,' she said, then added, 'Let's go downstairs and have some coffee while you tell me everything.'

They took their coffees into the dining room and sat down, side by side at the table. The old lady watched carefully as Tilly transferred her photos to her laptop. She told the old lady of the visit with Miriam at the *Fils et Filles des Déportés*, her official appointment with the Pavillon de l'Arsenal where Jean-Luc worked and all about Jean-Luc taking her to the Grand Synagogue.

Next, Tilly enlarged the photos of the butterfly gate, the courtyard and the outside of the buildings within the courtyard.

'What are those names?' Madame asked as Tilly was scrolling through the photos.

'Oh, that's the list of residents' buzzers outside the back

building which is where we are assuming your apartment is.'

Madame peered at the screen. 'Uumm, I seem to remember a name DeFoud,' she said.

'That's interesting, as she is a very old lady who we actually got to speak to; well, Jean-Luc did, I couldn't quite keep up with their French.'

As Tilly scrolled across to the photos of the hallway, Madame's bright eyes were still very focussed on the screen, but she was silent.

The atmosphere had changed. Tilly could sense Madame's apprehension: something she had seen had acted as a trigger.

Tilly placed her hand on Madame's hand. 'You don't have to say anything, just look away if you are finding this distressing and I will turn off the screen.'

Madame swallowed hard, paused, then spoke. 'I am all right, Tilly, but please excuse me, I just need some time on my own in my room. I want to see and hear more, but at my age I just need to digest these awakened memories one at a time.' Then she got up and left the room.

CHAPTER TWENTY-EIGHT

PARIS, 1944

Manon DeFoud is wearing a pretty dress. I see her in our courtyard. She is very strange now; when we used to play outside behind the butterfly gate, she would only talk to me when the adults weren't looking. I didn't understand why. Mama said just to ignore her. But, although she is a bit older than me, she is one of the two other children that I see. The other girl is the daughter of 'the guard at the gate' and I am forbidden to even look in her direction.

That long hallway: it is so scary because it is so dark. I always felt much safer once I am inside our apartment. Now Mama and I have stopped going out at all, I often wish if I could only run up that hallway, I would feel better.

Papa Hans has stopped polishing his boots and his buttons. It used to be so important to him. Now he is at home with us more. So, I must keep quiet and Mama says I must go and play in my bedroom.

Papa Hans came home late a couple of nights ago with a sheet of wood and some shiny tools. He has been busy with Mama and they don't notice me looking as I stay in the dark and the door is open just a small crack. But I can see. Papa Hans has got out the hammer that Mama keeps in the broom cupboard. He has a big thick roll of paper. I open the door a bit more to have a closer look. Then he sees me; but he does not tell me to go back to bed, but he tells me 'not to touch'. But I have already seen it was like the paper on the wall outside our door in the dark hallway.

The next night he comes home with a big tin of paint. I know it is paint because I can read that word on the side of the tin. I can hear Mama and Papa Hans talking for ages during the night. I can hear Mama crying; I want to go to her, but then I think I hear Papa Hans crying too. I didn't know big men could cry. I feel frightened, so I decide to stay in my room.

In the morning Mama wakes me and tells me we were going on a trip to the seaside on a train. She says I must pack, just my special things, into a small case. I am worried as my shoes don't fit. She said it will be a fun adventure, but I do not believe her.

TWENTY-NINE

MENTON

Tilly had updated Enid on all the details of her Paris trip as they prepared the evening meal. Madame, who hadn't been seen since Tilly showed her the photos, arrived at the dinner table with a renewed sparkle.

'I am remembering so much more now! What a mechanism the brain is; there is so much stored there; after eighty odd years I just need to find a way in.'

The younger women shared a curious glance.

Madame sat down then continued. 'I think something terrible happened to my Mama at the end of the war – as it probably did to a lot of people. So many Jews were killed; I'm not sure why we were spared. I think my memory loss is tied up with that.' She paused as she helped herself to the platter Enid had placed on the table.

They ate for a few minutes in silence.

'Do you remember the trip from Paris to Nice?' Enid asked.

'No. I'm not there yet. But I am confident it will come to me.'

'I have suppressed memories of what Karen inflicted on me as a child. I think there are devices our brain uses to enable us to survive the emotional pain,' Tilly added, then took a bite of the chicken Enid had prepared.

'When my young son was killed by that car, I blamed my husband as he was looking after him at the time. It was cruel of me, but I felt so much grief and guilt. I just feel sad now that I inflicted the blame on him. But it makes me realise what ever happened to Mama back then, she didn't want me to remember and whatever happened, I believe she would have only done it to protect me. As I would have, if I could, for my son.' The other two women stared at the old lady, then she added:

'You two will catch a fly if you keep your mouths open. I know I don't normally talk so much but now it is time for me to speak, and I think of you two as family.' She paused, then added: 'I did eventually resolve it with my husband; we had a few good years together before he died.'

As dinner went on and they all had a second glass of wine, they shared more information about themselves. Then, Madame steered the conversation in Tilly's direction and asked when they were going to meet Jean-Luc.

'Well, I agreed he could come here to visit me, but he can stay at a hotel as he wouldn't wish to impose on you,' Tilly said.

'Nonsense! The spare room only has a single bed, but it's

perfectly adequate if he is happy to share your bathroom,' the old lady replied as she raised her eyebrows above her twinkling eyes and offered a glance in Enid's direction.

The following morning, woken by the dawn chorus, Tilly opened her curtains and caught sight of a few butterflies fresh from their chrysalises. Her eyes followed the flutter of their shimmering wings – she couldn't quite make out where in the garden they had emerged from. She threw on her dressing gown and hurried down the stairs and out of the back door. She stood perfectly still and watched where she had seen the butterflies from upstairs. She hadn't ventured down to the farthest end of the garden before as it was full of overgrown shrubs around two ancient olive trees. With her bare feet she stepped carefully into the bushy area and immediately spotted three butterflies hovering near a butterfly bush. She recognised the shrub instantly – a Buddleia.

Forgetting her unprotected feet, she crept closer so she could observe the beautiful creatures as they flirted with each other in the glory of the early morning. After a few focussed minutes Tilly looked up and spotted the corner of what looked like an old shed covered by out-of-control ivy at the very rear of the overgrown section.

Having already felt something stinging her bare foot, she retreated to the house to shower and dress.

Tilly especially enjoyed Saturday mornings as Enid didn't have to rush off and the three of them shared a late, lazy breakfast of fresh croissants, orange juice and coffee. They were all seated on the battered cane chairs under the big old tree.

'I thought there was a stampeding elephant on the stairs this morning, Tilly. Where were you going in such a rush?' Enid said attempting to look stern.

'I saw a Monarch butterfly from my room and figured there may be more. I found it over there, playing with potential mates by the butterfly bushes.' Tilly pointed to the overgrown section of the garden.

'Ah yes! The butterfly tree is what my husband used to call it; he used to potter around down there but I'm afraid I've let it go in the last twenty years,' Madame added with a dreamy look clouding her bright eyes.

'Is that an old garden shed I spotted near the back fence?' Tilly asked.

'Oh yes, it is; I had forgotten all about it. My husband used to store stuff in there.' As Madame spoke the other two proceeded to reply at the same time.

'That could be the answer!' Tilly said.

'Well! There may be more of your mother's things in there,' Enid had chipped in as both younger women simultaneously rose and walked briskly in the direction of the shed.

It was a trek through prickly bushes, overgrown weeds and tree roots. The shed itself was almost entirely encased in ivy. They eventually found the door and ripped the ivy off only to find an ancient rusted padlock.

They pulled at the lock and rattled the door, but it didn't budge.

'Do you remember where your husband kept the key to the lock?' Enid asked, once they arrived back at the breakfast table.

'Well, it might be in his toolbox, the one Enid has commandeered, so let's go inside and have a look. I can see we are all thinking the same thing,' Madame said as Tilly and Enid scooped up the plates on to a tray.

They found the metal toolbox where Enid had left it, in the laundry. She was the one who did minor repair jobs around the house. All her obvious tools like the hammer, pliers and fuse wire were on the top-level tray. She lifted the box up on to the washing machine then lifted the top tray out. There was a mangle of rusty screws, old nails and lots of loose wire. The two women started going through it bit by bit while Madame leaned on the door.

'Here it is!' Tilly called as she held up an insignificant looking silver-coloured key.

They were all off again, out to the garden and back through the maul of shrubs to the shed.

'*Merde*! The lock is too rusted to allow the key to turn,' Enid said as she tried the key for a second time.

'Shall we kick open the door?' Tilly said as she gave it a big shove with her foot.

'Being practical, I think we should get someone a bit better equipped to take it off its hinges as there may be things stored close to the door. Also, we wouldn't want the whole place to collapse,' Enid replied as they stepped back to the grass where Madame was waiting.

Madame agreed she would pay a local handyman to come and either break the lock or take the door off safely.

As Tilly tidied the dishes in the kitchen she considered that if Madame had forgotten about storage in the shed, what else had she forgotten about? The key to the Paris apartment had to be somewhere. She was just about to voice this to Enid when her phone buzzed.

'Tilly, I can come to visit you for three whole days next weekend as it is a French holiday on Friday; if it suits you I will fly to Nice on Thursday evening,' Jean-Luc said before Tilly had a chance to say hello.

'If you hold on, I'll just walk through and check with Madame.'

It seemed like an age before the old lady responded; Tilly could hear Jean-Luc breathing into the phone.

'He is welcome – on one condition…' she paused, and looked across at Tilly, then continued, 'as long as he agrees to take the door off the garden shed; it will save me some money.'

Tilly laughed and told Jean-Luc the details of the shed.

'I can be practical, if I put my mind to it!'

THIRTY

Tilly and Enid collected Jean-Luc from Nice airport. He appeared awkward as he chatted in a formal fashion to Enid in French. Because his diction was very precise, Tilly was able to capture most of the conversation.

During the week, Tilly had tidied up the small single room on the other side of her bathroom. Enid had made some cheeky comments as she observed Tilly ironing the sheets and the pillowcases as well as a newly purchased nightdress.

'This is very pleasant! What is the fragrance?' Jean-Luc asked, still in 'polite' mode as Tilly showed him to his room.

'I was afraid it may have been a little musty, so I put a fragrance stick over there called "Enchantment" to try to help freshen things up. You will be sharing the bathroom with me; it's next door.'

Jean-Luc finally smiled. 'Well, I am sure I will enjoy that!'

The three of them were seated at the dining table nattering, when Madame arrived. She had visibly put some effort in. She wore a pretty dress Tilly had never seen before, printed with red roses. Her hair was more orderly than usual, and Tilly was sure the old lady was wearing lipstick.

Jean-Luc immediately jumped to his feet, walked towards Madame and offered his hand. She shook it firmly and welcomed him to her home.

'*Enchanté*!' Jean-Luc replied.

As the meal progressed and everyone had agreed on a second glass of wine, Jean-Luc appeared to relax a little. Madame Pollock's eyes sparkled as she introduced some humour into the conversation. Enid and Tilly had chosen to give the matriarch the lead, as she was clearly enjoying her interview with Tilly's beau.

By the time they were eating Enid's impressive crème brûlée dessert, Madame led the conversation to her quest and her search for the elusive apartment key.

'Now young man, we are all relying on you to be able to gain safe access to the old shed. My late husband used it as his "den" – probably to get away from me.' She smiled, then added, 'Are you good at this type of thing?'

Jean-Luc shifted uncomfortably in his seat and then cleared his throat. Tilly could see he was nervous.

'Well, I have brought what I believe is an appropriate tool with me, and I may need Tilly's assistance with it, but yes, I am sure I can satisfy your request.'

He had been speaking in English out of respect for Tilly. Both younger women stifled their laughter. Then Enid quickly asked everyone if they wanted coffee and

Tilly followed her out into the kitchen where they both fell on each other giggling.

'Oh! I am sure he has an appropriate tool!' Enid said as she ground the coffee beans.

Madame left the table first. It had been a late night for her, but it was obvious she had enjoyed it. Jean-Luc helped the other two clear the table, then he and Tilly made their way up the stairs.

'I will see you in the bathroom in five minutes,' he said as he walked off to his room.

Tilly slipped into her new white satin nightdress; it had cost a bomb, but the French did lingerie so well and she couldn't resist it. The satin slid down her body and the intricate lace trim just skimmed her knees. The sweetheart neckline showed far too much of her breasts, but she figured that was the point!

She quietly opened the bathroom door and Jean-Luc was right behind her in his boxer shorts. He took her shoulders and gently turned her around.

'I know what you two rude women were laughing at! What a cruel thing to do to a friend who is struggling to fit in!' he said as he slid his hands down the soft satin.

'My God! You look so beautiful in this!' He kissed Tilly who fell into his arms.

'I will make love to you in this avocado green bathroom if I have to, but I am sure Madame won't suspect or hear a thing if you slip into my small but cosy bed so I can look at your new nightdress at close quarters.'

Jean-Luc didn't stir when Tilly snuck back into her own room around midnight.

He arrived at the breakfast table next morning with a heavy-looking black plastic box. The three women looked at it expectantly.

'This is my power drill; it can do most things so when you are all ready, I will commence my task,' Jean-Luc said, then sipped the fresh orange juice Tilly had just placed in front of him.

After breakfast they all walked down to the end of the lawn. Tilly carried one of the garden chairs and placed it as near to the action as she could for Madame. She wouldn't be able to see everything because of the overgrown shrubs, but at least she could hear.

Jean-Luc wore his 'casual' clothes but even his T-shirt was immaculately ironed as well as the signature crease in his faded jeans. Tilly had carefully chosen a pretty lemon-coloured sundress to impress her lover. Enid looked far more butch; she had pulled on her overalls and wore her Doc Martin boots.

Jean-Luc examined the rusted lock, then looked carefully at the hinges on the door. He opened his black box and connected an appropriate screw head to his battery-powered tool. Enid raised her eyebrows as he placed a pair of plastic protective glasses on.

Tilly and Enid supported the door as slowly he managed to get all four screws out of each of the two door hinges. The door was so stiff from years of being closed it took a huge pull to lift it off.

The smell hit them first; it was a mixture of musty air and dry rot. There were shelves full of jars of nails, screws and assorted bits on the two main walls and a cracked window covered in ivy at the end. Tilly spotted two big trunks on the floor under the bench. Enid bent down first to take a closer look. As she pulled one trunk forward there was an almighty crack and before any of them could move, the jars on the shelves started falling, as the wall on which they were stored began to collapse. Jean-Luc yanked Tilly back and pushed her in front of him back outside, then he quickly turned to grab Enid, but it was too late.

They heard an almighty scream as the wall hit Enid's arm. Madame's call of concern followed, but Tilly could only try to push past Jean-Luc to get to her friend.

'Tilly!' he shouted. 'I will get Enid; we don't want everyone injured.' He grabbed her arm. 'Stay right here!' Then he slowly picked his way through the now shattered shed and gently lifted Enid up. As they emerged, Jean-Luc had his arm around Enid's shoulders; she was covered in dust and cradling her left arm. Tilly felt a sense of relief as her friend was up on her feet and there was no sign of blood.

Madame stood anxiously holding the back of the cane chair when the three arrived at the lawn.

'It's going to be OK Madame; I think it's just my arm,' Enid mumbled, but she sounded very shaky.

Tilly didn't know why, but for some reason she hadn't imagined Jean-Luc could drive. Most people who lived in central Paris, and in central London, either walked or caught public transport. But once they had carefully helped Enid into her car, he confidently drove them to Menton Hospital. Enid's arm was fractured. It was set in plaster and she was given a shot of some sort of pain relief.

Madame was adamant that no one was to go near the shed until they had talked through a plan to dismantle it safely. Once Enid was comfortable on her bed resting and Madame had gone for a nap, Tilly and Jean-Luc headed off to the market to sort something for dinner.

It was a perfect Menton day. The locals were enjoying the long weekend, mingling around the main plaza; children were lined up with grandparents to ride on the small carousel that created the heartbeat of the square.

'What a charming town! I can see why you love it here. It seems so far removed from Paris,' Jean-Luc said as they circumnavigated the indoor food market, surveying all the delectable options on offer. They agreed that the easiest options would be preferable and set off home with a selection of pâtés, fresh bread, pre-made salads and some ham cut fresh from the bone.

Enid sat in the salon with a cushion propped under her arm.

'Oh Enid! How does it feel now?' Tilly asked as she sat down beside her.

'It's a bit sore; but let's be positive – it could have fallen on my head!' She managed a laugh, then added in a whisper, 'But we really need to get those two trunks out before Jean-Luc goes. Now the wall is actually fallen down I am sure we can navigate a safe way in to drag them out.'

'For God's sake! There's no "we" in this; you are not moving for several days!' Tilly replied.

'She's right Enid; it must be me who assesses the situation with the shed; but I will have to gain Madame Pollock's confidence first,' Jean-Luc said.

Enid only picked at her food and excused herself early from the dinner table. Once she had left, Tilly could tell by Jean-Luc's body language and slightly nervous conversation that he was building up to saying something profound or confrontational. But she was wrong on both accounts, he was telling a lie. Telling it in English, so that she would back him up.

'It was terrible what happened to Enid, but she was at the far end of the shed. The two trunks are right at the front near the doorway. I feel very confident I can safely pull them outside, away from the shed. It would really make all our efforts worthwhile if we could look in those trunks. There may be more information or even the key stored inside,' he said as he offered Madame Pollock a smile.

There was a prolonged pause before Madame responded.

'It's late now, and it's been an upsetting day; let's discuss this in the morning.' Then she thanked them for the meal and wandered off to her bedroom.

After they had cleared the table and stacked the dishwasher, Jean-Luc asked Tilly if there was a torch somewhere.

'What for?'

'Well, I think we should take a stroll in the moonlight in the garden.'

'Look, I don't want to disrespect Madame in any way.'

'It's not disrespectful. I just want to assess the situation before I speak to her again in the morning. Come on, Tilly, where is the torch?'

They found one in the drawer that housed all things

useful. Jean-Luc took Tilly's hand and quietly opened the back door. He didn't switch on the torch until they were out of sight of the house. One side of the shed was still upright, as was the open doorway. The frame was obviously quite strong.

'Please don't go in! Not only don't I want you injured as well as Enid, I really don't want to upset Madame Pollock,' Tilly said as Jean-Luc flicked the torch around the old shed.

The smell had dissipated now that the site was opened to the fresh air from outside the door, and they could see the corner of one of the trunks which was strewn with old nails and screws.

Jean-Luc studied it all for several minutes. 'I am confident I can pull that out and then when Madame agrees to me doing it in the morning, I will be halfway there to accessing the other trunk.'

'I am totally against this!' Tilly said.

'I will take full responsibility and not even acknowledge that you were with me,' he stated as he carefully stepped into the shed.

Tilly put her phone light on to help illuminate the area. They both jumped as a few jars fell on their side. Jean-Luc reached the corner of the trunk and very strategically began to ease it out. Tilly stifled a squeal as a few more things fell, but she could see it was only loose screws and nails that were on the top of the trunk. Jean-Luc stepped back and handed Tilly the torch as he needed his two hands and all his strength to pull the heavy trunk out of the door.

Tilly let out a big sigh, as Jean-Luc flopped to the ground beside the trunk. He took out his pristine ironed handkerchief from his jeans pocket and wiped the dust off the top, revealing the word NICE in large faded print. Tilly sat down beside him, and their attention was directed at the lock.

'I'm not going to crack that lock tonight!' Jean-Luc said as he rubbed the dust off his hands.

'Thank goodness for that!' Tilly said.

'Have you forgiven me, *ma Cherie*?' Jean-Luc leaned over and kissed her cheek.

'Well, for an architectural geek who has a weird ironing habit, you've been acting rather "butch" as Enid would say,' Tilly said, then returned the kiss with a peck on his cheek.

The following morning Jean-Luc had layered on the charm with Madame, but initially to no effect. By hardly responding she was making it clear she didn't want them re-entering the shed.

However, after she had eaten a croissant and had her coffee, she warmed up a little.

To Tilly's surprise she did a complete about-turn and for the second day in a row, they all walked the length of the lawn to the shrub area at the back. Tilly sat Madame on the chair and offered one for Enid.

'It's my arm that's broken, not my legs!' she said as she followed the other two into the bushes. Then in hushed tones added, 'Or my brain – what are you two up to?' As she spoke, they had arrived at the shed.

'Ah! I see you had a midnight excursion. You pulled one

of the trunks out; no doubt I would have done the same.'
She bent over, cradling her sling to look at the lock, then
added, 'That's a professional locksmith's job I think.'

'I think you are correct, and I don't think we will
be able to achieve it on a weekend, if I know my fellow
French countrymen,' Jean-Luc responded as he pulled at
the lock.

'However, since we are here, with permission, I am
going in to see if I can drag the other trunk out.'

'I don't think you are,' Tilly said as she placed her arm
on his shoulder. 'It's very unstable, let's get a professional in.'

'So, are you telling me I'm not capable?' Jean-Luc
retorted without a flicker of hesitation.

Before Tilly could respond, Enid chipped in. 'If I was
able to, Tilly, I'd be going in myself; it's just a matter of
assessing things first and moving carefully; I'm with you,
Jean-Luc, let's do this!'

Tilly pursed her mouth; Jean-Luc ignored her. He
moved slowly into the shed and carefully lifted the
collapsed bench; a few more things fell, but nothing
major. He called back that he could see the second trunk
and bit by bit gently pulled it out from underneath.

Then, with a one final pull, he dragged it out through
the door. Enid took a used tissue from her pocket and
wiped the dust off the top and from around the lock.

'It's almost as if there was something hidden in there,
to have such dramatic locks on supposed storage chests?'
Tilly commented as she sidled up beside the two.

'Am I forgiven, again?' Jean-Luc said as he squeezed
her hand.

'Maybe,' Tilly replied and managed a smile. In truth, she was enjoying the camaraderie with her French 'bestie' and her boyfriend.

As they approached the lawn, Tilly experienced a visual surge of joy, as beside the butterfly bush several Monarch butterflies flew about, showing off their shimmering coloured wings and enjoying the pinnacle of their short lives.

Back at the house they phoned the only two locksmiths in Menton, but being a Sunday there was no way the trunks would be opened before Jean-Luc returned to Paris.

Apart from her broken arm, Enid was back to her normal self. Tilly followed her instructions in the kitchen as they prepared the evening meal. Jean-Luc sat chatting to Madame and both women were surprised at how forward he was with questions about what she remembered from the war, and how responsive she was.

'He has really embraced this mission with you, Tilly; he is a little unusual, but I can relate to your attraction,' Enid commented as they plated up.

'A bit like us two!' Tilly said and playfully tapped Enid's arm.

Once Madame and Enid had gone to bed, Tilly snuggled up beside Jean-Luc on the squishy old sofa. Here, cocooned in this bohemian Turret House with these two diverse French women, and her new lover, she had begun to believe she would be able to overcome the deceptions of her family and hurt from her past.

'What are you thinking about *ma Cherie*, you seem a million miles away?'

'Just thinking how lucky I am to have my three new French friends!'

Jean-Luc kissed her, then he sat back as if to announce something.

'I was talking to Madame while you were in the kitchen, and it is my opinion she has forgotten things that happened to her as a child in Paris; not because she has dementia, but because those events were so horrible for her. I believe we all need to prepare ourselves that when we find the apartment and anything associated with that period in her life, it may not be very pleasant for her.'

Tilly nodded. 'The same thoughts occurred to me when I heard what Miriam said at my visit to the *Fils et Filles des Déportés.*'

They tiptoed up the stairs and into the spare bedroom. Tilly fell into Jean-Luc's arms. That night, in this small single bed, in the old cluttered house, they made gentle love and Tilly drifted to sleep engulfed in a reassuring sense of total peace.

THIRTY-ONE

Tilly's heart sunk as he offered a restrained wave from the window of the airport bus. She still didn't feel entirely secure about her relationship with Jean-Luc. But all romantic thoughts were put on hold as she rushed back to the house to be there for when the locksmith arrived.

He was a big burly chap and Enid had pressed Tilly to ask him if he would help them to pull the trunks to the back of the house where they would be under the cover of the eaves and protected from the weather. Enid held the notion that a man would be more likely to be more agreeable to Tilly than to her.

He obliged, and once in place he had the old rusty locks prised off in no time at all.

Tilly pulled up a chair for Madame and the younger women took positions on cushions on the ground next to the first trunk.

Madame's late husband had firmly tucked a sheet of

strong black plastic over everything, clearly to protect whatever precious things were inside.

Sitting on the plastic was a sturdy brown envelope with 'Corrinne Estienne' written on the front.

Madame opened the envelope, which contained a neatly folded letter penned on white paper.

'It's my husband's writing,' she said and then read it out loud in English.

'My dearest Corrinne,

I will probably be well gone from this world if you are looking in these trunks. I have done what I can to protect the contents. Your mama confided in me before she died that she didn't know if you were ready to hear about some of the things from her past. She was hesitant that perhaps it was better you never knew. She didn't tell me much more, and I didn't ask. She just gave me some of the contents of these two trunks and said it was all she managed to bring from Paris at the end of the war. I do hope they will all still be intact. I have added the items I deem precious to us both and I am sure if you are reading this it will all be self-explanatory.

My love to you always.

Marc. Xxxx

Madame's eyes had welled up. She took a deep breath, then picked up a faded piece of paper on which was written 'PRECIOUS PHOTOS'.

Tilly carefully pulled the plastic off and revealed several bags of old black and white photos.

She gently passed the first bag to Madame. The photos were of Madame's wedding day. She studied each photo without commenting, then handed them on to her two younger companions.

It appeared to have been a simple wedding; Madame wore a mid-length dress with no frills and held a small bouquet. There were no attendants, but one photo featured an austere-looking older woman whom Tilly assumed was Madame's mother standing next to the bride.

As Madame passed the photo of the bride and groom cutting the cake, she commented, 'It was a delicious chocolate cream cake!'

As she slipped out the photos from the next bag, Madame's eyes filled with tears. They contained the story in photos of the brief life of her son. As she looked at each one, she gently touched the little boy's image with her thumb, staring at his face and feeling his living gaze.

In some of the photos he was on his own, his parents capturing him in playful situations; but nearly all the rest were of the small blond boy sitting on his mother's knee, or leaning into her, clutching her hand. It was obvious that a loving father had taken them.

'We especially bought a camera when Eric was born; we were so in love with each other and with our son, we wanted to capture all the moments. But then when he died, I couldn't bear to see anything that reminded me of him, even Marc my husband; so he stored everything away, then weathered the years with me until he died.'

The old lady dabbed her eyes and blew her nose.

'I'm going to make us all a coffee,' Enid said as she arose, a little lopsidedly.

'I'll come and help – a bird doesn't fly well with one

wing!' Tilly said as she followed behind allowing Madame some time with her memories.

The last plastic bag contained much older-looking photos; as Madame removed them Tilly could see they must have been a collection from Madame's mother, Elsie Estienne.

Most featured Madame as a child upwards from the age of eight, posing in popular locations in Nice; then as a teenager in Menton.

'Mother loved her camera and she seemed to enjoy photographing me. She worked hard all week, but Sundays were our special day together.'

'How old were you when you moved to Menton?' Tilly asked.

'Well, there was something unpleasant that occurred, which would have been four or five years after the war. My mother refused to discuss it with me, and I had learned from experience not to question her. She must have owned our Nice apartment as I remember her commenting we would be able to afford a house in Menton and she bought this house and I have lived here ever since.'

Under the photos was a box marked 'VERY IMPORTANT DOCUMENTS'; inside they were contained within a plastic bag. The first was Madame's husband's death certificate – it stated he had died from a heart attack.

'How on earth would that be here if he had packed the trunk?' Enid commented.

'Oh, it would have been his brother Frank, they were as thick as thieves and when after Eric's death I regressed into my own world, Marc turned to his brother for support. Marc would have given him instructions, and Frank would have locked the trunks.'

Next, were copies of Eric's birth and death certificates. Fresh tears flowed as Madame read them. Such a short life.

She then held up her marriage certificate – this was a revelation!

'I don't ever remember seeing this before; I had never even heard of the name "Jacob" until this quest!' she said as she handed it to the younger women to read.

It showed under father of the bride the name Jacob Estienne, deceased.

'So, who did you think your father was, who wrote this in?' Tilly blurted out.

'I have memories of a man in uniform – I called him Papa Hans.'

There was a protracted silence.

Finally, Enid spoke. 'Maybe Papa Hans was your stepfather?'

Madame was silent. She took the certificate and placed it on the top of the others.

The next was her mother's death certificate.

'Well, I don't remember ever seeing this either; but then my husband may have been given Jacob's name from Mama and just not told me, she was so protective. I left all the paperwork to him, and he dealt with everything to do with Mama's death. At that time I was in such shock.'

The certificate stated that Madame's mother's husband had predeceased her, and that she had only one living child – Corrinne Cohen Estienne.

The last certificates related to the sale of the Nice apartment seventy years ago, and the purchase of the Turret House the same month.

That completed all the certificates. There was no record of Madame's parents' marriage nor her birth certificate.

It took the rest of the morning to finish going through each paper and letter from the first trunk. After lunch Madame declared she would like to rest in her room and that they would start on the second trunk the following day.

As Enid was on sick leave with her broken arm, she and Tilly maximised the opportunity and took their coffees outside to Madame's favourite chairs.

'Jean-Luc thinks Madame may have some post-traumatic memory loss from the events that happened during the war,' Tilly said.

'But she was less than eight years old; maybe some people have memories earlier than others,' Enid replied.

'I have several traumatic memories from around the age of four; but I grew up assuming my stepmother's behaviour was normal as I didn't know any different. It's only since my late teens that I realised it wasn't normal and she clearly disliked me.' Tilly slumped back in her chair and sighed. Enid reached over and squeezed her hand.

'I think Madame must have witnessed something so terrifying to a young girl that it was best it was wiped from her mind, and it seems it may have been connected with her father as it appears her mother never did anything to restore those memories.'

'Yes, I think you are right. Her mother was protecting her the only way she knew how. But I feel a certain anxiety about what a revelation of any of this will do to Madame,' Tilly said.

'Tilly, I think Madame is not as frail as you think; she weathered the death of her son and has fought numerous other emotional battles. I believe she now wants to know what transpired back then and find some sort of completion before she dies.' The friends continued chatting, exchanging opinions on the old lady who had become like a special aunt to them both and adding their own experiences to the mix. Once the late summer sun had sunk behind the shrubs, they moved back inside to prepare the evening meal.

THIRTY-TWO

PARIS, 1941

I am little, maybe three or four years old. I can see my mama's face clearly; she smells so good and I can see her smiling at someone above me. It is a man, he smells good as well. Their scent is of 'belonging'. I know they both belong to me. I wish I could see the man's face. He scoops me up and throws me in the air. I hear Mama laughing, and I am giggling. My whole body is made of joy; it is a wonderful feeling. I reach out and touch the man's face; I still can't see it, but I can feel it. It is a bit scratchy, how a man's skin should be. Mama's is so smooth like mine.

I try to widen my eyes, it is as if there is a blindfold across them, but only when I try to look at his face.

Please, please God, let me see his face, let me remember him…

THIRTY-THREE

MENTON

'Madame, are you OK?'

Tilly and Enid heard the old woman call out and they arrived at her bedroom at the same time.

Madame slowly sat up; Tilly rushed to prop a second pillow behind her.

'Yes, I'm fine. I'm not in any physical pain. It was more a bad dream. I wanted God to help me, as no one else can.'

She let out a big sigh as she reached for her spectacles. Her intense blue eyes seemed so much larger through the lenses.

'I think I was remembering my papa, Jacob; I must have been three, maybe four, at the time. I could feel him, I could even smell him, but I just couldn't see his face.'

Madame had recovered her composure quite quickly

and joined them downstairs. However, during the evening meal she was subdued and didn't mention the episode again.

Tilly's phone rang just after dinner – Jean-Luc gave all the details of his flight back to Paris and enquired about any relevant discoveries from the trunks. Just after he said goodbye Tilly heard a very quiet '*Je t'aime.*' Before she could respond he finished the call. It was the first time he had told her he loved her.

The following morning Tilly wrote an email in English to Miriam at the *Fils et Filles des Déportés* requesting that she check Jacob Estienne against the records of those who had perished in the camps during the war. She forwarded it to Enid to translate into correct French. She had become very conscious about the bureaucratic French and knew the response would be better if she used all the formalities that the French preferred.

Madame appeared later than usual for breakfast and announced she was ready to proceed with the second trunk.

The mood had lightened from the previous evening as the three women took up the same positions.

The trunk lid was very stiff, and it took both Tilly's arms and Enid's one good one to pull it open. It seemed to be jammed with years of what appeared to be a mixture of rust and sticky dust.

As in the first trunk, the top layer was of strong black plastic that had helped preserve the contents for what must have been over fifty years.

The first layer was of books; they appeared quite old.

Some were children's books, beautifully illustrated, and, after Madame had flicked through the pages, she passed them on to the other women and they read the inscriptions. All were to Eric with love from Mama and Papa. It was Tilly's turn to cry. A huge tear wet her cheek as the thoughts of her small stillborn daughter filled her mind, merged with visions of the dead mother she never knew. The other women allowed Tilly her tears, then once the moment had passed, they moved on with the investigation.

The next lot of books appeared to be from Madame's husband's family, including an old album with photos of his parents. They all seemed to be at locations around the Côte d'Azur and the subjects wore very typical clothing of that era.

What appeared to be the final three books had been individually wrapped in brown paper and tied with a red satin ribbon. Madame very delicately unwrapped the paper of the first one to reveal a small book with gilt-edged pages and a dark red flocked cover. The title was *Les Chants du crépuscule* by Victor Hugo. There were small pieces of paper acting as bookmarks on several of the pages.

Madame opened the first page. Handwritten in beautiful script in blue ink it read:

Juin 1938. À ma précieuse épouse et âme sœur, Elsie, avec amour pour toujours, Jacob. X

Madame helpfully translated this for Tilly. "'June 1938. To my precious wife and soulmate, Elsie, with love for ever, Jacob. X.'"

Enid whispered that it was a book of poetry.

Madame turned the pages to the first bookmark, then lingered on the page reading the poem.

'My father must have been a very romantic man; Enid, please see if you can read this in English to Tilly?'

Enid nodded and took the book.

'I think I may be able to do better than that.' She went inside and returned with her iPad. She went into Google and in no time at all she had the translation. Enid read out loud with feeling; Tilly was transfixed as her friend voiced such poignant words of love, as she read a few extracts from the poem.

Let's love for ever! Let's love again!
When love goes away, hope runs away.
Love is the cry of dawn,
Love is the hymn of the night.

What the stream says to the shores,
What the wind says to the old mountains,
What the sun says to the clouds,
It is the ineffable words: Let us love!

Love makes one think, live and believe.
It has to warm the heart,
A ray of more than glory,
And this ray is happiness!

Love! let them be praised or blamed,
Always the big hearts will love:
Join this youth of the soul to

the youth of your forehead!

Love, to charm your hours!
So that we can see in your beautiful eye
Inner voluptuousness,
The mysterious smile!

All pleasure, flower barely hatched
In our dark and tarnished April
Flesh and dies, lily, myrtle or rose,
And one says to oneself: 'It is thus finished!'

Love alone remains. O noble woman
If you want in this vile stay,
Keep your faith, keep your soul,
Keep your God, keep the love!

For Tilly it felt like an exquisite moment of collective love. Over one hundred and fifty years ago this French poet wrote these loving words for some fortunate woman, then all those years later Jacob Estienne bestowed the same words on his young wife and then their daughter ,now aged eighty-four, was reading them as her first introduction to her papa she had forgotten.

After reading through a couple more poems, Madame put the book to one side and proceeded to untie the ribbon of the next book.

It looked even more delicate; it had the same gilt-edged pages; the cover was made from brown soft leather with the title written in gold: *Nouvelles Odes* by Victor Hugo.

Enid didn't need to translate this one; Tilly had briefly studied Victor Hugo's novels at high school but until now had not been familiar with his poetry.

Madame read out another beautiful handwritten inscription:

"*À mon très cher mari, Jacob, avec l'amour pour toujours de ton épouse dévouée, Elsie.*

To my sweetest most caring husband, Jacob, with love for ever from your devoted wife, Elsie."'

'Oh my!' Enid exclaimed, as she got up on her knees to read the book in Madame's hands. 'It's a first edition and signed by Victor Hugo; it will be worth a fortune!'

Madame beamed. 'It will never be sold while I still have breath, it is my treasure, for ever!'

Tilly carefully rewrapped the books and tied the red satin ribbons. Madame placed them by her side. 'I will keep them by my bed.'

The last was much larger than the other two, and as Madame removed the wrapping they could see it was some sort of album, the old-fashioned kind with a leather cover and a cut out where a photo or a title would normally be inserted. A pressed butterfly of the most magnificent colours had been carefully glued in the space.

It had a decorative lock. Tilly remembered seeing similar albums when she worked at the museum.

Each page was made of stiff paper, almost like cardboard, and had a transparent tissue page to protect whatever had been pasted or presented beneath.

The first page housed a mounted pencil sketch of a butterfly, side on view.

'I think this must have been one of my mama's early sketches; it appears a little juvenile, don't you think?' Madame stated and both girls nodded.

The next page featured a watercolour of what looked to Tilly like an *Attacus Beauconie Doris* butterfly with its wings at full span.

'She is progressing,' Madame said as she tenderly stroked the painting with her finger.

The next few pages were mounted with paintings of colourful butterflies, most of which Tilly was able to proudly identify to her friends.

They were nearing the end of the album when a pencil sketch appeared; it was the face of a young man; he looked about twenty years old. His hair was very short to the back and sides, but with a big curly flop on the top. His eyes peered out from underneath; they appeared to be looking directly at you from the paper. Madame scrutinised the image for what seemed an age.

'I think this is a drawing of my father; my sense is that it could have only been drawn by someone who truly loved him.'

Then she turned the next page.

All three women simultaneously gasped. Here was the same man, the same image but painted in oil in full colour.

Looking out from the page, were Madame's piercing aqua-blue eyes. The man's hair was luxuriantly black, and his skin had an olive tinge to it. His mouth was held in what Tilly termed 'a soft Mona Lisa smile'. Full of love and directed at the artist. But the startling portrayal of his magnificent eyes spoke volumes; the painter had captured the essence of who he was and revealed the genetic link to his descendant.

'He has to be your papa; look at those eyes! It's as if your eyes have been superimposed on to a man's face,' Enid blurted out.

Both younger women turned to the old lady. She wasn't tearful. It was more of a state of shock.

'God did hear me! I wanted to see my papa's face and now I have it for ever.'

They analysed every stroke on the page of Elsie's painting. Madame's entire demeanour lifted as she said the name Jacob several times. She glowed with approval as Tilly and Enid found different ways to reiterate the likeness of their eyes.

Next, it was Tilly's turn to light up as they turned to the second to last page of the album.

It was a pencil sketch of the butterfly gate at Maison Papillon – her special gate. Madame read her mind and didn't dally on the pencil sketch. Tilly was not disappointed, as when Madame turned the page it was all she hoped it would be. A full-colour, glorious oil painting of the butterfly gate!

'It's so beautiful! I feel sure it was your mother's design; it feels like such a reflection of her style!'

'From what Tilly told us,' Enid chipped in, 'the butterfly gate was added sometime after the building was first built. Your grandparents must have been rather wealthy to commission such an artisan piece.'

'I was dwelling on the subject of my grandparents'

wealth when we looked at the sale certificate of the Nice apartment. I remember we went straight there when we first arrived from Paris. I think it must have been my grandparents' holiday apartment.'

The morning's adventure had put a shine on the day. As they sat at the lunch table sharing cold ham and cheese with a fresh baguette, the three companions discussed the literary contribution of French poets to the world.

'We were taught at school that the French led the world when it came to literature about love. From the core of their souls to the summits of their hearts they examined and offered love in all its expressions,' Enid said, with a faraway look in her eyes.

After lunch they resumed their positions beside the trunk and with the layer of books removed, they could see what looked like three shoeboxes in the bottom.

The first box contained several pairs of gloves – delicate, glamorous gloves, the evening ones made in luxurious satin. A black satin pair had tiny shimmering seed pearls delicately hand sewn around the edge. Madame handed Tilly an olive-green pair that appeared to be made from a felt-like fabric.

'These were meant for you Tilly, try them on.'

The edge of the gloves had been meticulously embroidered with tiny exquisite colourful butterflies. Tilly slipped the gloves on; they were a perfect fit!

'I can't accept these Madame! Your mama will have embroidered them herself. They are for you.'

'I will never wear them! The mere fact they fit is a sign; besides, the signature butterflies mean they are yours.'

The next box contained a few pieces of dated costume jewellery – nothing that appeared of real value.

The women speculated that the family jewels didn't make it through the war, or Elsie had sold them off. Being a single parent at the end of the war would have been a massive challenge. Enid took a shine to a silver brooch of a cat, and Madame gave it to her.

'I will wear it with love,' she said as she kissed the old lady's cheek.

The final box had only a few bits and pieces of broken jewellery and a couple of fountain pens. Then as Madame rummaged, Tilly had spotted the key. It was large by present-day standards, made of what she thought was steel. She picked it up and laid it on her flat hand so they could all study it. A fine piece of black thread was tied to the loop at the top of the key.

'This could be it, Tilly! Do you recognise it, Madame?' Enid asked.

'No, but with what goes on in my memory that doesn't mean anything.'

Tilly put the key down and continued to trawl through the box. She spotted a very small piece of white card attached to what appeared to be matching black thread; she cautiously picked it up. The scrawled writing on the card had smudged and faded.

'There is a magnifying glass in the drawer; please go and fetch it, Enid,' Madame asked, forgetting about her broken arm. It didn't stop Enid; she was back in no time with the glass.

As they enlarged the card, the letters 'Par' became

apparent. As the P was a capital they assumed the word was Paris; then there were only the last three letters obvious from the second word, 'ent'.

'Oh! Do you think it says *Paris Appartement*?' Enid stood up.

'I jolly well hope so!' Tilly responded as she got to her feet.

'I'll offer up another prayer; they seem to be working!' The old lady added with a smile.

THIRTY-FOUR

PARIS, AUGUST 1944

The man I call Papa Hans is not unkind, but he has become grumpy and appears in a bad mood all the time. He used to appear happy and would make me feel good because he seemed so strong and would bring us yummy food.

I am confused. My mama will snap at me one minute and the next she is hugging me. Papa Hans has always been so tidy; now he has a shadow on his face which looks prickly and his shirt is hanging out. He doesn't bring food any more; Mama makes meals from the cans and jars in our pantry. They both sit up for hours talking; they think I am asleep, but I creep out and listen at the door.

Papa Hans is telling Mama she should leave as soon as possible, and he will go the following day to try to get her train tickets to Nice. She searches through her messy kitchen drawer where she keeps her 'junk' and declares she has the key for the Nice apartment. They talk about money, and she tells him she would sew it into her coat. I peer through the crack in the door; Papa Hans helps her unpick the hem of her winter coat. I watch as they roll up money and put it inside her coat; then Mama threads the needle and sews it up again. Perhaps she has to hide it from bad men. I am so scared; why won't Papa Hans be able to protect us?

I hear him say he will do all he can to protect the apartment. I am not sure what that means but is it about the roll of wallpaper and the paint he has already brought home?

When he leaves the apartment the next day, Mama wraps her arms around herself and asks what she should do if he doesn't return. He used to stand up straight, but he looks at his feet as he tells her he will be back, and that she must pack and be ready. She takes out two suitcases from the hall cupboard. She mumbles to herself as she looks in her wardrobe. There are so many beautiful dresses. Sometimes I sneak into her bedroom and look at the long sparkly ones. I imagine Mama is a queen and I am a princess. But she doesn't even look at the sparkly gowns. She takes out only three very plain dresses, and packs them, then she puts some books and her art folder in the case.

Next, she goes into my room and picks out the two dresses that still fit me. She tells me I had grown like a weed and when we arrive in Nice, she will buy me a new dress. I am puzzled at what a weed is. But she says it so kindly I figure it must be a good thing. She tells me I may only choose two toys and two books as I will have to carry my own case so it must be light. I choose my teddy bear and my blonde doll, who looks a bit scruffy, but I still love her. Mama makes sure I can carry my case. She tells me to pick it up and walk briskly down the hall. I tell her it isn't heavy, but it does feel heavy. I sneak in an extra book and a very small toy horse.

I trail behind her around the apartment. We go into the salon; she examines everything and has a strange look on her face. Her easel sits with an unfinished painting; she sighs and says she never really wanted to paint a boring old bowl of fruit, anyway. She sits for a moment on the gold-edged striped sofa and strokes the fabric. She tells me my grandmother chose it. Next, we go back into her bedroom where the two packed, brown leather cases sit on the bed. I sense they are our 'goodbye' cases.

Mama walks around the room and stops and stares at each painting on the walls. It is as if she is taking photos with her eyes so she can look at the pictures later when we arrive in the place called Nice. Normally the fur creature is kept in the wardrobe, but Mama takes it out and lays her treasured lush grey fox fur over the back of her red velvet chair. She strokes him and pats his head as if he is a pet dog that she is saying goodbye to.

Next, she tidies her dressing table, lining up the silver brush and comb set alongside the silver and glass hat pin containers and her powder bowl. I always feel so special when she brushes my hair with that brush; I ask if we can pack it. She just shakes her head. The top drawer of her dressing table is where she keeps her treasured gloves. She opens the drawer, and tenderly strokes the top pair of gloves. I have a long-ago memory of her wearing them, but my memories of things have faded now. We haven't left the apartment for such a long time. She closes the drawer and I can see her eyes are all wet. She lets out a big sniff. Then she quickly returns to the drawer, gathers up the gloves, opens her case and hurriedly puts them in.

Our tour continues through the hall and into my bedroom. Here, she takes down a picture of a pink butterfly from the wall. It's my favourite; she said it wasn't a real butterfly, but if I wanted a pink butterfly, then I should have one. She places the painting on my bed and tells me to wait, then returns with a big envelope and tapes it to the back of the painting before placing it back on the wall. Her tears drop on to the dark blackish circles under her eyes. She plonks down on my bed and clutches me in her arms; I cry. I don't really know why, but everything feels so sad in this apartment and I hope in the new place called Nice my mama's eyes will sparkle again.

Papa Hans comes back; I can see Mama's relief when he gives her the two train tickets. I wonder why we only have two tickets; how will Papa Hans get on the train? But I don't ask, as I think it will be better if I do exactly what Mama tells me. They send me to bed early; I feel hungry, but I see that Mama eats nothing, so I don't ask for anything; my tummy rumbles as I lay in my bed. I can smell something weird, so I sneak to look through the crack in the salon door; Papa Hans is painting the glass windows with thick white paint. It has a funny smell.

THIRTY-FIVE

MENTON

That evening Tilly emailed Jean-Luc the details of what had transpired during the voyage of discovery into Madame's forgotten trunks. She would need to wait until Miriam responded about any record of Jacob, but she felt confident now that they would find a way to gain legal access to Maison Papillon.

Tilly drifted off to sleep with visions of Madame's talented mama painting butterflies, intertwined with dreams of her own mother and what might have been, if circumstances had been very different.

Enid and Tilly were pleasantly surprised as Madame bustled to the breakfast table earlier than usual with a spring in her step, her hair neatly done and a subtle touch of lipstick on.

'What happened to you during the night?' Enid said.

'I have remembered so much more, not all of it pleasant, but just to be able to remember makes me feel like I am solving my own puzzle. I can clearly see the Paris apartment in my mind's eye now; however, I am realistic enough to understand, my memories are through the eyes of a seven-year-old.' Madame chatted away as she sat down and began to butter the piece of baguette Tilly had toasted.

Tilly's phone beeped with a text from Jean-Luc: 'Call me when you can JLx.'

'He's early!' Madame remarked with a smile.

'How do you know it's not my Aunt Lucy calling?'

'Because it is only 6 a.m. in London, and we all know this is a mad "keen" French man who is your lover!' Enid added, laughing with a mouth full of crunchy toast.

Their cheerful banter continued over a lingering coffee; they were making the most of the revelations from yesterday's venture and the fact that Enid didn't have to rush off to work.

When Tilly finally called Jean-Luc he sounded much more assertive than usual; he almost demanded to know what had taken her so long to return his call; then, he checked himself and apologised.

'It's OK, I understand, and I'm pleased to know you were desperate to hear my voice!' Tilly said, still in a very playful mood.

'Now that we have Madame's father's name and the key, that should help with our search. I will see if I can have an unofficial word with the man I know in that department at work; but I think if Jacob was killed in one of the camps, Miriam will be the one who can assert authority. Give me a couple of days to see what I can find out,' Jean-Luc said. Then he added, 'Besides, I want to get you back to Paris.'

The three women were still in high spirits over lunch, when suddenly Madame clutched her chest and appeared to gasp for breath. Enid was about to call an ambulance, when the colour began to return to the older woman's cheeks and her breathing calmed.

'Best we get you to the sofa and you put your feet up. Can you walk?' Enid asked once they could see her breathing had normalised.

'Don't fuss, it is probably only indigestion,' Madame replied, as she slowly got up. Her companions supported an arm each and guided her to the sofa. Tilly lifted her feet on to the footstool, then removed her shoes.

'Perhaps it is angina; you had it last year. I'll go and get those pills you were told to take,' Enid said as she left the room.

Tilly sat down beside Madame on the sofa and gently took her hand.

'Is the pain bad?'

'It has subsided now.'

'You never told me you had heart problems?'

'Don't look at me that way! As far as I'm concerned, I don't have heart problems; this has only happened once before. I'm not dying anytime soon; I want to find my parents' apartment first,' Madame said as she patted Tilly's hand.

Once she had taken her tablet and rested a little, they

escorted her to her bed, and she slept all afternoon. That evening, Tilly served them a light meal upstairs in the Turret room, so Madame didn't have to do the stairs.

'I have made you an appointment to see the doctor tomorrow; I can't drive with this arm so Tilly will take you in a taxi,' Enid said.

Madame began to protest, when Tilly butted in.

'I mean no disrespect, Madame, but Enid is right, there is no harm in having the doctor give you a "once over"; please do it for us.'

After the meal Madame brightened a little. 'As we are going into town and Monsieur Dupont's office is close, can you please make me an appointment with him. Now I have seen how my husband kept everything in order, I may just make a few provisions with the advocate for when I do leave this world.'

Tilly and Enid were taken aback.

'Don't look like that! I have told you I'm not leaving anytime soon. I still have my quest to complete; I just feel it is fair to put things in order,' the old lady said with a smile.

The next day when they arrived at the surgery, Madame made it clear she would see the doctor on her own. Tilly felt a sense of frustration as she was concerned that if anything was wrong, Madame would not be forthcoming with the truth.

The old lady said nothing as she returned to the waiting room, just pointed her walking stick towards the door and took Tilly's arm. Once they were on the street she stopped and faced Tilly.

'Well, he said it was most likely an angina attack and I shouldn't excite myself too much.' Then she smiled and they both laughed. 'He doesn't know the half of it!' she added.

Although privately Tilly felt worried.

The lawyer, Monsieur Dupont, looked nearly as old as Madame. He was very formal towards Tilly, but warmly greeted his client with a kiss on both cheeks.

Tilly waited for nearly an hour in the small reception area thumbing through dated law magazines she couldn't really understand before the old lady reappeared. 'Sorry to take so long, Tilly, but he is so old it takes him ages to do anything.' Tilly shot her a look, as he was standing directly behind her.

Madame smiled. 'Don't worry, he can't understand a word of English!'

As they left the building Madame asked Tilly if she was happy to walk slowly with her for a bit out on the promenade.

'It's been ages since I have smelt the sea; in my younger days, we always used to swim, usually early evening in the summer,' Madame said as she guided Tilly to a beachside café. The café was elevated on the raised footpath so patrons could look over the beach and out to sea. The water lapped gently against the stone wall offering a salty fragrance and the unique sense of calm that an ocean brings.

They ordered a pot of tea and Madame enquired if they had any pastries. The waiter returned with a large white china pot of tea and two chocolate eclairs. Madame chuckled to herself.

'What's so funny; do you want to share the joke?'

'Well, the other thing the doctor said was I should be careful what I eat and to watch my weight!' Then she added, 'It seems I am regressing to childhood; I never really felt like eating a pastry until I was told I couldn't!'

One of the things Tilly enjoyed about the old lady's company was that she didn't have to talk all the time. Growing up, Tilly had spent a lot of time alone and enjoyed her own company. It felt as if a good ten minutes had passed watching people and enjoying the sound of the sea before Madame spoke again.

'Tilly, please stop me if you think I am going a bit far with this; I know you prefer to keep your own counsel and value your privacy...' She paused and looked to Tilly before she continued.

'Please go on.'

'I just want to tell you how much you have brought to my life since you came to live at the Turret House. I had been wallowing in self-pity and repressed grief for years – ever since my son was killed. When I met you, I recognised deep pain, but you conducted yourself with such restraint and still allowed Enid and I to find joy in your company. Then, when you shared with us the torture from your stepmother, your papa's death coupled with his deception and the loss of your baby, it nudged open the door to my memories. I can now see I was very unfair to my husband. He suffered as much as I did. Our Eric's death was bigger than both of us.' Madame paused to study Tilly's reaction. The girl was difficult to read. Tilly gave a half smile and she continued.

'If I ever had had a daughter, I would have loved her to be just like you, to deal with things as you do. Although we tease you about Jean-Luc, I really think he is an excellent man. I can see he is a bit unusual in some ways, but there are so many other faults he could have. He shows nothing but love in his eyes for you. It is rare in this busy world to find a man who is a gentleman.'

Tilly gulped and forced a smile.

'Don't worry! I had such a bad boyfriend last time, the one good thing I took from it is that I now appreciate a good one when I see him. I will treasure him, Madame, I promise you.'

The bright sun that had filled the afternoon was nearing its end, and they walked towards the taxi stand in the square. Tilly gave Madame's arm a gentle squeeze. 'Madame Corrinne, if my mum was alive, I would want her to be just like you.' Then she kissed the old lady's soft powdered cheek.

When they arrived home, Enid had managed to prepare the evening meal with her one good arm; but Madame ate very little and went up to bed early.

'She must have been exhausted; we walked to the beach and then to the taxi stand in the square,' Tilly commented.

'I feel sure she has something brewing and there is more to come from that dear old soul that we aren't expecting,' Enid said before she turned the television on and slumped down on the sofa.

THIRTY-SIX

A week had passed since Tilly had emailed Miriam; when she eventually responded it was difficult news.

Madame was sitting on her favourite wicker garden chair; she had a light rug across her knees.

Tilly positioned her chair, so they were facing each other. 'Miriam rang from Paris. I am so sorry to tell you this, but a Jacob Estienne of the same age as your father was listed as being taken to an internment camp at Drancy, France in 1942 then moved to Auschwitz where he was gassed in 1943.'

Tilly paused to allow the information to sink in. Madame sat silently for a few seconds before the first single tear rolled down her powdery cheek.

'It was so long ago, and I hardly remember him, but right now, right here I feel his presence and his love, also now I understand my mother's pain.' She tapped her heart as she spoke.

Then she continued, 'Does this mean we can have

access to the apartment?'

'No not yet, we need more documented evidence of ownership,' Tilly replied.

They sat contemplatively for a few minutes, then Tilly spoke.

'I wonder if this is what became of my two grandfathers, they never made it to England with my grandmothers.'

'I have to assume my grandparents ended up with the same fate, my mother never spoke of them and I have no memory of them at all,' Madame added as she dabbed eyes.

'Once we have solved the quest for your apartment, my next mission could be to research their history,' Tilly replied and smiled.

Later that night Tilly received a call from Jean-Luc.

'So, I don't think my contact within the department has any legal ability to allow us into a building where we believe Madame's apartment is. Madame's doesn't currently exist. On the ownership papers in our files from 89 years ago, it exists, but there is no documentation since then. I have found out who the managing agents are. Of course, they weren't helpful, but did say there was no apartment 59 and no one on their list called Cohen or Estienne, but if there was, they would need to be paying them the yearly service charge.'

'Oh wow! That would be over seventy years of fees; there may be a fly in the ointment down the track,' Tilly said.

'What do you mean…a fly?' Jean-Luc asked.

Tilly laughed. 'It's an English saying; can I explain it another time?'

She went on to tell him about Jacob's fate and Madame's reaction.

'So, what do you intend to do next?' Jean-Luc asked.

'Tomorrow I am going to suggest to Madame that I come back to Paris with the key, and copies of the certificates, and the ownership file from your department as well as the emails from Miriam, in case we are caught. Then probably sneak into Maison Papillon again to see if the key works in any of the doors on the fifth floor.'

'So, it will be a real adventure! If that is what it takes to have you back in my arms, then count me in,' Jean-Luc said before they finished their call.

The following morning Madame appeared at breakfast very bright, she looked taller with her back very straight, she didn't have her walking stick.

'I feel so good, I am confident I can walk some distance without the stick,' she stated as she sat down to the fresh croissant.

'So, what has brought this on?' Enid asked.

'I feel as if the burden I have been carrying is lifting. I have decided, if Tilly is willing, I will go to Paris with her!'

Tilly looked up from her coffee and didn't quite know how to react.

'Now, before you both make comment, let me say this is my quest, my Paris apartment and the building has a lift. We can fly there, catch taxis and I am sure Jean-Luc will help. Enid, it is not that I wish to exclude you, but you do have a broken arm, so I feel in this case you won't be of much use.'

There was a pregnant pause as Tilly and Enid absorbed this information. Enid responded first.

'I don't have an issue with not going, but what about

your heart? Considering you haven't even been as far as Nice in the past twenty years, this trip to Paris would surely constitute "excitement"?'

'That doctor hasn't got a clue! Look at me, I am in better shape and feeling more alive than I have in thirty years.' She took a bite of her croissant, then Tilly felt the gaze of the old lady's bright eyes shining in her direction. 'Well Tilly, are you up for it?'

Tilly hesitated, and she continued chewing her croissant to allow herself a little more time. 'Well, I guess I can't see why not; but if I may, I would like to state a few things that you would need to agree to so that I know I could cope.'

'Well, what are they?'

'First, you must bring your stick, second, allow me to book you a wheelchair at the airports, and third, consider us hiring you a wheelchair in Paris as if we need to sneak in to the building we may need to move swiftly, but also a senior lady in a wheelchair may gain us some sympathy and thus help with the quest.'

'I will agree to having my stick and the airport wheelchairs but I'm not agreeing to being pushed around like an invalid all over Paris!'

Tilly and Enid knew better than to react; if it was a deal breaker she would eventually have to come round.

They discussed where they should stay; they all agreed separate bedrooms would be best, as Madame snored and needed her privacy, but Tilly needed to be close at hand. Tilly looked up accommodation on her phone and read it out to Madame. She found something near to Maison

Papillon that had all the facilities; it sounded as if it was a fully serviced apartment within a hotel. In the photos it appeared to be an old building, but it had a roomy lift which would be useful for Madame. There was also a kitchenette along with optional room service.

Enid said very little; as Tilly took the plates into the kitchen, she followed her and pushed the door closed.

'This is not a good thing, Tilly; she is far too frail!'

Ever since Tilly had known Enid, she had never seen her friend so agitated, bordering on angry.

'I don't disagree, but she is on her final journey and this is the only thing she really wants to do. I understand what it means to her. She doesn't have dementia; she is of sound mind and knows the risks. I will ask Jean-Luc to take some days off work so he can be with us whenever we leave the hotel, and of course, I will book a wheelchair and make her use it. Please let's not fall out over this?'

Enid let out a sigh. 'You are right, it's her choice and we must respect that.'

That evening Tilly phoned Jean-Luc and explained the plan. Like Enid, he was aghast at first, but then agreed to take some leave to assist them in every way possible. Tilly had already considered he would be reluctant to say no to her at this stage of their relationship. After a few protracted silences, he offered to sort a wheelchair and meet them at the airport. He also said he would see if he could investigate what day the old concierge who policed Maison Papillon had off as it may be easier to bluff entry if she wasn't around.

Tilly remembered the American girl in the holiday let

in Maison Papillon so after trawling through a few holiday rental sites online she found a studio in there to rent. She quickly called Jean-Luc with the news.

'What a great idea. How about I rent the studio, and then as you say I will obtain legitimate access to the building and the door fob. I'll go online now and come back to you'

'That would suit as I will need to stay somewhere with more facilities to deal best with Madame's needs,' Tilly said, then added, 'Be assured Madame will pay you back the fee.'

It took some explaining and demonstrating to Madame on the laptop how Airbnb worked, but she eventually got her head around it and kept reassuring Tilly that any payments were not a problem.

They decided to fly out four days before the day they would have access to the short-let studio. Tilly wanted to give Madame time to adjust to her new surroundings and to give herself time to work out how to manage her old friend in the new environment.

Tilly and Enid had spoken out of earshot and agreed that once they had located Madame's apartment Enid would join them in Paris for a few days.

THIRTY-SEVEN

Madame had clucked around in her bedroom for almost two days pulling various garments out of her wardrobe; there were clothes strewn everywhere. Tilly finally went in and offered to help.

'I have been trying to do it on my own, but, Tilly, what does one wear in Paris these days?' Madame said tongue-in-cheek.

'Well, as an attractive eighty something-year-old, you must wear what you are comfortable in and what you can move around in easily. So, I would say your shoes are the first thing to address.'

After a couple of hours, Tilly had managed to condense the old woman's choices down to five dresses, two cardigans and a glamorous wrap in case they went out in the evening. They were booked for ten days in the apartment but, depending on the outcome, they could extend their stay.

Tilly booked a taxi to the airport and although Madame was fine about paying, she had no idea how much things cost. So, 80 euros for a ride to Nice airport had been a bit of a surprise. Enid insisted on travelling with them, assuring Madame she would catch the train back.

'Oh Tilly, please keep her safe!' Enid whispered in her friend's ear as they hugged goodbye.

Madame proudly positioned herself bolt upright in the wheelchair, silently taking it all in as Tilly pushed her towards the departure gate. Her blue eyes captured every nuance of a whole new world of travellers. Once they had passed through security, weaved their way through the illuminated bustling duty-free area, and were sitting at the gate, she finally spoke.

'You were so right about the wheelchair; I never would have coped with all that chaos. The world has turned upside down since I last travelled anywhere.'

Because of the wheelchair they were in the first group to board the plane. Madame confidently walked from the door of the plane to her seat. Tilly put her next to the window, anticipating no one would knock into her there.

The old lady loved every minute of it. She ate the snack the hostess offered her and marvelled at the fact there were male attendants.

'There were never men waiting on me last time I flew!' Madame said.

Tilly laughed.

It was a brief trip and within an hour they were descending towards Orly airport with Madame giving her young companion an ongoing commentary about what she could see from the window.

As they emerged from the arrival gate, Jean-Luc was waiting with his hired wheelchair folded beside him and a luggage trolley. He bent down and kissed Madame on her cheeks, then kissed Tilly full on the lips and whispered, 'You smell beautiful.'

Madame stood up. 'You may give that back now, Tilly.' She gestured at the airline wheelchair with her stick, then turned to Jean-Luc. 'I am sure I may need your one at some point, but just now I need to stretch these old legs to keep them moving.'

Tilly pushed the luggage trolley with the folded wheelchair on the top. To any onlookers, they were an interesting group. A smart clean-cut Frenchman whose blue jeans featured an ironed central crease, accompanied by a striking English rose with a glossy head of shoulder-length walnut brown hair, walking alongside an old lady whose wrinkled face was illuminated by her piercing aqua-blue eyes.

The reception area of the chosen hotel was pleasant but looked a little tired. It didn't faze Madame; she still managed to walk with aid of her stick. Along with the two cases and the folded wheelchair, they were all able to squeeze into the lift. Their apartment, which was more of a suite, was on the sixth floor at the top of the building. The living room had a little balcony and the two bedrooms were small but adequate. The furniture was a little worn, but everything was clean and appeared comfortable.

'If you feel up to it, I will come and accompany you to

a small restaurant nearby around 7 p.m. But if you feel too tired, Tilly will phone me and I will bring a selection of casual food from the delicatessen around the corner,' Jean-Luc said to Madame before she went in to inspect her bedroom and Tilly walked him to the door.

'I can't bear not to be "with" you *ma Cherie*.'

'You are "with" me, it's just you are with Madame as well! See you at seven,' Tilly replied, kissed him on lips and playfully pushed him out of the door.

The dated furniture in the suite didn't bother Madame; she was delighted with the simple things, like the toiletries supplied in her bathroom, and the minibar and chocolates in the fridge. Tilly persuaded her to relax in a comfy chair in the living room. She positioned the chair so that the old woman could look out through the open glass doors, across the rooftops of Paris. Tilly took the opportunity to unpack both of their cases.

By the time Tilly returned to the room Madame was sound asleep. Tilly gently lifted her feet up on to a footstool and draped her wrap over her shoulders.

'Shall we take up Jean-Luc's offer of eating here in the suite?' Tilly asked once Madame had awoken from her nap.

'Absolutely not! I'm quite refreshed now and besides I'm not leaving you two alone at this early stage of our visit! Come on, show me what should I wear?'

Once Madame was dressed and Tilly had helped her with her hair, she slipped into a new red dress she had picked up in the Menton Saturday market. She teamed it up with some red bead earrings and a pair of black sandals.

'Why, Tilly, how impressive; you look lovely in red!' Madame said when Tilly appeared from the bedroom.

As they arrived in the foyer, Jean-Luc was waiting for them. He greeted Madame first, complimenting her on her beautiful shawl, then turned to Tilly and kissed her, whispering, 'You look perfect.' Tilly blushed. Madame smiled.

'The brasserie is just a five-minute walk, so Madame, I am sure you will manage with just your stick.' The old lady straightened, then slipped her arm into Jean-Luc's. 'Old age has its compensations!' she said as she smiled at Tilly.

The brasserie, called Chez Antoine, appeared very unassuming; a red canopy that had enjoyed better days sagged over slightly grubby windows that displayed several dated 'recommended' stickers. The centrally located door clattered each time it opened. However, when they entered, they found that it was almost full. Jean-Luc seated Madame with her back to the wall so she was facing the rest of the tables and the bar beyond. The atmosphere buzzed, filled with lots of locals and a smattering of tourists who had done their research and hadn't been put off by the street appearance.

Madame studied the blackboard menu intently and questioned Jean-Luc about what was typical Parisian food before she made her choice. The old lady was relishing every moment of her excursion. Tilly excused herself to go to the loo, then sent a quick text to Enid: 'Our darling Madame has taken to Paris like a duck to water!'

Tilly chuckled at Enid's swift reply, 'Just make sure the old duck doesn't slip!'

Madame didn't offer much conversation; she was too busy eating. They all had the pâté de foie gras for a starter. Madame had the escargots in butter and parsley for a main and managed to eat half of her favourite pastry chocolate eclair for dessert. In between mouthfuls she was totally engaged watching the antics of two old chaps who appeared as if they had been holding the bar up since World War II.

'I thought we might catch the Batobus tourist boat tomorrow so Madame can be seated but see all the main sights. What do you think?' Jean-Luc quietly asked Tilly.

'I need to see how she is in the morning, and we will have to take the wheelchair; you will need to insist on that. She responds to your charm.' Tilly squeezed his leg under the table. 'Then there are only two more days until we have access to Maison Papillon. I am thinking we might take her past the building the day before, so she can familiarise herself, and maybe it will throw up some more memories,' Tilly added.

When they returned to the hotel, Tilly ensured Madame was orientated to the new surroundings in her bedroom. It had been at least twenty years since she had last slept anywhere but the sunken bed in the Turret House. She thanked Tilly and before Tilly had even left the bedroom the old lady was snoring loudly enough to wake the dead. As she pulled the bedroom door closed her phone beeped with a text.

'Open the door!'

'What on earth are you doing here? How did you know she would be asleep?' Tilly asked as Jean-Luc walked in.

He took the phone from her hand and placed it on the table and kissed her.

'It was the most excitement she has had in years; I just knew she would go to sleep, *tout suite*!' Holding Tilly close, he moved them both towards her bedroom.

'Now show me your room please?' he asked as he undid the zip of her dress.

They made gentle all-consuming love very quietly.

'I love you Jean-Luc,' Tilly said for the very first time. As they sat naked on the bed with only the moonlight illuminating their faces, a large tear ran down his cheek.

'I didn't mean to upset you!' she said as she wiped the tear with her finger.

'They are tears of happiness; I am French, don't you know by now we feel deeper than the English,' he replied with a soft warm smile. 'I think I have loved you since the night we sat in the park together on a very similar moonlit night and you spoke so honestly.'

Around midnight Tilly insisted that her lover left and go home. She felt it was necessary that Madame didn't know he had been there. Besides, this trip was all about Madame.

THIRTY-EIGHT

Tilly quietly opened Madame's door around 8 a.m. to check on her, but she slept on till almost 9 a.m.

'What a wonderful night we had!' she said as she emerged from her room in her dressing gown. 'What have you two got planned for us today?'

Tilly smiled and handed her a cup of coffee. 'Well, now you are awake, I will have the breakfast brought up and we can talk about it.'

Madame was fascinated with the miniature jam jars offered with the croissants. She managed to eat two of the pastries and consume two cups of coffee. Tilly told her about the suggested boat trip, then delicately led the conversation towards a trip past Maison Papillon for tomorrow.

'I can see you have been thinking this through, my dear. I think you are right; I need to do things in stages. Yes, we can pass by Maison Papillon tomorrow and see what I can remember.' Madame paused, then added 'But today I am happy to take the boat trip.'

They would never have coped without the wheelchair. Finding a Batobus stop that had disabled access was a challenge, but Jean-Luc had looked it all up online in advance. They only left the boat once, at Notre-Dame. En route, Tilly spotted a quaint patisserie, with a wide enough door for the wheelchair, so they enjoyed a refreshing coffee and shared a salad baguette. Then using the disabled access to the cathedral, they avoided the queues and moved slowly around the vast space.

'Stop here please!' Madame said as she looked through her purse for some coins. 'I may be Jewish, but in the early days of our marriage, I often went to Mass with my husband. I want to light four candles for my family while I am here.' She stood up out of the wheelchair, walked over and placed her coins in the slot, took four of the candles, lit them and placed them on the rack.

Jean-Luc handed Tilly a couple of euros. 'Why don't you join her?'

The two women stood in silence side by side in front of the line of flickering flames, both momentarily lost in their own thoughts. The air was rich with the fragrance of spicy smelling incense, while the whispered voices of the many visitors created a bee-like hum throughout the sacred space. Tilly listened as Madame told her that she hoped her parents were up there somewhere with wee Eric and her husband, waiting for her. Tilly tried to imagine her own mother, and what she would make of this scenario if she was looking down on them all.

Tilly squinted as they moved out into the sunlight. Sometimes it was as if she was alive in a dream. Here in Paris, the city of love, doing amazing things with a wonderful man and a special old lady, both of whom she believed loved her.

As Madame positioned herself comfortably in the wheelchair, Jean-Luc squeezed Tilly's hand and mouthed, 'I love you.'

Tilly was relieved when Madame announced she was ready to return to the hotel. It had been another massive day.

Once they had ensured she was comfortable, Madame had agreed that the two women would order room service for dinner. Tilly walked Jean-Luc to the door.

'Please don't feel hurt, but it's best you don't come back tonight; we all need our sleep!' For a moment Jean-Luc looked at his feet, then quickly recovered. 'I understand.' He kissed her and walked off towards the lift.

Although Madame was worn out and had said what a great day it had been, Tilly could see a thread of anxiety growing as they talked at the small table eating the salad and fresh ham from the room service menu.

'I know as yet I haven't said anything about why this Papa Hans man was in our lives; I am realistic enough to know it may not have been out of the goodness of his heart,' Madame said, then popped a piece of tomato in her mouth.

'I am reluctant to comment; there have been so many stories about civilian life in World War II, and many of them with no witnesses to substantiate the truth. Miriam said there were hundreds of babies born to French women from German soldiers during that time and many mothers altered the age of the children and passed them off as French. But when I saw the painting of Jacob, there was no way anyone else in this world could be your papa, except him.'

'I agree with you, Tilly; I felt an instant connection to the man in Mama's painting. I think I have prepared myself for the worst in this quest; so hopefully whatever it all throws up at least I will finally have the truth. The one thing I am sure of, after seeing the poetry books my parents exchanged, is that they were madly in love.' Madame let out a big sigh.

Tilly stood beside her, offered her arm and led her to the bathroom, then waited and helped her undress and get into bed. These almost intimate moments when Tilly assisted Madame with her personal care had added to the bond the two friends now shared.

These were personal duties a mama might expect of a daughter and Tilly felt privileged to have that role.

Tilly decided to make good use of her solitary time. She lit a candle, put a restorative mask on her face and lay in the bath deep in thought. Now that time had moved on, she was comfortable with considering the dynamics and the history of her relationships. The one with her father, her stepmother, with Giovanni and up to a point Aunt Lucy. But Tilly knew she would stay connected to her aunt. Time was already repairing that wound.

Then her thoughts shifted to her new life and her new friends. The truth was, they were more than friends, they were the most like 'family' that Tilly had ever experienced. Growing up, she had totally missed out on a mother's true love, and yet somehow, she knew there must be more as she caught glimpses of her schoolfriends' mothers in action.

As she cleaned her mask off in front of the mirror, a memory of Karen passed through her mind: the woman who adored her own reflection. In the past, mirrors had only been associated with the horrors of her stepmother; it had been no mean feat for Tilly as she grew up avoiding her own reflection.

That evening she progressed. She experienced a new sense of comfort in the dated 1970s bathroom. Focussed directly on the mirror, studying her scrubbed face with all its faults and freckles, she was curious, rather than frightened about the future.

The following morning Tilly woke suddenly hearing her mobile beep, rushed up and checked on Madame. Once she heard the old lady's familiar breathing noises, she calmed down and checked her phone. It was 8 a.m. and there was a text from Jean-Luc.

'Call me when you wake up, please.'

'I missed you last night, *ma Cherie*,' he said as soon as he answered her call.

'Well, that's a bit rich, I spent the entire day with you!' Tilly laughed.

After they had exchanged the banter that is exclusive to new love, Jean-Luc moved on to the plan for the day.

'Even though I will have access to the apartment from tomorrow, when we make this preliminary visit today, I think it will still be best to try to avoid the old concierge. My research shows she has lunch around 12.30 p.m. most days so perhaps that's a good time for us to visit.'

'Madame was very tired last evening so I think that should be our only excursion today,' Tilly replied.

Once she had eaten her breakfast, Madame was bright enough, but Tilly could see that physically she was fading when she got into the wheelchair of her own accord.

Jean-Luc pushed the chair. Tilly walked behind holding Madame's walking stick, the streets mostly too narrow for her to walk beside them. As they passed by a park that was about five minutes' walk from Maison Papillon, Madame asked Jean-Luc to stop.

'I can remember this place.' She pointed towards the old iron gates. Jean-Luc glanced at Tilly who nodded, and they pushed her into the park.

'Those swings are modern, but I am sure they are in the same place they were when Mama used to bring me here to play. She would push me high, and I remember her laughter. It was usually at dusk when there were no other children about. It must have been late autumn or winter as I remember Mama had a headscarf and I wore a woollen hat.'

They pushed her around most of the park; she commented on snippets of memories, she mentioned that people she vaguely remembered were wearing a yellow star on their coats. Then they moved on towards Maison Papillon. Once outside the large doors that led into the paved area in front of the gate, Madame requested her stick. She got up out of the wheelchair and stood looking along the street, then towards the doors and the building. She was totally absorbed in her surroundings.

One of the large outer doors was slightly ajar. Tilly pushed it open and Madame walked slowly through; there was no sign of the concierge. Her apartment door was closed, and there was no flicker of lace curtains. Madame stood quite still, taking it all in. When her gaze finally rested on the ornate butterfly gate that heralded entry to the groomed courtyard beyond, Tilly could see the tears welling in her eyes.

Both Tilly and Jean-Luc moved closer and stood either side of her.

'This is as far as we can go today, we can explore once I have checked into the Airbnb studio, Madame.' Jean-Luc spoke with kindness.

Madame slipped her free arm through Tilly's. 'It is coming back to me; I remember this gate so very well.' She walked over to the gate and peered at the manicured garden courtyard on the other side.

'I used to play in there with the concierge's daughter and an older girl who also lived in an apartment here. But then suddenly one day, with no explanation, I wasn't allowed to play or see them again.'

Tilly had become concerned; it was apparent her dear friend was visibly affected by whatever she was remembering from living at Maison Papillon so long ago. Her whole expression had changed. Tilly gently guided her back into the wheelchair, and they pushed her off in the direction of a café Jean-Luc had spotted that looked a suitable place to have lunch.

Madame said very little and barely picked at her food. Then, she requested they return to the hotel as she felt she needed to rest.

THIRTY-NINE

PARIS, 1944

Papa Hans has painted the windows in our apartment and turned off the electricity, so the rooms are darkened as he carries our suitcases to the door. Mama has tied on a dull brown headscarf. It is the height of summer, but she pulls her coat on as well. It is the coat I saw her sew the money into. They hardly speak or touch. Papa Hans gives Mama a key. Which is strange as he says he will get rid of his own key once he has completed his task and left the building.

Mama has a large tote bag slung across her shoulders; she gives me a handbag with a long strap and puts it over my head and across my shoulders the same way as hers. Then she places her hands on my shoulders and looks me directly in the eyes and says no matter what happens, I must not let anyone take my handbag. It contains very precious things that we will need in Nice. Now, I feel the first wave of raw fear.

It is early morning; Mama explains to me we are going to catch the Métro to the big train station called Gare du Nord, then catch a steam train all the way to Nice which is a city beside the sea.

As we walk outside, the courtyard seems messy and everything looks dry; not like it used to be when I could play there. I cannot hold Mama's hand as she is carrying both our suitcases. I walk as close as I can beside her. The street is quiet, but as we turn the corner, I recognise the grumpy lady who lives in the studio by our butterfly gate and guards the apartments. She is pulling her grocery wheelie bag. All of a sudden she points at us and starts yelling *'Collaboratrice, salope, elle vit avec un Nazi! Salope.*

Suddenly, as if from nowhere, two men appear in front of us. One grabs both my arms, he smells bad. Mama drops the suitcases and rushes towards me, the other man punches her in the face, then a third man arrives. I watch as Mama is dragged ahead of me up the street; she is screaming my name. I can't speak, I open my mouth, but no sound comes; the terror has paralysed me. We are dragged into a barber's shop. It is one we have walked past many times. I am pinned against the wall. The man who has grabbed me holds me upright with one arm. He shouts, 'This is what happens to sluts who sleep with the enemy!' I watch in horror as they push Mama to the ground; they both kick her in her side. Then the barber steps over, he roughly lifts her head up and begins to hack off all her beautiful glossy hair. It is impossible for me to turn my head away; the man holding me forces me to watch. Hot urine stings down my legs; I have no control. Huge hunks of Mama's hair fall on to the shiny black and white tiles. Once most of her hair is off, the barber takes his razer and begins to shave her head. My mama screams, his hand slips, and blood spurts up from her scalp all over his white jacket. He swears as he drops her head and I hear the crack as my beloved mama's head hit the tiles.

I feel the man who holds me loosen his grip. My mama lies still on the floor, her spiky shaved head is encircled by a halo of bright red blood. Her eyes are closed and her face is still. I run to her. I reach out to touch her. She still has the tote bag over her shoulder. I touch her arm, it feels warm. As I bend down to see her face, her eyes flutter, then open. Once she can see it's me, she whispers, 'I will be OK, get ready to run, my love.'

Now I hear a lot of strange shouting and two men in uniforms come in, yelling in a foreign language I have never heard before. They are like avenging angels. One of them gently picks Mama up, then he carefully winds her scarf around her head. The bleeding seems to have stopped, but she has blood trickling down her neck, and I have it all over my hands. The bad men stand there with their hands on their hips still calling Mama those horrible names.

A lady I recognise from the market comes into the barber's shop carrying our suitcases. She nods to Mama as she places the cases in front of her. One of the men in uniform, speaking the strange language, picks up the cases, then they guide us outside. I can't understand their words, but their meaning carries a weight of reassurance. They are our saviours. Mama holds my hand and whispers, 'It's all right Little One, my hair will grow back.' They put us in a funny car which has no roof and a flag with stars and stripes fluttering on the front of it. Then they drive us away from that terrible barber's shop.

Then we are in a bathroom at the big railway station. Mama has washed the blood off her neck and off my hands and has taken my knitted woollen hat out of my case. She stretches it as far as she can and pulls it on to her head. She looks very weird. I look down at my feet as we walk to our train, it is as if I have left my body and I am looking back at myself and it isn't really me. We are squashed into a carriage with four other people. Mama tells me not to talk. Just to sit quietly. She promises me we will soon be safe.

After a few hours' travelling and a few stops down the line, the other four passengers have left the carriage and we are finally alone. Mama pulls the blinds in the carriage so no one can see in. Then takes her tote bag off her shoulder and removes a bottle of water she has wrapped in one of her blouses to stop it breaking. I drink some. Then she tells me to take my pants off. I realise the smell in the carriage is me. She uses more of the water and the blouse to wash me, and then opens the case and puts me in fresh pants. Then she has a sip of the water herself. Her face has turned all blue on one side and her eye is so swollen it has closed over.

We don't speak; she just holds her arm around me the whole time. I am careful not to move, as I know under her dress where the men kicked her must be very sore. There is an announcement that we will soon be arriving in Nice. Mama tells me to stand at the door to block it if anyone comes in, then she swiftly and subtly turns the hem of her coat over and pokes her finger into the stitching to pull it apart and make a small hole. She puts two fingers in and pulls out some money and puts it in her pocket.

It is dark when we arrive in Nice. The station is busy, and everyone seems to be shouting. I watch as Mama winces in pain, trying to lift the suitcases. I take one of them, and she half drags the other on to the platform. She calls out to a man with a trolley; he takes one look at her face and walks off towards another woman who was calling for a porter. It seems an age as we stand in the dark on the platform trying to get someone to help us. We have to go down one lot of stairs then up another to get into the station building and Mama is so sore and stiff she can only sit on the case and hold my hand.

A big man with black skin appears at the stairway; he is wearing a porter's uniform and has a trolley. I have never seen a black man close up before; he smiles at me with a neat row of very white shiny teeth. He puts the suitcases on the trolley and gently guides Mama to the handrail on the stairs. 'Just go slowly,' he says, 'I only get to work after dark and there are no more trains tonight.' I walk beside Mama; it takes us ages. The big black porter is waiting with our cases when we finally reach the station foyer. Mama asks him if he knows a hotel that would take us. He writes something on a bit of paper, then walks us outside and finds us a taxi. She tries to give him some money, but he says, 'No, you be safe.'

We arrive in a dark narrow street outside a building I assume is where we will sleep. The taxi driver won't help Mama with the suitcases. He just sits there while we struggle and drag them out of the taxi.

I am hiding in behind Mama as she knocks on the hotel door. When someone finally opens it, the hotel lady looks at Mama and pulls the door shut. I find my voice, and scream! The lady hadn't noticed me before that. I start to cry. I am so tired, so hungry, and more frightened for Mama and me than I have ever been in my life.

The hotel lady softens, she takes us inside and helps us with the suitcases into a lift that looks like a cage. We go up to the top of the building. It smells musty and there are no lights in the hall. She shows us to a room with bare floorboards, a big old bed and a chest of drawers. She tells Mama not to leave the room for a few days until she heals. There is a lot of anger and blame about and she does not want any trouble in her hotel. She returns with a tray; it has two mugs of hot tea and some bread and cheese. After we have eaten, I follow Mama down the dark hall to the shared bathroom; she fills the basin from our room with hot water. She is in too much pain, and it is too heavy for her to carry, so I walk slowly back making sure I do not spill a drop. I watch as Mama removes her clothes, she is bruised black all over and I help dribble the warm water over her body as she stands naked on a towel. Next, she starts to peel the woollen cap off her head. She cries out in pain as the cap has stuck to the dry blood. Once it is off, she puts her head over the basin and gets me to dribble the water over her head. I watch in horror as the basin of water becomes pink with the blood from my mama's head. I help her on with her cotton nightdress, then put my own on. We fall asleep side by side in the dusty big bed.

The hotel lady's name is Madame Bruton; she is frightened to attract any trouble, but she is kind and brings us food twice a day. She also gives Mama some medicine for the pain. It makes her sleepy, which frightens me at first, but then as the days pass, I can see Mama is getting better. Her face is healed up, her eye is back to normal, but I can still see the blue tinge of bruising on her cheek. I play with the few toys I had brought with me. In the evenings after she is sure there are no other guests around, Mama washes our clothes in the bathroom. We hang them to dry around our room. I am not sure how many days have passed. Madame Bruton tells Mama if she covers her head with a scarf, she should be OK to go out on the street.

I don't want to go; I clutch at my mama and beg her to just stay in the room. She could just keep paying Madame Bruton. It is safe in our room. What if we are attacked? Eventually she persuades me. The first time we step out I am terrified, but Mama takes it very slowly; she is wearing a summer dress and a brighter coloured scarf that she had in her case. She tells me we need to blend in. She has a map in her hand that Madame Bruton has lent her, and I cling to her dress as she needs both her hands to read it. We walk for ever, then Mama finally says, 'Here it is, just like I remember!'

We walk into the foyer of the building; an older lady comes bustling over and carefully studies our faces. I freeze. She reminds me of the lady who guards our Paris apartment.

Mama calls out, 'Hello Frances, it's me Elsie!' The old woman rushes up to Mama and hugs her. 'My God, my God you were spared!'

Although I am relieved, I have lost my tongue again. But it doesn't matter, I just follow them; the old lady called Frances natters the whole time. Mama takes out the key from her bag and opens the door to what is to be our home.

FORTY

At 6 p.m. Tilly was concerned. Madame hadn't stirred for a few hours. She opened her bedroom door.

'Madame, are you OK; would you like some soup?'

The old lady looked awfully pale as she slowly sat up and reached for her glasses.

'I think I will be all right, Tilly; seeing Maison Papillon, especially the gate, triggered all my lost memories. They rose up from their locked cupboard in my brain and seeped swiftly into my consciousness. Let me splash my face, then come out to the living room.' She took a breather, then added, 'Yes, I'm hungry – soup would be wonderful!'

Some of her colour had returned as she sipped the delicious French onion soup. 'The Parisians really do this the best,' she commented.

Tilly had been patient, but really wanted to cut the small talk and hear about what her companion had remembered.

When they had finished the meal and Tilly had placed the tray of used plates outside the door, Madame finally cleared her throat and began her story. She articulated about the forgotten fear she had experienced as a seven-year-old, she even recalled not only the sense of loss of her real father but faded memories of her older grandparents who had left suddenly. It had been installed in her by her mama and her memories that it was not safe to be Jewish. She told her whole story from the escape from Maison Papillion to arriving in Nice.

By the end, Tilly was in tears, and it was Madame who was comforting her.

'Oh, I am so sad and so very, very sorry that you had to endure such hell! I feel so pathetic that I felt sorry for myself about what happened to me. Your experience was beyond bearable,' sobbed Tilly.

Tilly sniffed back the tears. Madame held her hand. Once Tilly had calmed Madame began to speak again.

'I don't think the experience that I endured was any worse than yours; I found a mechanism to block mine out and I am sure my mama welcomed that. God only knows what she went through!

'I believe that you and I, Tilly, have been drawn together for a reason; we have both suffered childhood trauma and the loss of a child; so, for my part, I can fully empathise with you. I am not up to retelling all this to Enid on the phone, so perhaps tomorrow after we see what happens at Maison Papillon, you will call her for me.'

Tilly nodded and blew her nose.

Their conversation became circumspect, speculating

about what they had to assume had been collaboration. What was patriotism, and what was survival?

'Clearly there was no joy for us with the liberation; we couldn't afford to be patriotic during the Occupation; the only thing us Jews could strive to do, was to survive.'

As Madame spoke, Tilly began to consider how all this had played out with her own French Jewish grandparents; nothing was straightforward, and there were obvious reasons as to why survivors chose to repress the past and move on with the future.

However, at a certain trigger-point, life as it is sometimes ceases and something else drives us forward towards our future. An incident, a query or a trauma could become the catalyst that leads us to pause, to reflect and ask, 'Why?' Then we have to turn and acknowledge our past.

Tilly wasn't up for any more conversation; Madame's story had devastated her; she was emotionally drained. She sent Jean-Luc a short text and said she would explain tomorrow when she brought Madame to Maison Papillon at 1 p.m. as they had arranged.

Both women woke early and enjoyed the leisurely, indulgent breakfast from the room service menu. Tilly texted Enid to say a lot had transpired, but that it wasn't appropriate to chat, and she would call after they had visited Maison Papillon. She wanted Madame to rest up as much as she could before their afternoon excursion.

Madame had agreed that Tilly would push her. She sat upright in the wheelchair; both their handbags rested on her lap as she clutched her walking stick. They both felt familiar with the short route, passing the park then heading along the bumpy footpath towards the large doors of Maison Papillon.

The doors were ajar. Tilly texted Jean-Luc to alert him that they were downstairs. He said to push the door buzzer marked 'Bengue'. Tilly wheeled Madame over to the row of names and buzzers. Then, as she pushed the designated buzzer, the butterfly gate clicked, stretching out on its long steel hinges. It glided open and Tilly pushed her companion into the courtyard where all those years ago, she had played with her neighbours, where she had sat with her parents, and possibly her grandparents, and from where she had escaped.

Jean-Luc arrived from the Airbnb studio. After greeting them both, he leaned down and spoke in a hushed tone. 'The old witch is watching; she has eyes like a hawk. My studio is in the other block, so let's hope she doesn't notice we are going into the wrong building.' He took Tilly's position behind the wheelchair and quickly pushed it in the direction of the main door of the building at the rear of the courtyard.

The key fob was the same for each of the three entry doors. Once inside the building, Madame got out of the wheelchair and took her stick.

'Let's leave that here; I wish to go the rest of the way on my own two legs.' As she spoke the foyer door opened and the old concierge woman stepped in. It was a small foyer, and they all stood very close to each other.

'The Airbnb apartment isn't in this block, it's next door. Please leave, you are not permitted in here,' she announced in French as she placed her hands on her hips.

No one reacted, no one spoke. Tilly could see Madame was intently studying the woman's face.

'Well?' said the concierge and shifted on her feet.

'Well what! I know your type; your type has been policing this building for generations. I own an apartment in here and I intend, along with my friends, to find it,' Madame said, then turned to Jean-Luc. 'Please call the lift down.'

The concierge appeared to have been struck dumb.

The three friends got into the lift, leaving her standing in the foyer. They went directly up to the fifth floor. As they stepped into the hallway it looked even more barren and neglected than their last visit. Madame stopped and meticulously surveyed the hallway. She crossed to the wall opposite the lift and ran her fingers along the wallpaper. Next, she began walking along the hallway; Tilly and Jean-Luc followed her. She walked towards the apartment at the end where they had encountered the Asian nurse and the confused Madame DeFoud. Then she turned and looked back.

'I used to go and play with the girl who lived in there.' She pointed at the door. 'Then I would walk back to our apartment,' she said as she retraced her steps, past the second door to the other end of the hall.

'It's behind this wallpaper somewhere!' She started running her hand along the wall.

'This wallpaper is a special type called anaglypta. It has a raised pattern, mainly used in old buildings to help cover up defects in walls,' Jean-Luc commented as he went on ahead feeling the walls as well.

'Can you two stop for a moment please?' Tilly called out.

'If you go and measure the distance from the last apartment door at the other end to the next door, that should give us the place where Madame's door was or should be.'

Jean-Luc motioned for Madame to stay where she was; he walked back to the other end of the hall and paced out loud to the second door, then counted the paces from there along towards where the others were standing. He arrived about metre further along the hallway.

All three of them began running their fingers along the wall.

'I can feel a seam of some sort!' Tilly called. She tried to rip into the paper, but it was too tough.

'We need a knife!' Madame said.

'I don't know if we should do that? It could be interpreted as wilful criminal damage,' Jean-Luc stated.

Tilly glared at him.

He frowned, then answered: 'Well, I brought this, as well as a knife.' He pulled out a pair of pointy pliers and a folded pocketknife from his jacket pocket.

He unfolded the knife and dug it into the heavy-duty wallpaper. Then, he managed to rip it away. There were two layers to peel off. Someone had been in a hurry and just papered over the existing wallpaper. But the original layer had sunk along what now looked like a door seam.

He pulled and scraped most of the wallpaper off – the top half of the door and the keyhole were obvious. However, there was the dado rail and the painted plywood below it.

This was a little more difficult. Jean-Luc dug his closed pliers under the dado rail; the wood was cheap, old and brittle; it snapped off. Then he had to push the pliers in behind the painted plywood which now, missing its stabilising edge, he was able to grab hold of. Tilly stepped in to help. She yelped as she broke her fingernail, but kept going until all the wood was removed and the door was ready to receive Madame's key.

At that moment the concierge arrived in the hallway. She stood and stared. She did nothing to stop them. Madame took the large steel key out of her handbag and placed it in the lock. Her old hands shook as she attempted to turn it. Jean-Luc was standing directly beside her. 'May I?' he said. She nodded and stepped back.

It took him a bit of wiggling and pulling at the door before he could get the key to finally turn. Then, before he pushed the door open, the old concierge spoke.

'Is that you behind all those wrinkles Corrinne Estienne?' Tilly and Jean-Luc turned and looked at Madame.

'Yes, it is Isabelle! And you have turned out just as rude as your mama and your *grandmère*!' Then she turned back to the task. 'Jean-Luc, please open this door!'

FORTY-ONE

Jean-Luc pushed open the door; the entrance was dark with a strong musty smell. His companions followed; the old concierge lurked in the hallway. He felt for a light switch on the wall. It didn't work. Then further along at eye level, he opened a small cupboard and miraculously it was a 1940s equivalent to electric mains. He flicked the switch. Although the hall light didn't come on, through a door which he assumed would be the salon a faint flicker from an ancient light bulb illuminated the space. Tilly took Madame's arm and the three of them walked in. It took a few seconds for their eyes to adjust. Jean-Luc pulled open one of the heavy brocade drapes that shrouded the window. They all placed their hands on their mouths as the dust flooded down and flickered in the light from the solitary working bulb.

'The windows have been painted over; I'll see if I can open one,' Jean-Luc said as he started to turn the stiff window handle.

Tilly could see Madame was waning; she had been on her feet for almost an hour. She led the old lady to a nearby chair. Madame sat down, then with a sense of familiarity she stroked the gilt-edged carved wooden arms of the chair, then put her hand to the seat which featured a padded tapestry.

Tilly joined Jean-Luc at the window; they both heaved at it; eventually it moved, and they threw it open. The afternoon sun flooded into the salon.

The room was a time capsule – the belle époque era at its Parisian best. Cobwebs danced softly in all corners of the room, swayed by the gentle breeze that breathed into the room for the first time in over seventy years.

Despite the thick layer of dust coating every surface, it was evident that every piece of furniture, each object was a work of art; they all had a story to tell. Tilly stood in a museum of perfectly curated furniture, art and curiosities. Madame was totally absorbed in her surroundings. The old lady had dropped her stick and handbag on the floor and was gazing from one painting to another, to a vase or ornament, and studying each piece of furniture.

Tilly acknowledged the significance of the moment. A shiver swept over her, as if angels were tapping her bones. Together they had reached the pinnacle in Madame's quest.

She left the older woman to her survey and followed Jean-Luc down the hall where he was prising the main bedroom window open.

'It will take solvent to remove the paint from the windows, but at least by opening them a little we may get rid of some of the dust, and it will give us enough light to see most things.' Then he stepped over to Tilly and took both her hands. 'This is the most exciting thing that has ever happened to me,' he said, then tenderly kissed her lips. Tilly hugged him and kissed him back.

'I had better go back to Madame, I am sure she will want to look in here next.'

When Tilly returned to the salon the concierge had walked in and was attempting conversation with Madame.

Tilly didn't quite catch what she had said, but even in French Madame's response was clear.

'Isabelle, I hold no grudge against you, you are not responsible for the sins of your mama, but please, allow me this time. Please leave us alone. I will talk to you once we have worked through things here.'

Tilly followed the concierge, whom she now knew was called Isabelle, out of the apartment; the woman was about to say something, but thought better of it. Tilly stayed silent. She took the key from the door and pulled it closed.

'Jean-Luc has opened the windows in the bedrooms, when you are ready to come through,' Tilly said to Madame.

'Oh Tilly, I have returned to my past; I half expect a young version of my mama to walk in any moment. These beautiful vases and paintings belonged originally to my grandparents; it as if the family are all here in the room with me.' She pushed herself up from the chair; Tilly bent down to give her the stick. They walked into the hall, then into her mama's bedroom where Jean-Luc had opened the window.

The curtains were a stunning ice-blue brocade with

large navy beaded tie-back tassels hanging on either side. Crowned above were the perfectly swagged pelmets, made in matching brocade, edged in gold fringing and anchored in place above the floor-to-ceiling windows.

The kidney-shaped dressing table was made of what appeared to be either solid walnut or maple wood; the surface was protected by a grey-white marble top. A vintage brush, mirror and comb set were obvious, even under the layer of dust. The legs of the dressing table were elaborately carved and stood on four claw-like feet. An oval carved mirror sat comfortably at the rear of the dressing table, reflecting the activity of the room.

'Mama always sat there to brush her hair, sometimes she would let me brush it for her,' Madame said to no one in particular, as she walked over and started rubbing the dust off the objects on the marble top with her handkerchief.

The bed had been covered in a dust sheet, which Tilly carefully rolled up to avoid the dust going everywhere. The bed was swathed in a rich brocade bedspread in a shade of blue that worked with the colour of the curtains, and it was edged with the same gold fringing and scattered with several tapestry cushions.

'That will be just as Mama left it; she was always so specific about where the cushions sat, and my *grandmère* did all those tapestries especially for Mama when she married.'

Tilly was fascinated with the luxurious fox fur that was slung over the back of the second chair.

'Mama loved that fox! I always felt sorry for him; but here he is, as alive as he was then!'

Jean-Luc was very comfortable taking the practical role of this journey into the magical place of Madame's past. He recognised the quest was almost over but he was very keen to remain involved in every aspect. He had opened the window in the second bedroom, and as the light filled the room, it revealed the most lovingly decorated child's chamber, displaying an array of feminine vintage toys and treasures.

Madame gasped with a mixture of delight tinged with sadness as she walked in. On an ornate child-sized chair next to a small bed sat a stuffed bear with a glass eye missing, a stuffed monkey wearing a fez and a doll with long blonde plaits.

'They are just sitting where they were when I said goodbye to them; at the end they were the only friends I had. I felt so guilty as I was only allowed to choose one doll to take with me.'

Madame had plopped down on the small bed; she propped her stick up against the carved bed end. Tilly sat down, close beside her. She could see and feel the emotion radiating from her special friend. Their eyes both settled on a stunning oil painting of a fantasy pink shimmering butterfly that had been hung to be viewed by whoever was in the bed.

'Now, I do know Mama painted that especially for me; she usually only painted "true to life", but she did that as an exception, as pink was my favourite colour.'

'There must be many happy memories here as well as the challenges?' Tilly asked as she gently placed her arm around Madame's shoulder.

'Oh yes! Many memories coming to light, of Mama and a few faded ones of a kind man who must have been my papa. It will all just take me a bit of time to digest. I'm happy here, Tilly, on my little bed. Why don't you two explore and perhaps you could text Enid and update her; she'll be anxious.'

They left her to her memories, and as Jean-Luc scraped at the paint on the salon window, Tilly phoned Enid. They agreed that as Enid was still off work and had already asked the neighbour to look in on the Turret House each day, she would get the next available flight to Paris to join them.

'This paint is going to need solvent to remove it,' Jean-Luc said as he walked into what appeared to be the kitchen and, using the light from his phone, started opening the cupboards.

'I doubt we will find anything in here that would be usable now.'

Once their eyes had adjusted to the light, they could see the kitchen was quite roomy; it featured an oblong scrubbed wooden table, with six vintage chairs tucked in around it. They shone the light around the room: one wall featured three still life paintings of bowls of fresh fruit. At first glance Tilly had thought they were photos, they appeared so real.

'Madame's mama was a prolific artist, if we are to assume most of the paintings are hers. Although a couple in the salon pre-date even her grandparents. Before the war they must have been serious collectors,' Jean-Luc commented.

A small window at the rear of the kitchen sink

materialised in the light from the phone; Jean-Luc pulled a chair over, climbed up and managed to push it open. It allowed some natural illumination in, but still the kitchen was the darkest room in the apartment.

They returned to the bedroom where Madame still sat on the small bed. She looked weary.

'I spoke with Enid, Madame Fleury is going to look in on the Turret House each day, and Enid is on her way to join us. If she can get to the airport on time, she should be here later this evening,' Tilly said.

Madame nodded, then replied, 'I think I need to return to the hotel now and rest; I'll come back tomorrow, and we can all look at things with fresh eyes together.'

As Tilly helped her up, Jean-Luc cleared his throat and moved awkwardly to his feet. Tilly stood still supporting Madame with her arm to give him space to speak. He looked directly at Madame and spoke to her in French.

'Madame, with your permission I would like to engage an emergency electrician today; as well, I will go and purchase some solvent. If you give me until tomorrow afternoon before you return, I can remove the paint from the windows and hopefully have enough power connected to vacuum the dust so you can be more comfortable here.'

'Thank you, Jean-Luc, that would be wonderful.'

They locked the door and Madame leaned on Tilly as they slowly walked to the lift; once on the ground floor she willingly sat down in the wheelchair.

Although feeling very concerned at Madame's pallor and exhaustion, Tilly's heart lifted as the butterfly gate gracefully swung open in front of them.

On the walk back to the hotel, Tilly was impressed as she reflected on the practical solutions her eccentric awkward boyfriend had come up with. Jean-Luc said he would call and engage his parents' handyman to come over and help him, as well as an electrician he knew. If the electrics in the apartment were unsafe, he suggested that they could use a small generator and some temporary lights.

FORTY-TWO

It was late afternoon when the threesome arrived back at the hotel. Madame went to her bedroom for a lie-down. Before Jean-Luc went off on his mission, he embraced and lovingly kissed Tilly. They agreed to speak later in the evening; Jean-Luc was keen to fulfil his commitment to have the apartment ready for Madame the next day.

After he had left the room, Tilly experienced such clarity of feeling towards him, it practically overwhelmed her. In this moment, the only person she really wanted to always be there, and never leave her, was this attractive odd French man with the ironed jeans.

Madame woke up around 6 p.m. from her nap; by 7 p.m. Enid had arrived; all three enjoyed the bond of being together again. They ordered room service food and a bottle of excellent Chablis to have with their dinner. Tilly sat enjoying the warmth of friendship while she listened as Madame told Enid all the details of the apartment.

'So, this Isabelle woman, how did she know you?' Enid asked.

'Well, she was about two years younger than me and either her *grandmère* or her mama was the concierge. And before Papa Hans came on the scene, I used to play with her in the courtyard garden. I would never had recognised her if she hadn't spoken to me. I am fairly sure it was her mama who gave us up to the men who attacked us. Papa Hans paid her mama money, I have clear memory of that. Now I can only assume it was to stop them reporting him shielding a Jewish woman and child. She was just as much a collaborator as my mama.' As Madame said the word 'collaborator', her voice began to falter.

'We do not know all the facts yet; just because he was German, he may not have been a bad person. As with the English, the Germans had no choice; they all had to participate in the war.' Tilly attempted to soften the blow.

Tilly could see Enid needed the gaps to the story filled in, but it was best just to let Madame keep speaking.

'There is something playing on my mind; it's connected somehow with that painting of the pink butterfly in my bedroom. Maybe when we visit tomorrow it will come to me,' Madame said before she unexpectedly kissed both women goodnight and went to bed.

Tilly made a pot of camomile tea and told Enid the entire sad horror story of Madame and her mama's escape from Paris. When she had finished, they were both in tears and talked through all the issues of lost memory and how a lot of the old lady's past vagueness and unsociable behaviour could all be explained.

The following morning the three women continued to enjoy each other's company in their new environment with an unhurried breakfast. The younger women mainly listened while Madame recalled many more childhood memories.

Jean-Luc had texted to say the apartment was as good as he could get it, and for them to arrive anytime from 2 p.m.

Isabelle was on patrol when they arrived in front of the butterfly gate. She and Madame greeted each other in a civil manner and she kindly handed Madame a key fob so she had free access to the building.

It was with great pride that Madame, from her wheelchair, swiped the pad with her new fob and electronically opened the magnificent butterfly gate. The papillon gate. Many years ago, her parents would have done it manually with a large key.

As they approached the apartment door, they could see how much work Jean-Luc had achieved. The door had been stripped of all the wallpaper and paint and was all tidy and ready to be restored to match the other apartment doors in the hallway. Tilly noticed a small decorative container on the right side of the door post. Madame reached out and touched it. 'This is our Mezuzah; it contains the prayer to bless our family home.'

Jean-Luc greeted them in a brightly lit hall. There was the gentle hum of a small generator he had organised in the kitchen. Temporary lights had been set up in each room, and now the paint had been removed from the windows, the sun streamed in.

'Oh, my goodness!' Enid exclaimed. 'What a divine apartment!'

The bulk of the dust had been vacuumed from all the obvious surfaces, and they could all view the wonderful furniture and works of art more closely.

Madame rose from her wheelchair and walked into the kitchen. As she passed the paintings within her reach, she lightly stroked them as if taking back ownership. Then she turned her attention to opening every cupboard and every drawer. At first Tilly assumed she was just exploring, then it occurred to her that she was searching for something.

After the kitchen, Madame opened the hall cupboard which was stacked full of neatly ironed and folded linen. Nothing much to see there.

A large walnut chiffonier took up most of one wall in the salon. It had been ornately carved and had two large drawers above its two cupboard doors. She struggled to open them.

Jean-Luc was quickly at her side and with a strong pull opened the first one for her. It contained the most exquisite silver cutlery service, but Madame didn't linger on that. Leaving that drawer open, she indicated for Jean-Luc to open the second one. Madame's eyes lit up this time. It was typical of a drawer most family homes have. It housed a bit of everything, including a ball of string, a corkscrew, a pair of scissors. Madame went straight for envelopes that were tucked in one of the corners. She opened each one and read the contents. Clearly, they weren't what she was looking for; she hastily threw them back in and commenced with the cupboards. Here, there was a stunning eight-branched candelabra; it was silver and in the Jewish design, called a menorah, mostly used to see in the Sabbath dinner ritual.

As the old lady walked towards the main bedroom, Tilly asked, 'What exactly is it you are looking for? I am sure we can all help.'

Madame sat down on her parents' bed and sighed. She looked tired.

'I'm not exactly sure. I know my mama would have left an explanation of why and how things happened with my papa and maybe the man I called Papa Hans. Somehow, I feel she told me; but I just can't remember what she said.' Then she got up and commenced probing through each drawer of the dressing table.

The three friends hovered nearby, assisting the old lady where they could. Enid and Tilly could see her complexion was fading and she needed to rest. Once they had all arrived in Madame's childhood bedroom, Tilly insisted she stop and have a big drink of water. Madame sat on her small bed, and Enid swung her legs up, so she was in a resting position, then propped a couple of cushions behind her.

Now it was so much lighter in the rooms, so many more wonderful treasures were revealed. Tilly spotted a doll's house; she had missed it yesterday. She bent down and opened the doors to disclose a perfectly formed eighteenth-century French house in miniature. It was seriously detailed, including a grand piano and beaded chandeliers.

'That was my mama's before me; I was only allowed to

play with it when she was with me. It's more of a piece of art than a toy.'

Enid and Tilly knelt as they examined each room of the doll's house, taking out small pieces of furniture as well as the tiny people, and handing them to Madame on the bed. Lying with her legs up and holding a glass of water, she rallied and gave a commentary of reminiscences about her mama, her *grandmère* and the doll's house. Then she closed her eyes and drifted off for a few minutes. Waking suddenly with a start, she sat bolt upright. 'Enid, Tilly, I remember, I remember!' She was practically shouting.

'What Madame? What do you remember?' Tilly responded as both women were up on their feet beside her. Jean-Luc arrived at the other side of the small bed.

'There! There! The butterfly painting!' she said pointing to the painting at the end of the bed. Now with the room fully lit, the painting had so much clarity, the delicate pink wings shimmering in a magical way.

'Jean-Luc please take the painting down and bring it to me.'

Jean-Luc did as he was summoned.

'Put it face down, here beside me please,' Madame said as she swung her legs down to make room for the painting beside her on the bed.

On the back of the painting was a large brown envelope with the name Corrinne written on it. Madame pulled at the envelope which had only been attached with a little tape. Jean-Luc took the painting and returned it to the wall.

Madame's hands shook as she opened the envelope.

'Enid, I think you should read this out loud. You have all been here for me, through all the stages of this quest, and I'd like you all to hear what my mama says.'

Tilly and Enid sat on either side of Madame on the small bed. Jean-Luc filled the space on the floor the other two had vacated beside the doll's house.

My dearest Corrinne,

As I write, you are seven years old. I have to visualise that if you are reading this, you will be an adult. I will write this all down just once, then I will never speak of it again. I must believe that you and I will arrive safely in Nice and that there will never be another war like this. I will do all I can for you to forget the final tragedy of this apartment and I pray you are young enough to only have memories of the happy times here.

We should have heeded the warning we were given as Jews, to leave France, but we just never believed anything would happen to a wealthy respectable family such as ours. My parents had moved to a smaller apartment and one day they just disappeared. Things were getting bad; most of our friends had already escaped Paris. Then, it was too late! On 16 July there was a banging at our door. I thought it was the concierge and answered it. A tall man in a Nazi uniform stood there and asked to come in. He was exceptionally polite and spoke excellent French. As your Papa Jacob walked into the hall, the colour drained from his face.

We ushered the soldier into the salon. He took a good long look around the room, then stared at me for what seemed like ages before he spoke.

He told us he was under orders to confirm that the occupants of our apartment were Jews, then to alert the local authorities who were working with the occupiers. They would take us to the velodrome where we would be 'reassigned'. Then his German compatriots would appropriate our apartment. My Jacob cried out, no, that we would give him the apartment if he let us go. You heard your Papa's fear and came running from your bedroom and ran to him.

The Nazi had a gun in a holster at his side. Your father gently pushed you aside and dropped to his knees in front of the German. He begged for my life and your life. He offered the man anything he wanted to save you and me. Eventually the German said there was nowhere for us to go, but he would do a deal, on the basis that I must agree to be compliant on all fronts with his wishes otherwise at any time he would send us to the camps.

Tears streamed down your papa's face; his eyes pleaded with me, willing me to agree. It was the hardest thing I have ever had to do. It was the last thing your papa ever did. The soldier said he would take your papa away, and confirm he was the only Jew at our address; he would personally appropriate our apartment, then he would visit us regularly.

I only had a few minutes to say goodbye; Jacob told me that we had chosen to bring you into the world and that we must do all in our power to ensure that you lived. He kissed us both. The German asked for the apartment key, then ushered my Jacob, your precious papa, out of the door; Papa did not make a sound; he didn't want to frighten you. Then the German locked the door from the outside and we never saw Papa again.

The Nazi was a high-ranking officer called Hans and we agreed you would call him Papa Hans. Children adapt, and so if I acted as if everything was all right you would not know anything different. You asked about Papa for weeks, but I told you he was away working. You seemed content enough. Hans wasn't a violent man. I obliged him as a wife would. He had a wife and child of his own in Germany, whom he missed; he didn't approve of the war but had no option. I believe when he first saw me, that he wanted to save me. In one way I was grateful, also I had absolutely no options. All the time I carried out the duties of the deal we had made, I was slowly dying inside. There were many times I felt you and I would be better off dead. But then I would think through that Jacob had given his life for us and somehow, I would manage to keep going. It is now the end of the war and from what I can gather the Americans and the English have liberated France. I have been stuck in this apartment with no radio, so only have Hans' version of events. He is frightened for himself and for us. He is attempting to board up and conceal this apartment, so hopefully no one will remember it. I am going to take you to my parents' holiday apartment in Nice on the Riviera. I don't want to ever return here, but Hans has convinced me one day you may need to know these things, and that I may need the money that this apartment may provide in the future. So, he is doing all he can to hide the apartment before he returns to Germany. And I am writing this letter to you.

Please forgive your mama and papa for what we have done, but you probably will have a child of your own, so I am sure, like us, you would choose to give your own life, to allow them to survive. You are the most precious thing that ever happened for us; you are the most adorable child, and you have my Jacob's eyes. So, while I have you with me, I will always have a part of him as well.

I have no idea what the future will bring for us both, but please know and believe how much we have loved you.

Ever yours

Mama. x

Enid clutched the letter; the four friends sat mute, without a dry eye amongst them. Madame was the first to break the silence.

'I can't bear to think how horrific this must have been for my parents; I am trying to rationalise what I would have done in the same circumstances. What I do understand now is the reason why my mama never spoke of my papa; why she never remarried and why she had very few friends.'

Tilly placed her hand on top of the old lady's. Madame's companions were stumped as to what to say.

Madame seemed to need to talk. 'Mama survived only for me to live, and I never knew this. But I often felt a sense of shame and couldn't understand why. But, if I reflect on why we left Nice, I realise my mama's so-called collaboration followed her, as it did many people in the early years after the war.'

Jean-Luc looked uncomfortable; Tilly agreed when he offered to go out and fetch some takeaway coffees.

Once he had left Madame got up to her feet and walked through to the salon. She sat down on the largest armchair which had obviously been for the master of the house. It had a soft squishy cushion seat, padded armrests and a high supportive back.

'I can just imagine your papa sitting there!' Enid exclaimed.

'Yes, I was thinking the same; Mama would have been over there.' Madame pointed to a smaller chair. 'And I am sure I would have been sneaking into that wonderful doll's house that I was only meant to play with under supervision.' She turned to face her young friends.

'Thank you both for all you have done, I knew in my heart this quest was going to have a painful finale, but I actually feel a type of peace and completion, if that makes sense. You have both been like daughters to me. My old age has taught me that love is bequeathed via all different channels. Both your mamas' losses have been my gain.' She sighed and leaned back in the chair.

'Hand me the letter again please,' Madame asked Enid.

Tilly and Enid could see she needed her space. She tenderly caressed the words on the page; it was as if her mama's love was flowing from the ink. They heard Jean-Luc return and they slipped out to the kitchen.

'How is she?' Jean-Luc asked as he handed out the coffees.

'I think she just needs a few minutes to herself; if we keep the lid on the coffee, I'm sure it will stay hot.'

After a few minutes of quiet exchanges about the latest revelation, Tilly popped her head around the corner to check on her elderly ward. She could see the letter had dropped to the floor. At first Tilly thought Madame must have dozed off. Then she heard a strange mumble come from the chair. She rushed in, the other two right behind her. Madame clutched her chest with one hand, a strange noise came from her mouth. Then she dropped the hand and raised the other one upwards and whispered, 'Mama I'm coming, I'm coming!' She gave a deep final sigh, dropped her hands, her head drooped, and her body slopped into the chair.

Enid picked up Madame's wrist. There was no pulse; her eyes were closed. Although pale, there was a last glow of peace on the exceptional old lady's face as her final worldly breath gently slipped away and her heavenly journey began.

EPILOGUE

PARIS, TWO YEARS LATER

Tilly cradled a welcome cup of coffee in her hands as she reflected on the amount of time Jean-Luc had taken to choose a new coffee machine. She had come to accept that any new appliances they bought would be scrutinized for both the efficiency of how they would dispense, and how they looked; these would be Jean-Luc's decisions.

Tilly didn't mind, as what she termed all the 'really important' decisions had been down to her. Like, where they were married, and where they would live.

She regularly experienced a mixture of sadness overlaid with joy as she remembered Madame. She often felt the presence of Madame and Madame's family alongside her here at number 59 Maison Papillon.

Enid and Tilly had been gob smacked when the old Menton lawyer had called them to his office. Tilly was the beneficiary of the apartment in Maison Papillon and Enid of the Turret House.

It had taken a lot of persuasion for Tilly to convince Jean-Luc to rent his apartment out and move into Maison Papillon. He said although he didn't believe in them, he felt they would be living with ghosts. Once Tilly had agreed he could put a modern architectural spin on some aspects of the apartment, he eventually agreed, and they moved in.

Jean-Luc had completely redesigned the kitchen and the bathroom, selecting stainless steel taps and fittings, choosing an Italian bathroom suite, but a French-made kitchen. Although 'edgy' it all worked sympathetically with the sumptuous, vintage curated main rooms of the apartment. He had convinced Tilly it was all in the same design principle as the glass pyramid in front of the ancient Louvre museum.

They had married in London, only because they had found an open-minded rabbi who would officiate the marriage of a Jewish woman and a Gentile man. The French had become more difficult in these matters. Tilly was emphatic that she would carry her late mother's religion on to her children, even if it was in name only. She had worn a simple cream, sheath, ankle-length dress to allow her mother's stunning embroidered veil to be the show piece of her ensemble. Enid was Tilly's attendant and Aunt Lucy gave her away.

Their move into Maison Papillon was delayed when Tilly discovered she was pregnant. She didn't want to live amongst the dust and upheaval while all the renovations were happening.

The twins, Estienne and Ruth, had turned one and the new family of four had been comfortably ensconced in their permanent home for the past six months.

At mid-morning on most sunny days a ray of light shone across the twins' cots. Tilly's butterfly collection hung in pride of place on the nursery wall. Tilly believed Madame was smiling down and delighted to know her childhood bedroom had been adapted to accommodate two little souls that were named after Tilly and Madame's families.

They had also discovered that the apartment had a 'maid's' room up on the sixth floor. so Tilly had decided to spend some of her mother's inheritance on renovating it and hiring a daily nanny. This gave her time for herself. Time she had spent researching her mother's French family. It transpired that her great-grandfather and her grandfather were both jewelers at the famous Georges Auger Parisian jewelry store. Her grandfather had made the butterfly jewelry that she had inherited. The family home was on Rue Hassock which was only a block from Maison Papillon, and so she believed it was highly probable that Madame's family the Goldsmiths and her family would have known each other.

Cocooned in her special home behind the security of the unique butterfly gate, Tilly gazed down on her sleeping daughters with an abundance of pure love. She had finally rid the shackles of the shame her stepmother had heaped on her; she had forgiven her father. In the process of completing the quest of an old kind woman, she had experienced the love of a mother, made new friends and married the love of her life.

Also by Merryn Corcoran

THE PEACOCK ROOM

CHAPTER ONE

FULHAM, LONDON 2011

It appeared to be one of those rare perfect days when Allegra had the opportunity to be self-indulgent; both children had left for school without any of the usual teenage angst or guilt-fuelled parental torment. She had cleaned and groomed the house to the minimalist standard that her husband Hugo goaded her to deliver. Making the most of her unaccompanied day, she pulled on her much-loved colourful Biba vintage dress and slipped into a pair of comfortable flat black pumps.

The Wallace Collection beckoned. The preserved 18th Century stately home in Manchester Square just off Oxford Street was a special place where Allegra loved to lose herself. The inspirational mansion offered charisma, beauty and mystery of what had gone before. She appreciated the manner in which the rich furnishings framed the massive rooms; the opulence of the furniture and lavish paintings, encased in their luxuriant frames, always reignited her love of art from the past.

As she locked her front door the fragrance of the potted lemon grass nudged Allegra's deliberations of lunch. The delicate smoked salmon they served in the conservatory café, a modern addition to The Wallace Collection, was one of her favourites. Then she remembered the dry cleaning. "Hugo's suit! Shit, he'll be mad if I forget that again!" She rushed back up the stairs and grabbed the suit along with her Missoni silk dress. As she walked out to the car, she instinctively checked through the suit pants and jacket pockets and was about to discard what looked like a scrappy receipt when she spotted 'Hilton Hotel' on the crumpled paper.

Throwing the clothes onto the back seat of the car Allegra clasped the paper, as she sat down at the wheel. It was clear a room had been paid for on March 12 at the Hilton Hotel, Park Lane. The itemised list showed the customer had a room service dinner for two, as well as an in-house adult film and room service breakfast, also for two. There was no doubting the recipient. Hugo O'Brien's name leapt out from the paper where he had swiped his Amex card.

Allegra reached for a tissue and wiped her forehead then took the battered leather Filofax from her handbag. Her hands trembled as she frantically flicked the pages back to March, hoping like mad this was all some mistake and it wouldn't be one of those nights her Hugo had been away on business. There it was, written clearly in blue pen. H. away in Birmingham.

Rushing back inside, she just made it to the downstairs cloakroom before she fell onto her knees on the cold tiled floor and vomited into the loo. After rinsing her mouth, she caught her reflection in the mirror. Her mascara had run. There were grey flecks showing in her jet-black wavy hair. Hugo had always said alongside her wide, brown Italian eyes her hair was her best feature. Both those attributes seemed to have abandoned her. Probably her weight gain hadn't helped, either. She was ugly. Past it. By the time she reached the landing at the top of the stairs, she was sure her heart would break.

Clutching her head in her hands, she sat on the edge of the bed, their bed, the one she had shared with Hugo for twenty-two years. Her home had always been under Hugo's roof. She had never once considered being with another man. Her children, Kirsty and Harry, gave her all the happiness she expected. Had that all not been enough for Hugo?

A numbness set in. Her instinct was to call her best friend, Julia, but realising she'd be at work, it would have to be her second choice - her mother.

All thoughts of her day-out abandoned, Allegra barely registered the road as she drove the short distance to her mother's house.

"Allegra, I wasn't expecting you. I have to be at my yoga class soon. Why are you crying? What's happened?" Her mother put down her coffee cup and embraced her daughter.

"It's Hugo. He's having an affair."

"What? Hugo! Are you sure?"

"I'm sure, Mum. Look at this." Allegra handed her the receipt.

"The bastard! All the support you've given him, and all you gave up for his career, not to mention your two beautiful children –"

Allegra stopped her.

"Mum, I know all that, but clearly I'm not getting it right. I think maybe I've let myself go. Maybe it's my fault." Her eyes welled up again.

"Well, yes, the weight is becoming a bit of an issue and your hair definitely needs updating."

Allegra let out a huge sob.

"Oh, sorry, my darling, that came out all wrong. I know you think I'm vain and spend too much time and money on myself, but I do have my admirers!" Her mother smoothed her hair, sucked in her cheeks and widened her eyes as she caught her reflection in the window. "However, a lapse in grooming is no excuse for Hugo to go off and shag somebody else."

Maria, Allegra's mother, gave birth to her only child at age nineteen after a shotgun wedding. Allegra's father passed away when Allegra was only twelve, so she was familiar with her mother's need to be seen in a youthful light. With the aid of Botox, a great hairdresser and a disciplined exercise regime, as well as inheriting some wonderful Italian genes, Maria was confident she safely passed for a woman in her early fifties.

Their conversation was interrupted by a bell ringing.

"Oh, I do hope Grandpapa didn't hear me!" Allegra sniffed and wiped her eyes.

"He's so deaf these days, he won't have even heard our voices," Maria said as they followed the sound of the bell up the stairs to his bedroom.

"Look who's here, Papa. It's Allegra come to say hello." Maria exaggerated her condescending tone as she entered the room and straightened the rug on her father's lap.

The ancient, stooped man with his grey moustache and wiry hair motioned for his granddaughter to sit on the chair next to him and offered her a toothless grin. At ninety-nine, he had lost most of his teeth and couldn't walk, but he still occasionally spoke a few words. Grandpapa wore his days like a faded suit, an empty man whose passion arose from thoughts of a magical folly he knew many years ago. A rather tatty peacock feather lay on his lap. It had been his talisman ever since Allegra was a tiny girl, when he would enchant her with stories of the peacock room in a faraway Italian castle.

As Allegra planted a kiss on her grandpapa's unshaven cheek, she inhaled the familiar scent of Novella Melograno cologne. Her mother at least allowed him that indulgence; she would visit the Santa Maria fragrance boutique in Walton Street every few months and buy him a bottle.

Grandpapa viewed Allegra through his thick-lensed spectacles with an intense stare, and she recalled that he had always played the major parenting role in her life. Her mother was mostly preoccupied with some new man and her social life. And when Allegra was at university, Grandpapa would happily spend time listening to her latest view of interiors and the use of colour in the fourteenth century.

He waited till his daughter had left the room before he spoke. "My precious Bellisima Allegra, every day you grow more like my Mama Cosima. For someone with only a quarter of Italian blood in your veins, I can see all the passion and artistic temperament of a full-blooded Italian woman from Donnini." He touched his constant companion, the peacock feather, with his wrinkled hand and looked intently at his granddaughter. "Why have you tears in your eyes, my sweet Allegra?"

"Oh, Grandpapa, I feel so betrayed. Hugo has been cheating on me." Allegra took the old man's free hand as tears rolled down her cheeks.

"I'm so sorry, my precious girl… But let me tell you something. We all have it in us to let others down. I chose to marry your grandmamma against the advice of my own mama, who was right. It was a terrible marriage, but I wanted to get as far away from Italy as I could, and marriage to an Englishwoman was my passage." He put his hand back on his lap and sighed.

"But why did you want to leave so much, when now all you speak about is your village of Donnini and Florence?" Allegra asked.

He lapsed into Italian babble. "Il Pavone, the magic castello. My papa, the peacock room." This was what occurred most times. He would appear perfectly lucid, then the dementia would take over and although his words made little sense to Allegra, they were clearly full of regret.

After a minute or so, Grandpapa's eyes flickered shut. The peacock feather dropped to the floor and she placed it back in his wrinkled hand before she quietly left the room.

"So, did the silly old man say anything useful?" Maria asked as Allegra walked into the kitchen.

"No, just the usual about how I look like his Mama Cosima, and the romantic peacock room in the magical castle."

She took a sip of the coffee her mother handed her. "So now I guess I have to go home and confront Hugo."

"Will you forgive him?"

"I have no idea. I want to hear what he has to say first. I guess." Allegra sighed, kissed her mother, and drove home to face her new reality.

Merryn Corcoran was born in New Zealand but lived a lot of her life in the United Kingdom and Europe. She spends her time divided between her homes in London and the French Riviera with her husband Tim. Merryn is an accomplished entrepreneur and has been writing for the past ten years. Behind The Butterfly Gate is her fourth novel. She also works with her daughter Emily's film company, Cork Films as an executive producer and publicist. Merryn is a keen supporter of UNICEF and for over a decade, chaired and organised an annual celebrity gala ball which raised approximately a million pounds for the charity. Merryn was made a UNICEF Honorary fellow (UK) in 2002.

Printed in Great Britain
by Amazon

44996347R00189